ONE MINUTE TO MIDNIGHT

JACK EMERY 4

STEVE P. VINCENT

PROLOGUE

Professor Denise Danuto hated the constant flashing of the cameras, but the video cameras were worse. They stood like black-eyed sentinels on tripods at the back of the room, ready to record her place in history. Danuto was still getting used to the fact that she would soon be on news reports all around the world. Though she was an expert in her field, the press conference was bigger than anything else she'd ever done.

She looked over her shoulder at the other members of the *Bulletin of the Atomic Scientists* Science and Security Board standing behind her. A few of her colleagues gave smiles of encouragement, and one gave a thumbs-up, filling Danuto with a little more confidence.

As she turned back to the front and gripped the lectern, the journalists sitting in the first few rows slowly quieted down. Danuto looked at one of the video cameras, took a deep breath, and began. "Since 1947, the *Bulletin of the Atomic Scientists* has proudly published world-leading articles about global security issues. More famously, since our first edition, we've also maintained the Doomsday Clock."

She glanced down at the journalists, most of whom were a half-century younger than Danuto and her colleagues. She doubted they understood how important the Doomsday Clock had been during the Cold War or how close the world had been to nuclear catastrophe only two years ago. She hoped her announcement would spread across the globe and shock world leaders into action.

"The Doomsday Clock has been the most recognized symbol of Earth's safety for over seventy years. The most ominous portent the clock can deliver is to strike midnight, which would signal a global calamity. Sadly, although we've had periods when the clock has ticked away from that deadly warning, too often, we've been perilously close to disaster. To track this, each year, the *Bulletin's* Science and Security Board analyzes the progress the world has made toward nuclear disarmament, addressing climate change, and dealing with the other threats the globe faces. Unfortunately, all too often, the movement has been in the wrong direction."

Danuto paused. The journalists were still comatose, sitting back in their chairs and looking like the troublemakers in the back of the class. She sighed and continued. "A year ago, amid peace negotiations between Israel and Palestine, we saw a group of Zionist terrorists almost succeed in using stolen nuclear weapons to destroy the peace and the world. Before that, the United States and China ripped themselves—and each other—apart. In both instances, the world was barely saved from devastation, and the Doomsday Clock remained at two minutes to midnight. We had faith that the world's great leaders and nations would restore sanity."

Danuto glanced back at her colleagues, who all wore

somber faces, then she turned back to the journalists. "Unfortunately, while it would be easy to think we've seen the worst the world can throw at us and fool ourselves that everything is back to normal, that would be wrong. Recently, we've seen Russia assert itself in Ukraine, which has prompted NATO to flood troops into Eastern Europe in scenes reminiscent of the Cold War. In our estimation, the world is in great peril. That is why, with a heavy heart, the Board has decided that the Doomsday Clock must be reset. For the first time ever, the world is one minute to midnight."

Danuto went quiet as heads shot up and shouts filled the theater. The journalists were more interested now that they had a sensational headline. She waited until the wave of excitement had calmed a little. Once it had, she would answer all the questions they could throw at her. She only knew one journalist in the crowd, and Danuto was saving her question for last. First, she pointed to a young man who'd put his hand up first.

He lowered his hand. "Phil Dodds, *Los Angeles Times*. We've heard similar warnings before, and we're not glowing in the dark yet. Aren't your actions today alarmist?"

Danuto smiled. The accusation was leveled against her organization frequently, and the answer was so ingrained that she didn't even have to think about it. "Thanks for your question, Phil. Just like a volcano or an earthquake, just because we haven't had 'the big one' for a while doesn't mean we won't in the future."

Dodds cut in again before another journalist could ask a question. "Do you see a clear path for moving the world back from the brink?"

Danuto smiled. "Of course. What's currently being done can be undone. We'd like to see a negotiated reduction in nuclear arms, a global moratorium on the testing and acquisition of nuclear weapons, for Russia to reduce its incursions into Ukraine, and for NATO to de-escalate. All of that would give us a much greater chance of avoiding chaos."

The questions kept coming. Danuto answered questions about who sat on her board, how they'd come to their decision, and if they'd spoken to any national leaders before making their decision—a whole lot of predictable stuff. The questions were all fine, but in Danuto's mind they were placeholders. It wasn't until much later in the press conference that she pointed at the journalist she'd wanted to call on first.

"Celeste Adams from the *New York Standard*." The flame-haired woman with a British accent twirled a pen in her fingers as she spoke. "The timing of your announcement seems odd. Why did the board consider it necessary to move the Doomsday Clock so close to midnight at this exact moment? Is there new information that led to the decision?"

Danuto smiled. The same journalist who'd armed her with the bomb was now giving her the opportunity to detonate it. She stood tall, because her next statement would make the news everywhere and would be replayed for decades to come. "Because we only just learned a group of terrorists very nearly succeeded in launching nuclear missiles from a British submarine."

Danuto gripped the lectern as the wave of noise from the journalists became overwhelming.

ACT I

1

The Bulletin of the Atomic Scientists *has set the symbolic Doomsday Clock to one minute to midnight. Speaking in Chicago, the head of the Bulletin's Science and Security Board, Professor Denise Danuto, stated that the world has never come so close to nuclear catastrophe as when terrorists almost succeeded in launching nuclear weapons from a British submarine. Although the White House has not commented on the explosive revelation, British Prime Minister Graeme Egan has confirmed such an incident occurred a year ago, although he was adamant the threat had been dealt with.*

—*New York Standard*

Jack Emery's eyes widened as an explosion lit up the room and the violent chatter of automatic weaponry assaulted his ears. Next to him, Celeste Adams cleared her throat. She was lying on the sofa with her legs splayed over his lap and a laptop resting on her thighs, not at all interested in the low-budget television show Jack was watching. He ignored her at first, until she cleared her throat again.

Jack turned his head to face his fiancée. "What?"

Her eyes were boring into him. "Some of us are trying to work."

"This is work!" Jack failed to sound convincing. "You're regretting the television, aren't you?"

"What do you think?"

Jack laughed. Even he had to admit the seventy-inch LCD was a little over the top. They'd purchased it after buying their house in Washington, DC, their place in the capitol to go with Celeste's townhouse in New York. Given he still worked for President McGhinnist and she still worked in New York for the *Standard* newspaper, they'd split time between the two houses since becoming engaged a year ago.

"You're just upset the show undersells your role in stopping the Zionists." Celeste smiled and jerked her head toward the TV. "Oh... he's attractive."

"Anyone watching it will think a muscle-bound Neanderthal foiled the dumb and predictable terrorists." Jack scoffed. "It's a fabrication of what happened!"

Celeste's features softened. She sat up, put her laptop on the coffee table, and leaned in to hug him. She was one of the few people who knew his role in stopping the terrorists from unleashing nuclear catastrophe. A day ago, she'd broken the news about the near miss with the British submarine, and it had spread like wildfire around the world.

"Nobody will ever know what you did." She squeezed Jack tightly. "At least Egan admitting the sub almost launched will set the record straight."

"Nice work on that."

"I don't know what you're talking about." Her face was

the picture of innocence as she let go of him and returned to her previous position. "I asked a question and got an answer."

Jack nodded. Although Celeste had helped Professor Danuto expose the truth, they could never reveal he'd told Celeste everything she'd needed to open the floodgates on the biggest story of her career. He'd broken more than a dozen laws to do so, but he didn't regret his actions for a second. He was still a journalist at heart, and the world needed to know the truth.

Jack turned back to the television and kept watching the dramatization of events he'd lived, although he was portrayed as little more than an advisor to the president. He wished that was the case. Instead, in real life, he'd found himself in the thick of the battle against Aron Braff, one of the few people who'd survived the fight to stop the nuclear launch from HMS *Vigilant*. Jack hadn't heard from the other survivors—Anna Fowler or Chen Shubian.

With a sigh, Jack turned off the television and resolved to do some work himself. He climbed out from under Celeste's legs, moved to the dining table, and sat in front of a pile of papers. He'd been back at work for the president for six months, but his mind hadn't been on the job, and he'd struggled to move on from the terrible events the TV show was dramatizing. He'd been a liability since his return to work, but he hoped to change that.

He now had a focus—nuclear disarmament—and he'd resolved to use every drop of his power and influence to achieve it. Jack's pleas to President McGhinnist had fallen on deaf ears, as he had an ambitious domestic agenda to deliver in his second term, so Jack had taken matters into his own hands. His first salvo had been giving Celeste and Danuto what they'd needed to tell the world. The next part would be much harder.

The papers on the table were a draft of President McGhinnist's speech for the State of the Union address, when he would up the ante on nuclear disarmament after Jack's leak had put the issue firmly on the agenda. It was no longer a question of a few small backpack nukes falling into the hands of terrorists—now the world knew a nuclear power had been critically compromised and that the vast nuclear stockpiles across the globe couldn't be properly safeguarded. All Jack had to do was make sure the speech was a killer and convince his boss to spend the last few years of his presidency fighting for something that might be impossible.

He reflexively touched the deep scar on his cheek, where Aron Braff had sliced him open. Then, sensing Celeste standing behind him, he asked, "Will he go for it?"

"He might." Her voice betrayed a lack of confidence. She massaged his shoulders then leaned in to kiss him on the cheek, right on his scar. "There's no shame if you try and fail."

Jack nodded. He had to try. He owed it to the men and women who'd died saving the world from catastrophe.

DMITRY KHARLOV STARED out the window and saw nothing but inky blackness. He was riding in the first truck in a convoy of four, somewhere near the border between Russia and Ukraine. The darkness matched his mood. His ass had gone numb from sitting all night, and he was getting impatient. The only thing that made the drive tolerable was knowing there was a fortune at the end of it.

Kharlov turned to the driver. "How much longer?"

"Ten minutes." The driver shrugged. "Maybe a little longer."

Kharlov grumbled then settled back into silence. He wished he could conduct his business in the sunshine of the day, but instead he was driving through pouring rain in the middle of the night. It was that kind of enterprise. The ten minutes passed uneventfully, as boring as the hours that had preceded them, until finally, they pulled to a stop on the side of the road. The driver pulled on the handbrake, shifted the truck into park, and kept the engine running.

"Right on time." Kharlov smiled as his customers pulled up in a mix of sedans and SUVs dwarfed by the trucks in Kharlov's convoy.

After checking that his pistol was secure in its shoulder holster, Kharlov put the hood of his raincoat over his head and exited the truck. With two of his associates alongside him, Kharlov walked forward to meet with the same number of men from the other side. The rain was battering all of them, and the headlights of the vehicles illuminated the neutral ground, which the rain had turned to mud.

As the two groups drew closer, Kharlov saw the men on the other side had pistols holstered at their sides. That was the first sign he was dealing with professionals, because if they had tried to bring more firepower than their pistols to the meeting, Kharlov's sharpshooter lying prone in darkness on the roof of a truck would not have hesitated to take them out. His instructions had been clear, and he expected them to be followed to the letter.

The leader of the other party held out his hand. "Mr. Kharlov. It is wonderful to finally meet you."

Kharlov shook the proffered hand. "Let's get this done quickly so we can all get out of the damn rain."

"Were you able to get what we requested?"

Kharlov rattled off the manifest from memory. "One thousand assault rifles and ammunition, one hundred machine guns and ammunition, two thousand fragmentation grenades, thirty RPG launchers and ammunition, and an assortment of mines and other explosives. You can have three of the four trucks, as well, if you want."

The Ukrainian smiled, lifted his hand to his mouth, and let out a sharp whistle. On cue, two more men approached the neutral ground, one carrying a duffel bag and the other carrying an umbrella. Kharlov watched the new arrivals, alert for any hint of betrayal, although he didn't think the men were that stupid. They needed the cargo in his trucks more than he did the money that should be in their bag.

Kharlov was the most prominent arms dealer in Eastern Europe, North Africa, and the Middle East. He'd made a fortune supplying rebels, militias, and terrorists with the gear they needed to do their work. He didn't care for causes, only for currency. If there was a buyer, he would always be the seller. He'd had no trouble sourcing the equipment for these buyers, a group of Ukrainians who were tired of Russian incursions in the southeast of the country, where they were based.

For years, Russia had been butting up against NATO states and acting belligerently with those not protected by the NATO umbrella—Ukraine, in particular. Russian troops had found themselves on the wrong side of the border dozens of times, and Russian-backed partisans had gained control of many towns and cities. Kharlov's customers hoped to resist, though their government's efforts had proven inadequate.

Although Kharlov was Ukrainian, his family lived away

from the fighting, and he had certain other... protections. These men were customers, not comrades.

Kharlov watched as the new arrivals stood next to their boss. The man with the umbrella held it up, then the bag carrier put his bag on the ground and unzipped it. Kharlov felt uneasy when he saw how much money was in the bag, open to the elements with only a cheap umbrella to shield it. He wanted the transaction done with quickly and gestured for his deputy, Natalya Zima, to inspect the bag's contents. She nodded and moved in closer.

When Natalya reached the bag, Kharlov spoke loudly enough to be heard over the rain and the still-running vehicles. "Well?"

"Looks good." Natalya gave him a thumbs-up. "US dollars. The stacks seem fine. Want me to check them all?"

Kharlov was about to say no, then he noticed the leader of the Ukrainians tense a little. He didn't think they would screw him, but he couldn't be sure. "Yes."

Natalya nodded and began to inspect the money closely. A moment later, she looked back over her shoulder and shook her head at Kharlov. "They're short."

The Ukrainian leader drew his pistol as fast as a flash, pointing it at Kharlov and shouting in his native tongue for everyone to freeze. "You couldn't just take the money, could you?"

Kharlov sighed. Though his heart rate had quickened, he remained calm. This wasn't the first fool he'd dealt with in his business. "Put down the pistol, and we can complete our deal."

The pistol was shaking as the Ukrainian leader faced Kharlov and his men, even as his own followers began to shout at their boss to stand down. "We don't have enough money."

"We can amend the order." Kharlov forced a smile, despite

his growing anger. "But if you keep being stupid, you'll all bleed to death in the mud."

"No!" The Ukrainian leader glanced at his men. "They won't shoot while I've got a gun aimed at their boss. We'll take all of the guns, and then we c—"

Kharlov had heard enough. He tapped his leg. A split second later, the distinctive crack of a supersonic rifle round cut through the night, and the Ukrainian leader's head exploded in a mess of gore. As the man's body fell to the ground, Kharlov and his men drew their weapons and pressed their advantage, shouting at the Ukrainians to stand down. The Ukrainians were clearly surprised by their leader's actions and surrendered without another shot being fired. None of them wanted to be the next target of Kharlov's sharpshooter.

Having avoided a firefight, Kharlov gestured in the direction of the trucks. "Do you want to complete our business, or do you all want to die?"

The Ukrainians looked at each other, seemingly surprised that he still wanted to do a deal. But he was a businessman, and he had no use for four truckloads of weapons. He hadn't driven for hours to leave without money. The treacherous one had been punished, and judging from the reaction of his men, he'd been acting alone. If they were smart, they could conclude the business that had brought them here.

"Uh, we would still like to buy the guns off you, Mr. Kharlov." The man holding the umbrella seemed to have appointed himself leader. "Or as much as our money will buy, anyway."

Kharlov nodded at Natalya. As she stepped forward to take possession of the bag, Kharlov stared at the man with the umbrella. "I'll give you a discount for being smart."

Kharlov turned and walked back to his ride. The deal was

made. He had his money, and they had their gear. He knew his men would keep him covered and that the Ukrainians wouldn't be stupid enough to try anything. His shooter had shown that he could splatter any of them over the road at any time. Though he was glad the deal had survived a messy situation, he didn't care what happened to his customers afterward.

Chaos was his business, and business was good.

JACK TAPPED his foot as he waited in the office of the president's secretary, right outside the Oval Office. Waiting to see the president was a different experience for Jack. For the entire time he'd been an advisor to William McGhinnist, he'd enjoyed free and open access to the president's inner sanctum, but for the moment, he had to make an appointment like everyone else. That was one of many things that had changed in his relationship with McGhinnist lately.

As he waited, Jack thought about those changes. After stopping the Zionists, Jack had been burned out and retreated from his work for almost six months. In that time, McGhinnist had fought another election and won another term as the most powerful man in the world. It was only natural that during Jack's absence, he'd been replaced by other advisors and lost some of the access he'd previously enjoyed. He hoped that would change soon enough.

"You can go in now." McGhinnist's secretary, Clara, looked up from her desk and smiled at him. She had a hint of sadness in her features. "It's good to see you, Jack."

"Thanks." Jack smiled back, acknowledging the obvious look of sympathy. It was one he received often recently from the people who'd worked with him for a long time. "See you later."

Jack pushed open the door to the Oval Office. The place still overawed him. An Australian journalist being appointed a senior advisor to the president of the United States was a story that would last well beyond the life of McGhinnist's administration. The fact that he'd also saved America several times was even more amazing. Jack was sure he would reflect on it years from now, but he didn't feel he was done adding stories to the collection. He had one more to go, at least.

Jack waited just inside the office until McGhinnist looked up from his desk, where he was reading a report. "Good evening, Mr. President."

"It's been a while since you called me that, Jack." McGhinnist gestured Jack to the sofas in the middle of the room. "Let's sit."

Jack nodded and moved to the sofas. He knew the president was worried about him, just like Clara and many other staff at the White House. He'd vanished from their lives without warning after helping to secure the peace deal between Israel and Palestine, and not many people knew why. The president was one of the few who did. He'd given Jack time away when he'd needed it then welcomed him back when he was ready.

McGhinnist sat opposite Jack. "Before we talk business, I want to know how you are, Jack. I've been worried about you."

"I, uh..." Without thinking, Jack touched the scar on his face. "I probably came back to work too early, but my head is back in the game now, sir."

"Glad to hear it." McGhinnist crossed his arms. "You're always welcome on the team, and we've got a very busy agenda."

Jack knew that was an understatement. Fresh from securing peace between Palestine and Israel, McGhinnist had taken an aggressive domestic reform program into the election. Along with his successes in defense and foreign policy, McGhinnist had focused on education, health, entitlement reform, and other issues that appealed to a broad cross section of voters. He'd won the presidency, and the Democrats had won a majority in both houses of Congress.

"Thanks." Jack smiled as he dug into his satchel bag for the speech he'd written and placed it on the coffee table. "There's what I'd like to work on. It has all the info you need."

McGhinnist didn't even look at the papers. He kept his eyes locked on Jack. "I don't want to read it, Jack. I want you to tell me about it."

Jack hesitated. He knew the proposal was anathema to everything McGhinnist was focused on in his second term, so he'd hoped the president would agree to read the speech and the arguments it clearly outlined. His proposal would be almost impossible to negotiate with the other nuclear powers, staggeringly difficult to get through the House and the Senate, and unpopular with a sizeable slice of the public. It would be career suicide for a career political advisor, but Jack wasn't one of those. He'd joined McGhinnist's administration to right wrongs, and he would walk away from the job if necessary to pursue the thing he was committed to.

Jack held the president's gaze, hoping he might change his mind, but McGhinnist didn't budge. He was going to have to fight for the change he wanted. He sighed. "We avoided global nuclear disaster by a second or two. I don't think we can abide that. We need to do something about it in this term, while there's an opportunity to do so."

McGhinnist's eyes narrowed, and he leaned forward,

resting his elbows on his knees. "What exactly are you asking for?"

Jack swallowed hard. He knew McGhinnist's reaction would be so blisteringly negative that his proposal might not even last long enough for him to finish explaining it. That was why he'd wanted McGhinnist to read the speech, to see the logic and be ready to discuss it when the proposal had sunk in a bit. Jack wouldn't have that chance anymore. "Global nuclear disarmament."

"I didn't know you'd taken up comedy, Jack." McGhinnist scoffed. "I've got Russia nibbling like rats on anything we're not watching closely and more domestic issues I want to solve than there are days left in my term, and now you want me to add something that is impossible *and* unpopular into the mix?"

"People thought the peace deal with Israel and Palestine was impossible, but we achieved it. And popular doesn't matter, because you'll never face another election." Jack kept his voice even, trying not to show emotion. "The time is right to negotiate a global deal, and we have the numbers to get it through Congress. There'll never be a better opportunity to do this."

McGhinnist's eyes were piercing. "The leak about the British submarine almost launching came from you, didn't it?"

Jack had never lied to McGhinnist before, and he wasn't going to start now. "I gave Celeste the information."

"I could have you arrested for that." McGhinnist sighed and took off his glasses. He looked tired. "I should at least dismiss you."

"You could, but I won't budge on this one. I held a dying British minister's head to a radio as he spoke the five words that averted a catastrophe." Jack's voice wavered slightly. "If I'd been a second late or he'd bled out a second earlier, we wouldn't be here discussing this. Nobody can be trusted with these weapons. If we don't try, you won't need to fire me. I'll resign."

Jack felt like he'd scored the point, because McGhinnist reached for the speech. He watched as the president skimmed the first few pages, knowing the threat to quit would have hit the target. He'd been through a lot with McGhinnist, and to walk away from that would be difficult, but Jack felt so strongly about this issue that he'd fight for it either inside or outside the administration.

McGhinnist got through a handful of pages before he looked up at Jack and laughed. "It's ambitious, isn't it?"

"It's more than that. Read the whole thing." Jack was relieved that the president was willing to listen. "Clara offered to get us some refreshments. Should I organize some beers?"

"Sure." McGhinnist looked back down at the speech and kept reading. "Better get a six-pack. We'll be here a while."

2

*T*he President will deliver his annual State of the Union address today, which he has previously used to announce his major policy priorities. In his first term, these included the abolition of NSA spying on US citizens and his signature achievement—negotiation of a peace agreement between Israel and Palestine. Though there has been speculation about the content of the president's address for weeks, the White House has refused to comment on what may be in store. Given the president's enormous domestic reform agenda, pundits predict the address will focus almost entirely on issues close to home.

—*New York Standard*

Yuri looked around the table at his four comrades. They'd planned this day for months, but he wanted to be sure the others were as committed as him. There was no room for doubt or caution—that would only get them killed—but his comfort level grew as each of his compatriots nodded or smiled at him. None of them spoke. They didn't need to. The time for talk had passed.

"The time has come." Yuri slapped his palm down on the hardwood table, pushed his chair back, and climbed to his feet. "Get ready."

The small cellar exploded with activity. Oleksandr left the cellar and went up the stairs to keep a lookout while the others made their preparations. Stepan readied the guns, Arsen communicated their readiness to the other cells, and Pavlo triple-checked their route to the target. That left Yuri, who had the most vital responsibility of all, without which none of the rest would matter—the explosives.

Yuri walked over to the wooden chest in the corner of the room and opened the lid. As he stared inside at his collection of explosives, he felt a heavy weight on his shoulders. He knew some of the men in the cellar and some of those who opposed them would not survive the evening. Whether they succeeded or failed, history would judge them as heroes.

He reached inside the chest and gripped the backpack inside. He'd made the device as well as he could with the materials at his disposal, but it wasn't up to his usual standards. He was careful to treat it with respect because he didn't want it to cook off before they'd even left the townhouse. He grunted as he put on the heavy backpack, wondering why he'd agreed to make the bomb *and* carry it.

With his deadly cargo secure, Yuri walked back to the table where Stepan had laid out all their guns. Yuri assessed the arsenal. "Which are mine?"

"Sawed-off shotgun and a pistol." Stepan lifted the weapons and held them out. "Are you sure you don't want more firepower?"

Yuri shook his head. He was happy with his choice. His

comrades were packing more heat—rifles and submachine guns—but they didn't have bombs strapped to their backs. He took possession of the guns, stashing the pistol down the front of his jeans and hiding the shotgun in the right pocket of his trench coat. He'd cut out the lining of the pocket a few days ago so the gun fit easily enough and would always be close at hand.

With his gear secure, Yuri was the first up the stairs and onto the street. He nodded at Oleksandr. "We're good to go."

Yuri tapped his foot impatiently as he waited for the others, knowing every wasted second increased the risk of being exposed or coming into conflict with the authorities. The Ukrainian security forces were on a short fuse after years of incursions and loss of territory to Russian-backed partisans. Though Yuri and his comrades hoped to continue those losses, the Ukrainian government wouldn't be expecting a strike in Kharkov, the country's second-largest city. It was a huge gambit, but it was necessary.

Russia's seizure of much of the southeastern tip of Ukraine had answered the prayers of millions throughout the country, who were tired of economic stagnation and political corruption under Kiev's control. Joyous protests had erupted on the streets in many towns and cities across eastern Ukraine, many of which had risen up and overthrown the local authorities. In each location, "people's committees" loyal to the Russians had turned over control to Moscow.

But for the last two years, the situation had stagnated. No new territory had been liberated from the bureaucrats in Kiev, and none of the Russian-controlled territory had been returned to Ukrainian hands. Yuri, his comrades, and hundreds of men and women in cells all across Kharkov were tired of the stalemate, and they had decided to take matters into their own hands by opening a new front.

When Yuri's team had all reached the street, they headed to the target. From Danylevs Koho Street, they headed southwest along Nauky Avenue, past the university medical center. It felt strange walking with purpose through the city at three o'clock in the morning, when everyone else was asleep. If everything went to plan, those same people would soon wake in confusion and learn their city had changed forever.

Near the Founders of Kharkov statue, Yuri spotted the first signs of the wave that was building and would soon overwhelm the city. At the foot of the stone statue, a single Ukrainian soldier was splayed on the ground, blood pooling around him. Yuri didn't know how he'd died or which cell had taken him down, but it didn't matter. The solider was the first casualty on a night that would be filled with them, a young man on the wrong side of history.

They passed the monument and continued down Nauky Avenue to Svobody Square—Freedom Square. The largest public space in the city, it was home to many museums, educational institutions, and government buildings. Since the start of the conflict with Russia, the square had also been used as both a monument to the fallen Ukrainian soldiers and an army recruitment station. A public square meant for all had been perverted and corrupted.

As they entered the square, Yuri heard gunshots in the distance. Though silence had aided them to this point, their gambit had been revealed. None of them were surprised or worried. Noise, blood, and carnage were inevitable if they were to achieve their goal, and their Russian allies had promised to take care of the police and the army. The noise just meant they had to move faster.

Yuri gripped the shotgun in his pocket as he saw the first of the soldiers in the square react to the dozens of men and women streaming toward him. Each cell had been responsible for securing a different part of the city, but Freedom Square was so important that multiple groups were pouring in from different directions. To capture Freedom Square would go a long way toward taking the city.

Yuri kept moving toward his target as another Ukrainian soldier took an interest in his group. The guard, a boy of eighteen or nineteen, peeled off from his post, gripping his rifle. He barked at them to stop and to go home. Yuri and his men ignored the order. The soldier raised his rifle and yelled again, his voice wavering. Yuri and his men pulled their own weapons from their coats. Then the Ukrainian soldier fired, and the streets ran red.

Yuri flinched as the assault rifle chattered and its muzzle flash lit up the square. Oleksandr fell in front of him, and Pavlo dropped beside him, but then the Ukrainian soldier's head and upper torso exploded in a mess of gore. Yuri lowered his shotgun, which had almost cut the soldier in half, then locked eyes on the army recruiting station. The loss of his friends and comrades had only increased his determination to deliver his deadly cargo.

He ignored the gunfire, screams, and carnage around him. More patriots were filling the square, overwhelming the soldiers posted to defend it. Yuri left them to their work and kept walking, focused only on his job. He shrugged off the backpack and carried it by the straps in one hand. Using his other hand, he raised his shotgun and aimed it at the glass door of the army recruiting station. He fired, shattering windows.

Yuri tossed the bag with all his strength and watched it sail through the window of the recruiting station. With a grim smile, he turned and ran from the building. He didn't need to shout to his comrades to keep clear, because each cell had received instructions about what was to be blown up—the recruiting station, the main government offices, and the monument to the fallen soldiers.

When he was a safe distance away, Yuri pulled the detonator out of his pocket and looked around. The Ukrainian soldiers were dead and the square was won, though several of Yuri's comrades had also fallen. They were the first casualties in a battle that would call for much more sacrifice. Though the pro-Western government of Ukraine had surrendered some territory in the country, it wouldn't give up Kharkov. The city would have to be taken by force.

"It begins!" Yuri's shout earned a cheer from the others, after which he lifted the plastic hood of the detonator and pressed the button.

The explosion lit up the night and set the world on fire.

ANNA FOWLER'S eyes shot open as she heard an explosion somewhere in the distance. Her mind took only a split second to process the sound, and her senses strained to find more information to feed her analysis. She was in Kharkov. It was in the earliest hours of morning. A bomb had gone off. She climbed out of bed and was half dressed when she heard another explosion—close enough to rattle the windows of her hotel room.

When she was dressed, she moved to the window and looked out into the night. It was carnage. Fires were burning across the city, accentuated by flashes of gunfire. Something big was happening in Kharkov, and her small team of MI6 agents was right in the middle of it. There was only one thing to do—get to the street, where she could find out what was happening and figure out if it was in Britain's interests to mess with it.

She grabbed her pistol from the nightstand and raced down to street level. Graeme Tanner was already waiting for her behind the wheel of their van. Tanner was the long-time MI6 man at the British Consulate in Kharkov. He knew the city well, and she was glad to have him along for whatever the hell was about to happen. He had one hand on the wheel and a cell phone to his ear, but he terminated the call when he saw her.

Anna leaned against the driver's side window of the van. "Do we have any idea what's going on?"

Tanner shook his head and tossed the cell phone into the vehicle's center console. "I've made some calls. There's an organized push going on and not much resistance."

"Okay." Anna rounded the van and climbed into the passenger seat. "I'll call the chief and see if she knows anything."

Anna dug into her pocket, pulled out her own phone, and dialed Louise Watkins, the chief of MI6. As she put the phone to her ear, the other two members of her team reached the street and climbed into the back of the van. Tanner got them on the road as the call rang for longer than usual, probably because Watkins was in London and likely fast asleep in bed at this moment.

Eventually, a woman answered the phone, her voice heavy with sleep. "This is Watkins."

"Chief, it's Anna Fowler. There's explosions and gunfire all across Kharkov. I think the Russians are making their move."

"I'll inform the prime minister." Watkins suddenly

sounded very awake. "I need you to find out as much as you can. Kharkov cannot fall to the Russians, Ms. Fowler."

The line went dead, and Anna sighed. She didn't much like Watkins. Since Anna had helped Jack Emery stop terrorists from launching nukes off a British submarine, much of the senior leadership of MI6 had been replaced. MI6's failure to detect that the captain of that British submarine had gone rogue had cost them their jobs—and almost cost the world everything. Watkins had been installed to clean up the mess.

Whether she liked the boss or not, Anna was glad to have the green light to act. It was time to strike back at Russia. The country had been busy in the region for years. After capturing Crimea, Russian-backed partisans had waged civil war with the pro-Western government of Ukraine and effectively taken control of a chunk of Eastern Ukraine. The current border reached from Muripol to Donetsk and Horlivka then shot northeast to Luhansk and the Russian border.

The Russian game plan had been incredibly simple: arm partisans in areas where the populace overwhelmingly supported joining Russia, wait for those partisans to rise up, support the puppet governments that spring up behind the revolution, then annex the territory. It had worked well for Russia, until the Ukrainian government poured resources into holding the line. The situation had stalemated, and Russia had made no notable gains in over a year.

Russia's leaders had apparently decided to open another front in Kharkov. The city was the second-largest in Ukraine, home to about 1.5 million people and a major cultural, educational, and industrial hub. The authorities wouldn't give up the city without a fierce fight, because losing Kharkov would be a devastating blow to a country already reeling from massive losses.

"Okay, ten-second briefing..." Anna turned and faced her team. "Our mission is to gather information so the bosses back home can figure out what to do."

Tanner looked at Anna as he shifted it into drive. "I think Freedom Square is where most of the action will be."

"Then that's where we'll head."

Tanner pushed the van hard to get them to the square as quickly as possible. The streets were deserted, so they made good progress. The citizens of many Eastern European countries had hundreds of years of practice at staying inside when carnage engulfed their streets. It had kept them safe from dictators, revolutionaries, the secret police, war, and strife for generations. Only the Russian-backed partisans and the authorities trying to stop them would be on the streets...

Anna frowned as she processed the thought and looked out the window. "Why aren't there any cops? They should be out on the streets by now—"

Anna flinched as the van's windshield shattered. Then Tanner slumped forward in his seat, his head turned into a gory mess by a sniper's bullet. She reached out to grab the wheel and managed to keep the vehicle straight on. A second shot pounded into the hood of the van, and the engine started to spew smoke. The van slowed to a stop less than a mile from the square.

"Out!" Anna shouted at her team members—Patricia Evans and Tom Dalton. "We're sitting ducks!"

Anna and her team piled out of the van and took cover behind it. The sniper seemed to have been content to stop the van's advance, because no further shots came their way. The shooter was clearly posted to keep traffic away from the square while whoever was causing a ruckus there consolidated their control. She suspected shooters were on overwatch in other key parts of the city.

"These pricks are organized." Anna drew her pistol as she huddled behind the van with Evans and Dalton. "You guys okay?"

Evans nodded, despite the shock on her face. She was the least experienced member of the team. "We have nothing to take down a sharpshooter."

"No, we don't." Anna shook her head. "We need to find out what the fuck is happening here—who is taking over and why there's no cops or soldiers on the street to stop them."

Dalton jerked a thumb back over his shoulder. "There's a police station two blocks to the southeast. I've run past it the last few mornings."

"Then let's go."

Anna led them away from the van, and they headed toward the police station. When they were around the corner, they stowed their pistols. No matter what was happening, showing up to a police station with a gun in your hand wasn't a smart move. They turned the corner and found themselves at the bottom of the stairs of a large police station.

Anna saw no police, though. She frowned. Lights shined from inside, but there was none of the activity she'd expect to see with bombs exploding and bullets flying. Something was wrong. The station was quiet, and the streets around it were deserted. Anna drew her pistol again and led her team up the stairs. They reached the front door, and Anna tried the handle. It was unlocked. She opened the door and let out a gasp. All the cops inside the station were dead.

Several uniformed officers were slumped forward at their desks, while others were sprawled on the floor. None of them had visible wounds—they hadn't been shot or blown up—but all of them were dead. The cops at this station had been poisoned or taken out in some other way. If the same was true at the other police stations and military posts around Kharkov, that explained why no resistance had mobilized.

Anna turned to look at Dalton and Evans, who looked as stunned as she felt. "They've won. The city is lost. We need to go to ground and figure out our next move."

Dalton scoffed. "If there is a next move."

JACK SHOOK his head at McGhinnist, staring at the president in disbelief. "Please, sir, there's still time to reconsider."

"I know how much the nuclear weapons reduction meant to you, Jack." McGhinnist's hard features softened a little as he put a hand on Jack's shoulder. "You lost this one."

Jack sighed. He couldn't believe all the effort they'd put into crafting the State of the Union address speech into a landmark moment in American and global history had been wasted. For weeks, they'd written into the speech a plan to achieve the impossible. McGhinnist had been prepared to deliver it, until the hard heads from the State Department and the Department of Defense got their hands on it. Then they'd convinced the president to shift his focus.

"The whole world lost, sir." Jack held McGhinnist's gaze, not backing down. "Today could have been remembered for two hundred years, but instead, it will be forgotten by tomorrow afternoon. You had a chance to achieve something *else* that was great, on top of what we've already achieved, but instead, you're going to talk about healthcare, like fifty other presidents..."

McGhinnist winced and closed his eyes, as if Jack's words

had caused him physical pain. When he opened them again, his hard, granite look was back in place. "I have to go."

Jack nodded and watched as McGhinnist turned and walked away, escorted by Secret Service agents deeper into the Capitol Building, where McGhinnist would deliver his address in the next few minutes. Jack felt a small measure of regret for his cheap shot, which he'd taken more out of frustration than any malice, but he would have to apologize later. The president was about to give his speech.

Jack sighed again and headed through the Capitol Building until he made it to the House Chamber, which felt like it was buzzing with anticipation. He was one of the last to arrive, having been alongside McGhinnist until the last moment. Every member of the House and the Senate was already seated, along with McGhinnist's cabinet and his other key advisors.

Jack found his seat next to the president's national security advisor, Caleb Davidson. "Ready for the big one, Caleb?"

"It's an easier crowd than when the Republicans had a majority in this place." Davidson smirked. "Sorry if Russia derailed whatever you guys were cooking up."

"The Joint Chiefs and the State Department did that just fine on their own." Jack gave a bitter laugh. "Although the Russians moving into Kharkov certainly gave them more ammunition."

Jack sat back and crossed his arms. Though news about Kharkov hadn't been enough on its own to derail the speech about nuclear disarmament, when combined with the reservations of other senior administration officials, it had been enough to give McGhinnist cold feet. They'd reminded the president that the relationship between the USA and Russia was already tense and convinced him that adding nuclear disarmament into the mix wouldn't help things. Instead, the president was going to focus on the very safest of issues.

A chime sounded, signifying the president would be arriving in ten seconds. Jack stood in unison with everyone else in the room and started to applaud. McGhinnist waved as he walked into the room with a broad smile on his face. The president made his way to the podium then waited until the applause quietened.

"My fellow Americans." McGhinnist's voice boomed the same words presidents before him had said. "I'd like to talk about the basic issues that affect your lives—healthcare, education, and jobs—because, after years of turmoil in our country and abroad that demanded strong attention, I wanted these vital issues to dominate my second term."

McGhinnist continued to shift between teleprompters, reading the speech that'd been sanctified and sanitized by almost everyone who was anyone in the administration. He gave the key statistics on healthcare in America and started to outline his plan to improve things. As expected, each point the president made was met with riotous applause, because the same plan had already won him the election and won the Democrats a huge majority.

Jack watched and listened unenthusiastically, although he did applaud when etiquette demanded it. In truth, he felt empty.

Then the president paused, his eyes narrowed as he stared at one of the teleprompters, then another. Disquiet grew among the crowd as he remained silent. Jack looked at Caleb Davidson for answers, but the national security advisor appeared clueless about why McGhinnist had stopped speaking. Jack had worked with the president for five years, but he had no idea, either.

Eventually, after a few more seconds, McGhinnist shook his head and looked away from the teleprompter. He stared right at Jack. "Unfortunately, healthcare can't be the topic of my address, because there's another vital issue that needs airing. Several weeks ago, the *Bulletin of the Atomic Sciences* changed the time on the Doomsday Clock to one minute to midnight."

McGhinnist shifted his gaze. His next line would be the one played on the networks.

"At that same press conference, a near miss with a British nuclear submarine was also revealed. I can confirm that the terrorist aboard the submarine did almost launch its full arsenal. Cities were almost razed. Global catastrophe was barely averted. One of my closest advisors, Jack Emery, saved the world from disaster. Along with brave Navy SEALs and our British allies, Jack kept a UK government minister safe for long enough to prevent the launch." McGhinnist's usually booming voice softened. "Though many died, Jack and the others did their duty and saved us all."

Jack suddenly felt every set of eyes in the room turn to him. A secret he had expected to take to his grave had just become public. He kept his face blank, frozen in place, until Davidson elbowed him in the ribs. Snapping out of his trance, Jack raised a hand in acknowledgement of the attention and gave a small smile.

McGhinnist's voice hardened again. "But despite great bravery by all who worked to stop the launch, we should never have been that close to disaster. We can deal with an accident or attack on an oil rig or an airplane, but this incident displayed how spectacularly the same can't be said for nuclear weapons."

McGhinnist turned to face the House and Senate leadership. As he fixed them with a hard glare, the audience was so silent that a single cough echoed through the chamber. As he watched, Jack felt a tap on his arm. It was Davidson, a hard stare of his own fixed on Jack, as if silently asking Jack what the hell was going on. Jack smiled in response.

"The time has come." McGhinnist was back to facing the front and in rhythm. "The time has come for the political classes to do *their* duty and for me, as president of the United States, to do *my* duty. It is unacceptable that terrorists would get so close to unleashing the ultimate hell on our planet, and it is time to do something about the nuclear risk forever.

"We have been arrogant to think we were safe. We thought that because we're able to split the atom and unleash its destructive force that we were also able to moderate that power. History has proven us wrong. We have survived and thrived for no reason except luck, but I'm not prepared to gamble against fifteen thousand nuclear weapons.

"I'm ready to work with our allies and the other nuclear powers to collectively fold our hands and remove this blade from our throats." McGhinnist shifted his gaze onto Jack. "To negotiate a deal, I'm appointing Jack Emery as my special envoy for nuclear disarmament. The man who saved the world once will work to do it forever."

Jack swallowed hard. He'd been a reporter for ten years and a prominent advisor for five, so he was used to being on the periphery of public attention. With a few words, though, McGhinnist had thrust him into the spotlight. He didn't know why McGhinnist had changed his mind, but since the president had made the commitment, Jack had to be prepared to do the legwork.

After a second or two, McGhinnist picked up the speech again. "There is no bigger duty for an American president than to keep the citizens of this country safe. There is no bigger danger to those citizens than the Earth-killing weaponry that we're only one accident or hot temper away from seeing unleashed. It is not good enough.

"The world is not a safe or a peaceful place, especially at the moment. The events in Ukraine earlier today showed us that. The world is conflicted and divided. America isn't immune or blameless. No country is. That's why I'm asking all the nuclear powers to put this cause above all others. It is that important."

As McGhinnist smiled and held his hands out wide, applause ripped through the room. Not everyone was clapping and cheering, but Jack wondered if the president might just have enough support to complete his plan. The Democratic hold on both chambers, combined with strong leadership, might just be enough to secure passage for a bill of nuclear reduction or even disarmament.

All Jack had to do now was negotiate a reasonable agreement with the other world powers, some of whom were currently acting anything but reasonable...

3

---

*I*n the wake of the pro-Russian uprising in Kharkov, a significant number of Russian troops have massed on the border, as Moscow looks set to stake a claim over more Ukrainian territory. Though Russian Foreign Minister Veronika Oreshkin has called the deployments a response to increased NATO presence and exercises in the region, the move continues the doctrine of Prime Minister Nikolai Sokolov's government. Many NATO member countries have slammed the aggressive Russian deployment, although the United States has been more muted, which some analysts are attributing to US hopes of a global nuclear-disarmament agreement.

—New York Standard

Veronika Oreshkin looked down at her notepad and admired the flower she'd drawn. In her opinion, her handiwork was some of the finest art ever produced in Russia.

She sighed when someone asked her a question, stealing her focus. Veronika looked up and nodded. "I agree."

"Excellent." Russian Prime Minister Nikolai Sokolov smiled and moved to the next item on the agenda, something about industrial policy.

Veronika tuned out and started doodling again. Meetings of the Russian Cabinet seemed to be where she got most of her best artwork done lately. Though she was the foreign minister, the meetings rarely involved much more than listening to Sokolov charge through the agenda and call upon his cronies when he needed the number for a decision. It was a bad recipe —a man with dominant views and incredible power surrounded by yes men. Veronika was in the minority, and she had to pick her battles.

It wasn't all bad, though. Veronika was mostly left alone to do her job and only interfered with when the prime minister's attention was drawn to a particular issue. Over many years, she'd tended to the complex garden that made up a great power's foreign networks, pruning here and seeding there. She'd notched up significant achievements and mostly managed to limit Sokolov's interference in her space—with one notable exception.

"Now to our final item—matters in Europe." Sokolov's words roused Veronika from her restive state. "Sergey, can you give us an update?"

Veronika rolled her eyes at that. The prime minister's favorite lapdog, Defense Minister Sergey Popov, was in charge of Sokolov's obsession—reclaiming Russia's sphere of influence in Eastern Europe. The campaign had started a few years ago, when the Americans had been busy dealing with China and their own internal turmoil, and although she disagreed with the campaign, she had to admit that Russia had made impressive early gains.

The success in securing Crimea and much of southeastern Ukraine wasn't enough for Sokolov, though. Instead of taking what was already won and suing for peace, he kept pushing harder, and Russia was now bogged down. NATO was pouring money and arms into Ukraine, and Sokolov's resentment for them had only grown. Though he hadn't challenged the Atlantic alliance directly by attacking a member country, the situation was a powder keg.

For now, though, Sokolov had enough to chew on without bothering them.

"I'm pleased to report that our efforts to secure Kharkov are progressing well." The defense minister looked at the prime minister and smiled. "Everything went as planned—our spies took care of the army and the police, then the loyalists took to the streets and gained control of all key parts of the city."

"Excellent." Sokolov beamed. "What now?"

"We continue to arm and reinforce the loyalists." Popov smiled. "The intelligence services will also continue to disrupt Ukrainian efforts to re-establish control in the city."

Veronika spoke up for the first time. "Is there anything the Foreign Ministry can help you with, Sergey?"

Popov's smile vanished. "You can tell the UN if you want to, but the military and intelligence services will take care of all of the hard work."

Veronika kept her face passive, knowing she was about to jam her thumb into a sore point. "Is it possible Western resistance will intensify now?"

"Of course." Popov sneered. "But it's also possible that we'll continue to successfully devour Ukraine without issue. I propose we continue as planned. The president agrees with me."

Veronika snorted. Russia's president had been a puppet of Sokolov for almost a decade. He'd done nothing to check Sokolov's ambitions. Popov seemed content to remain in office, enjoying its perks, while Sokolov took care of the dirty work. Sokolov stating that the president agreed with him was no kind of real endorsement. Not that it mattered, because there were enough people around the table who *did* have power, and most of them agreed with Sokolov.

Sokolov and Popov looked around the table, but there was no disagreement. Just like that, the silent, consenting majority vaporized any pressure Veronika had hoped to put them under. She kept quiet and didn't push any harder. Nikolai Sokolov was not a man who accepted disagreement easily, and he was heavily invested in Popov's plan. She didn't consider the issue vital enough to end her career, especially without support around the table. In Russian politics, being pragmatic was far more important than being principled.

"Excellent." Sokolov knocked his knuckles on the table twice, as if he were a judge dismissing a court case. "Katerina will distribute the minutes."

As Sokolov nodded and turned to talk to Popov, the other members of the cabinet started to stand. Veronika clenched her teeth and stayed in her seat, annoyed that the prime minister had completely ignored the agenda's final item. At the start of the meeting, she'd asked for some time to discuss the American proposal on nuclear weapons, but Sokolov had simply ended the meeting without calling the item.

"Prime Minister." Veronika spoke the words loudly. "I'd like to discuss the American nuclear weapons proposal."

"An empty proposal that's not worth our time." Sokolov

waved his hand dismissively. "The Americans succeeded in neutering us before. They talked of peace and prosperity. We lost everything, and they gained it all. Now their alliance network pushes to our very doorstep, and they want us to give up even more. I won't waste our time on that insult, nor will you."

Veronika felt her face flush, embarrassed by the dressing-down. She found it hard to argue with Sokolov and his hardliners, especially when there were so few moderates around the table to support her. Men like Sokolov pined for the old days, when the Soviet Union straddled the world as one of two great powers while its people starved, waiting in line for bread. Such a view was anathema to Veronika. She wanted to help her country modernize, but she had to pick her battles.

Finally, she nodded at Sokolov, conceding the point and once again staying silent. She gathered her papers, stood, and left the room without talking to any of her colleagues. It was only when she was away from the main group that someone tapped her on the shoulder. Steeling herself, Veronika turned to find herself facing Yevgeny Mikhailov, the agriculture minister and another of Sokolov's sycophants.

Veronika plastered on a smile. "Minister, I didn't realize you wished to speak with me at the end of the meeting."

Mikhailov smiled. He looked and acted like a toad. "I wanted to warn you, Veronika."

"Warn me?" Veronika laughed, feeling some of her confidence return. "Is there a bad batch of beetroot in the stores? Some pork with an underwhelming flavor?"

Mikhailov's smile turned into a scowl, but he didn't relent. "You should be careful, Veronika. It's bad enough that you constantly speak negatively of our efforts to regain our influence in Europe, but now you seriously want to discuss the American plan to rob us of our nuclear arsenal?"

"I think it would be best if you focus on your job, rather than telling me how to do mine." Veronika crossed her arms. "I—"

"Just hear me." He held up a hand. "You need to tread carefully. You're good at your job and liked well enough, but you are replaceable."

Veronika said nothing as she watched him turn and depart. There was no point engaging him. His warning had been delivered, and he had no further role. With her fists clenched, she resumed the walk back to her office, though her mood had become dark. The dressing-down during the cabinet meeting and the not-so-subtle warning after it showed she was on thin ice with Sokolov. Although she knew she had to be even more careful in the future, she wouldn't stop her vital work. She'd done her best to maintain the status quo in Europe, both directly and indirectly through actions her colleagues weren't aware of. She needed to figure out how she could progress the nuclear negotiations without directly defying Sokolov's orders.

She pulled out her cell phone. There was a missed call from her ex-husband, but she ignored it. Instead, she fired off a message to her assistant, asking her to reach out to Jack Emery. Despite Sokolov's warning and the danger it posed, she wanted to be ready to act if the opportunity arose.

ANNA FELT her heart rate quicken as she watched the three men she'd been waiting for converge on the center of the park from different directions. She was on her stomach under a tree, dressed entirely in black and watching her targets through night-vision binoculars that showed them as clearly as if it were daylight. Her two remaining team members were also positioned around the park, drawing a deadly triangle around their targets.

"I have eyes on three men," Anna said into her headset. "Do either of you have a shot?"

"Negative." Patricia Evans's voice came in through her earpiece.

"I have a shot," Tom Dalton's voice followed. "Do I have clearance to fire?"

Anna considered the request. Though she was armed only with a pistol, the others were armed with scoped rifles and were good enough shots to take down all three targets in seconds. Ordering their deaths would be as easy as breathing, but her own orders were clear—identify the targets before taking them down. Chief Watkins didn't want any screw-ups now that she was in charge, and Anna wasn't stupid enough to defy a direct order.

"No." The words felt like acid in Anna's mouth, given what had happened to Graeme Tanner and the cops and soldiers posted in Kharkov. "We need to ID them first."

"Confirmed." Dalton didn't sound happy. "I'll wait for authorization before I split their skulls open."

Anna knew Evans and Dalton were angry. She was, as well. Graeme Tanner had been their colleague, and his death was the cherry on top of a giant cake made of shit. He hadn't been the only person to die on the chaotic night. As best as Anna and MI6 could tell, few soldiers and fewer cops had taken to the streets that night. They'd been murdered in their stations and in their barracks, leaving Kharkov to be taken by the pro-Russian partisans with barely a shot fired.

After leaving the police station with all the dead cops

inside, Anna and her team had scouted several others. In every one of them, they'd found the same thing—dead cops and no signs of violence. The cops had dropped dead writing reports, drinking coffee, and in one particular instance, on the toilet.

Anna and her team had retreated to their hotel to regroup. She'd contacted MI6, and the gears of the finest intelligence agency in the world had started to turn. Within hours, the agency had confirmed that the governor of Kharkov, Ihor Kutovy, had ordered all soldiers to barracks and all police officers to work overtime at their stations on the night of the uprising. MI6 had also uncovered an eight-figure deposit into a Cayman Island bank account linked to Kutovy. He'd been bribed to betray his country, and it hadn't been hard to figure out by whom.

Under orders from Chief Watkins, Anna and her team had kicked the doors in on a known Russian agent operating in Kharkov and squeezed him until he revealed he'd spent a year establishing cells of pro-Russian partisans in the city, assigned them targets, then set them loose. Kutovy had guaranteed success by ordering the troops and cops into position then having them poisoned.

Before Anna put a bullet in his head, the agent had provided the names and photos of his fellow agents and organized a meeting in the park. Once she had the names, MI6 had been able to rustle up some pictures, which was how Anna hoped to identify the two agents and Kutovy—the Ukrainian collaborator who'd helped to orchestrate the fall of Kharkov. If she could identify them, her team could kill them.

"Moving in to confirm their identities." Anna left the binoculars on the ground and stood. "Wait for my order."

Whistling a soft tune, Anna walked in the direction of the three men. She had her hands in her pockets, but her senses were on a razor's edge. She was ready to draw her pistol and deliver extreme violence, while two elite shooters with scoped rifles also had her back. As she closed the distance with the men, they turned to face her, and the air was immediately filled with tension. The two agents called out to her in Russian, while Kutovy kept quiet.

Anna recognized their faces in the pale light of the streetlamp. They were the men who'd orchestrated the takeover of a city. Even though Anna took down any target she was ordered to, she took special pleasure in erasing the mistakes of humanity. A group of men who would kill so many innocent people—and one of MI6's own—definitely fit that classification.

Anna stopped whistling. "Targets confirmed."

A split second later, the agents standing to the left and right of Kutovy dropped. Dalton and Evans had seen to them with their silenced rifles. Kutovy's mouth fell open, but no sound came out as Anna drew her weapon and aimed it at the traitor. Kutovy's initial shock at having his paymasters slump dead to the ground was replaced by the primal fear of having a gun pointed at him. She stopped three steps away from him, the pistol aimed between his eyes.

"You cannot do this to me!" Kutovy whimpered in broken English. "Do you have any idea who I am?"

"This is for all the dead soldiers and cops you let be murdered." Anna lowered her pistol and shot him in the knee, relishing his cry of pain as he collapsed to the ground. As his eyes flared with pain, he opened his mouth to speak, but she put two more silenced rounds into his skull. "And that's for their families."

Anna exhaled slowly as she pocketed her pistol and bent down to pick up the three shell casings. Kutovy's body had formed a neat triangle with those of the agents, though they had all slumped in strange poses with blood pooling around their heads. As far as the local authorities would be concerned, the men had been ambushed in the park. They would have no idea why these men had died or who'd killed them. But in Moscow, the message would be loud and clear.

Anna walked away from the bodies and returned to collect her binoculars, then she left the park and headed back into the city. Evans and Dalton were doing the same, packing up their rifles before disappearing into the night. They would rendezvous at the hotel in several hours, once they were certain they were clear of any heat. The operation had gone perfectly, but Anna had learned not to be overconfident. An incident with a British nuclear submarine had taught her that.

When she was a few blocks clear, she tossed the shell casings into a garbage can and put the pistol and binoculars down a storm drain. The gear was untraceable, but her training dictated her actions. With that taken care of, she pulled out her cell phone and dialed Chief Watkins. The MI6 director had personally ordered the operation and asked to be informed the moment it was complete.

When the call was answered, Anna spoke. "All three targets successfully identified and eliminated."

"Excellent." Watkins no longer sounded tired. "The prime minister asked me to thank you personally for your work tonight. Now we have another job for you—Jack Emery."

Anna frowned at the mention of Emery's name. She felt a tingle in her leg, right where she'd been shot on the night she'd helped Emery save the word. She'd been wounded so badly that it'd taken months of rehabilitation to get her back on her feet and back to work. She swallowed hard, forced down the feelings. She'd thought she was over it, but hearing his name dredged up the memories.

Watkins seemed to take Anna's silence as an invitation to continue. "The Americans have proposed a reduction in nuclear arsenals. It's something the PM wants to consider."

Anna stopped walking. "I struggle to see my role in this. Jack Emery is half a world away."

"Not for long. We have intelligence that he's headed to Moscow to meet with the Russians. We're pulling you out of Kharkov and sending you there to find out what's going on."

Anna frowned. It seemed like the prime minister picking up the phone to the president would be enough to figure that out, but she understood the hesitation. For a matter so serious, sometimes it was better to work through back channels between trusted friends and advisors. If she could talk to Jack Emery, she could help the UK government make an assessment about disarming or not. Besides, if he was headed for Moscow, she wanted to help keep him safe.

"I'll take care of it."

"IT's ABOUT TIME!" Kharlov glared at the waitress who'd brought food and drink for him and his men. "Keep it coming."

"Yes, of course." The waitress plastered on a fake smile, clearly afraid of the people she was serving. "Enjoy your meals."

Kharlov picked up his knife and fork. He was famished after delivering another huge shipment of guns and explosives to the Ukrainian militia. Things had gone smoothly. His buyers had handed over the money, and he'd given them the guns that would help the good people of Ukraine fight against those trying to steal their country. If his delivery led to a prolonged conflict and increased the chances of further orders, that was all the better.

Kharlov was about to start eating when he felt the tension in the room increase. He looked at his men, but their eyes were locked on something behind him. Kharlov's eyes narrowed when he saw Natalya, his deputy, reach into her coat and grip a pistol. With a sigh, he put down his cutlery and turned to face whoever had killed the mood. Of all the people he might expect, Kharlov hadn't expected to see the man standing behind him.

"Vangel Stevanovski!" Kharlov's voice revealed his surprise. "I never thought I'd see you again."

"Mr. Kharlov." Stevanovski held his hat in two hands, clutching it near his paunch like a child protecting his favorite toy. He seemed terrified. "May I speak with you a minute?"

"Of course!" Kharlov gestured for his man sitting opposite him to vacate the seat, untouched steak and all. "Sit!"

"Thank you." Stevanovski relaxed a little as he moved around the table to sit, though he still seemed uncertain.

Kharlov's eyes tracked Stevanovski as he moved. The Macedonian man looked nothing like he had twenty-five years ago, the last time Kharlov had seen him. Stevanovski had been a Yugoslav general during the wars that fractured that country. He was loved and hated in equal measure on both sides of the conflict. He'd also been a customer of Kharlov's until he'd accepted a weapon shipment, paid for it, then done the unforgiveable.

Kharlov picked up his knife and fork again and took a bite of steak. As he was chewing, he tried to figure out why Stevanovski would reappear after so much time. Kharlov had never managed to find the man, yet he'd come right to Kharlov. It made no sense. "So, Vangel, how have you been all these years?"

"Tired." Stevanovski wore a weary smile. "I have cancer. I know you've been searching for me. I want to end the uncertainty and make sure my family is safe before I die."

"The times are uncertain." Kharlov shrugged. He loved uncertainty. His business thrived on it. "But I'm prepared to talk about how you'd like to make them less so, given your health."

Kharlov flipped the steak knife and drove it into Stevanovski's hand as hard as he could. The sharp serrated blade penetrated right through flesh and bit into the hardwood table beneath. Stevanovski let out a guttural scream and grabbed at the knife, but Kharlov didn't release his grip on the handle. Instead, he looked at the man through cold and dispassionate eyes, enjoying the pain and the terror he saw on Stevanovski's face.

"I sell my goods to anyone who'll pay a fair price." Kharlov spoke softly, a contrast to the other man's loud screams and desperate pleading. "You owe me a great deal of money."

"Please!" Stevanovski's voice was more desperate, more visceral. "I—"

"Don't interrupt." Kharlov twisted the knife, earning an anguished howl. "We had a simple business arrangement. I delivered the goods, and you paid for them. Sound familiar?"

"Yes!"

"All was good, but then my man who had the cash was ambushed, and my money was stolen." Kharlov twisted the knife again. "Sound familiar?"

"Yes!" Stevanovski sobbed. "Yes!"

"Then, when I sought reimbursement, I was never able to

find you. The debt, plus the murder of my man, plus interest adds up to quite a bill. I—" Kharlov was interrupted when someone placed a hand on his shoulder and squeezed it. He turned to face the interruption with fury in his eyes. "What?"

Natalya was undeterred by her boss's anger. "Our Russian friends have arrived, Dmitry. You should finish this up."

Kharlov frowned, until logic penetrated the angry haze that had overcome him. It wasn't every day you had the chance to settle a score, but he knew time was of the essence when the Russians came calling. He nodded at Natalya and turned back to Stevanovski, who hadn't dared to move the knife. He looked like a caged animal—desperate and pathetic—and although Kharlov had planned to toy with the man, it was time to end this.

"My men will take you far away. You will dig your own grave and be buried alive." Kharlov's voice was softer now, almost tender. "I have a family myself. I love them very deeply, and I wouldn't want them punished for my mistakes. Nor should yours be. If you cooperate, our business will be done and your family will be safe."

"Yes." The relief on Stevanovski's face was clear, despite his pain. "Thank you, Mr. Kharlov. I'm going to die in three weeks anyway, but now I know my family will be safe."

Kharlov removed the knife from Stevanovski's hand and gestured for his men to take him away. Kharlov watched the man go, impressed by his stoicism in the face of a horrible death. He respected and admired a man who would front up to his doom to protect his family. Only then did Kharlov turn to face the new arrival, a man dressed in a business suit and tie.

"Mr. Kharlov." The Russian man clearly didn't care about the exchange with Stevanovski. "Nice to see you again."

"I'm popular today." Kharlov sighed. Whenever he saw the Russian, he knew his business was about to face disruption. "What can I do for you?"

Though Kharlov was in charge of most of the arms deals in Eastern Europe and North Africa, he didn't control everything. The Russian was Kharlov's messenger from inside the Russian Ministry of Foreign Affairs. He appeared sporadically to warn Kharlov when his business in Eastern Europe was about to be curtailed. Still, as annoying as it was, it was better to be told where Russia was about to hit than find himself in the middle of it all.

"I'm here to recommend you move your attention elsewhere." The Russian handed Kharlov a map. "We'll be pushing on the southeast front and consolidating our hold on Kharkov."

Kharlov frowned, his mind glancing back to his encounter with Stevanovski just a moment ago. "My family is in Merefa, near Kharkov. I assume you won't be pushing that deep?"

The Russian considered the name of the town for just a moment then shook his head. Kharlov nodded. Nothing else needed to be said. His family would be safe, but his business in Ukraine was done for the moment. He'd just been warned that Russia was going to direct even more attention into Ukraine and that anyone else playing in the area would suffer. That suited Kharlov just fine. Business was plentiful elsewhere, and he was happy to be agile.

As the Russian turned and made for the exit, Kharlov wiped Stevanovski's blood off the knife and took another bite of his steak.

4

eports have confirmed that Russian troops have crossed the border and are on their way to Kharkov, the second-largest city in Ukraine. Russia claims its troops are moving in simply to protect the interests of ethnic Russians in Kharkov, who have risen up and formed their own people's committee. Though Ukraine has no hope of throwing the Russians out, troops from many NATO countries, including America, have continued to flood surrounding member countries with boots and hardware, guarding against the possibility of Russian incursions deeper into Europe. Although the global community's patience with Russian Prime Minister Sokolov appears to be growing thin, he shows no signs of moderating his actions.

—New York Standard

Jack pulled his baseball cap down low over his head as he wheeled his suitcase through Sheremetyevo International Airport in Moscow. He was certain Russian agents were watching him, and that was fine so long as nobody else recognized him. Anonymity had been a strict condition of his visit to Moscow, and it felt like any chance of a nuclear deal rested on his ability to stay hidden.

He hadn't expected to be in Moscow at all, but sometimes his job required him to roll with the punches. The previous day, after hours of telephone discussions with representatives from the other nuclear powers, Jack had received a call from the Russian Foreign Minister, Veronika Oreshkin. It had been a surprise, because Jack had been trying to contact the Russian government for days without luck, and he could remember the conversation vividly...

"Mr. Emery, my name is Veronika Oreshkin." Her thick Russian accent was laced with urgency. "I don't have much time."

Jack frowned, confused by her tone, and decided to let her do the talking. "Okay. What can I do for you, Minister?"

"I'm intrigued by your proposal and would like to discuss it in person." She paused, as if her next words were going to be awkward. "I'm not authorized to do so officially..."

Jack selected his words carefully, certain the call was being recorded by the Russians. "What are you proposing?"

"If you travel to Moscow, anonymously, I can arrange for us to have discreet talks about your proposal. But there's to be no attention and no media..."

That was how Jack had found himself in Moscow.

Jack reached the exit and joined the line for a cab. Usually, he would have been met by a private car or a government escort, but Oreshkin had told him to catch a cab. He waited for only a minute before reaching the front of the line. As he waited for the attendant to assign him a cab, he noticed the man acting strange, directing travelers in line behind Jack into cabs and forcing him to wait.

A tingle shot down Jack's spine. Something was wrong. He was alone and anonymous in Russia, and it suddenly felt like Oreshkin had lured him to Moscow for something other than a discussion about nuclear disarmament. He was about to walk back inside the airport when the attendant finally pointed him to a cab. It looked the same as the others, and he had no idea why he'd been forced to wait, but he didn't sweat the issue.

The vehicle came to a stop, and the trunk popped open, but the driver stayed inside the vehicle. Jack sighed and hauled his case into the vehicle. It seemed Russian hospitality was as good as advertised. He slammed the trunk closed, rounded the cab, and took the seat behind the female driver. She didn't say a word as he handed her a card with the name of his hotel written on it.

As the car started moving, Jack closed his eyes and exhaled slowly. He was tired. The preliminary negotiations about the nuclear deal had been long and exhausting, but the results were promising. He was pleased no country had flatly rejected the proposal, although none had committed to a deal, either. Every leader and government on Earth now knew how close they'd been to annihilation, so they were listening.

The Russians were the most resistant. Until Oreshkin's call, the Sokolov administration had refused to discuss the matter. Worse, Sokolov had publicly berated the United States for attempting to weaken Russia while, at the same time, subverting its interests in Eastern Europe. Jack was fine with their bluster for the moment, given Russia hadn't flatly refused a deal and he was about to meet with their foreign minister to discuss it.

Other countries offered more promise. France and China were on board for negotiations, while both India and Pakistan were happy to talk if the other did. The biggest surprise was the United Kingdom. The United Kingdom, America's closest ally, had yet to reach out or offer a public statement on the president's proposal. It seemed strange he was going to be talking to the Russians before the British...

"Hi, Jack." A familiar female voice laughed. "Ha, funny, hijack. I'm hysterical."

Jack's eyes shot open at the sound of the British accent, which was ridiculously out of place in a cab in the middle of Moscow. His eyes darted to the mirror, where he saw a familiar pair of eyes in the reflection. He hadn't seen her in about a year, but he would never forget her after what they'd been through together. Somehow, Anna Fowler was at the wheel of the cab.

When he'd recovered from his shock, Jack shook his head. "I don't even know what to say, Anna. It's good to see you."

"Likewise." She swerved and pounded on the horn as another car cut the taxi off. "Now, Mr. Special Envoy, I hear you want to speak with a representative of the British government?"

"Uh, yeah, but I wasn't expecting to do it here. What are you doing in Moscow? How did you know *I* would be in Moscow?"

"I was in the neighborhood." Her eyes twinkled in the mirror. "And your friends at MI6 know everything—you should know that by now."

"Okay." Jack's thinking recalibrated quickly. Though the British silence on the nuclear proposal had been strange, Jack hadn't expected to hear from them quite like this. Sending Fowler to intercept him in Moscow instead of the PM picking up the phone was unorthodox, but it was better than silence. He had to work with what he had. "Well, let's talk."

"Great." Fowler pulled the taxi over on the side of the highway. "My leaders want to know if you guys are serious about this disarmament business?"

Jack had faced the same question from every leader he'd spoken to. The rhetoric of a State of the Union address was one thing, but the resources and trust the president had placed in Jack to pursue the issue gave meaning to the words. He didn't blame the British prime minister for being unsure or reluctant. Prime Minister Egan was a bit of a wild card, a new player in the game following the death of his predecessor.

"You can tell them we're as serious as we can be." Jack smiled. "We're trying to get it done, but if we're to have a chance at success, we need the UK on board."

"Sounds like a plan." Fowler shifted in her seat and turned to face him. She had a warm smile. "I think Britain will come along for the ride, so long as the other powers are in."

"They are to varying degrees." Jack chose his words carefully. "We're not going to get a deal done easily or quickly, though."

"Particularly with the Russians pushing so hard into Eastern Europe... I only flew in from Kharkov this morning."

"What the hell were you doing in the middle of that shit show?"

"A little of this, a little of that." Her features darkened. "I wouldn't count on the Russians playing ball, though. Sokolov is a madman."

"I know. He hasn't said a word to us, so I'm talking to his foreign minister tomorrow afternoon." Jack shrugged. "Are you sticking around for a while?"

"Nowhere else to be until my flight out tomorrow morning. Why don't we go someplace nice for dinner?"

"Is there somewhere nice in Moscow?"

YURI SMILED as he watched four Russian tanks roll into Freedom Square, their tracks scraping the road as they advanced in a show of might. He'd been waiting on the sidewalk for hours, since he'd first received word that two battalions from Russia's 8th Combined Arms Army had crossed the border and were headed for Kharkov. The sight of the heavy armor was worth the wait. His chest was bursting with pride.

On either side of the tank convoy, squads of Russian infantry were watching the civilians bunched on the sidewalk and on balconies overhead, ready to respond to the slightest hint of trouble. Such a powerful display of military force in the middle of the day wasn't something the people of Kharkov would soon forget, especially after Yuri and his comrades had taken power in the darkness of night.

For Yuri, it was what he'd waited a lifetime for. He and his comrades had been in control of Kharkov for several weeks. After that first bloody evening, the cells of pro-Russian patriots had secured their hold on power. The surviving police and military forces had been overwhelmed, and the city's politicians had been locked up. Within days, the populace had fallen into line, and many of Yuri's fellow revolutionaries had formed a people's committee. After receiving word the previous day that the Ukrainian Army was planning to retake Kharkov, the people's committee had invited Russian troops into the city.

Yuri sighed. As pleased as he was to see the Russian troops taking control of Kharkov and signaling to the world that the change would endure, he couldn't believe his role was at an end. He'd been a critical part of the uprising, but the Russian Army had made it clear that they would take over the military situation from here. Yuri yearned to serve further, until all of Ukraine was nestled against the bosom of Russia.

He waited until the last Russian soldier had passed then turned to Stepan and Arsen. "We need to go meet him."

Yuri led them north on the exact same streets they'd walked to take Freedom Square on that first fateful night. Days ago, there hadn't been a single Russian flag on the route, but now they were hanging in windows and draped over balconies, showing passersby that those who lived inside supported the change that had occurred. Yuri sported a smile for the entire walk, until they reached the cellar of the townhouse from which they'd launched a revolution.

Being back in the house was bittersweet. It made him think of their deceased friends. They headed back to the same table in the basement where it had all started, minus two men. No words were spoken. There was nothing to say. They'd worked hard, and they'd succeeded. It was time to see what came next. The instructions from their Russian contact had been clear. The same man who'd orchestrated their role in the uprising had told them to meet in the cellar at noon on the day Russian troops entered the city.

They sat down at noon, but there was no sign of their contact. They waited in silence for one hour... two hours... They waited until it was clear nobody was coming.

Arsen slapped Yuri on the back. "He's not coming, Yuri. I think the Russians are done with us."

Yuri turned his head slowly and stared at Arsen. He

couldn't believe the poison coming out of the other man's mouth. "He'll come."

Yuri held the stare until Arsen shrugged. More hours passed in silence, all of them staring into space or amusing themselves on their cell phones. Finally, even Yuri had to concede that their man in Russian intelligence had forgotten about them. The feeling that they'd been used then abandoned caused bile to rise from the pit of Yuri's stomach. It burned his throat and mouth.

It burned almost as much as the words he knew he had to say. "He's not coming."

Stepan and Arsen both nodded solemnly and looked around the table, seemingly lost. For so long, their focus had been on liberating Kharkov, yet nobody had considered the possibility that their role might end with that. They'd expected to continue working with the Russians to liberate all of Ukraine, moving to other cities and towns to share all they'd learned with other patriots.

Yuri closed his eyes for a moment, then he opened his eyes again when he heard the sound of chairs scraping. His comrades were standing. "Where are you going?"

Arsen looked at Stepan then at Yuri. "Our orders were clear. We were to win Kharkov, hold out until the Russian troops arrived, and then stand down and wait for further orders."

"There's no more orders." Stepan shrugged. "The army is here, and the Russians are in control now, Yuri. They're done with us. It's time for things to get back to normal. I—"

"You both expect me to go back to working in a gas station?" Yuri scoffed. "Are you going to go back to working at a school, Arsen? Or will Stepan return to his awful wife?"

"What do you propose, Yuri?" Stepan raised an eyebrow,

ignoring the jibe about his wife. "It sounds like you have an idea you're not sharing with us."

Yuri did have an idea. He and his comrades had done the impossible—taken Kharkov from Ukraine and delivered it to Russia. Even if they had been forsaken by their contact, their fight wasn't over. There were more places begging to be freed from the tyrants in Kiev, and Yuri and his comrades were ready to do the heavy lifting. They had more than enough guns, supplies, and money to get the job done. If the Russians were prepared to snub Yuri and the other men who'd bled to free Kharkov, then to hell with them.

"After all we've achieved, we're not stopping." Yuri looked at his comrades with fire in his eyes. "We have guns, bombs, and contacts in some of the other cells. We just need the courage to keep going! There's a hundred smaller cities and towns between here and Kiev. Why can't we help to liberate some of them, as well?"

"You've got balls, Yuri. I'll give you that." Stepan laughed. "You want us to forget about Russian support and freelance in the middle of a war zone?"

Yuri grinned. "Spread the word. We're leaving Kharkov."

VERONIKA FLINCHED as stones and bottles pounded the armored limousine, which she was riding through the streets of Kharkov with Sokolov. Though the Russian Army had control of the streets and there were members of the prime minister's security detail in the motorcade, she couldn't think of a moment she'd been more afraid in her entire life. She felt like she was a plump pig marching through a market full of starving people.

She wasn't wanted here. Russia wasn't wanted here. Yet they were holding a parade.

"Are you sure we're safe?" Veronika asked the agent who was also riding in the back of the limousine with them. "The locals seem on edge."

"Very sure." The agent was a senior man from Russia's internal security service. He spoke from behind dark-tinted glasses, never looking away from the window. "The Army is in control of the city, and we have plenty of firepower in this convoy. You're as safe as if we were driving laps of the Kremlin."

Veronika frowned. Given the warning she'd received after the last cabinet meeting, Kharkov may well have been safer for her. "Are tanks useful if we're dragged from the car and lynched?"

Sokolov laughed from the seat next to her. "Bottles can't hurt us! Give the locals their fun, Veronika! They're showing more resistance than their military! Cowards!"

Veronika crossed her arms and kept quiet. In truth, she was as afraid of Sokolov as she was the locals. He'd been jovial all day, since he'd ordered the Army into the city. Then once they'd taken it, he'd surprised Veronika by inviting her on a tour. The fact they were driving through Kharkov together when she'd been an outspoken critic of the continued aggression in Ukraine felt like another message from the prime minister.

For Veronika, it was only the start of her problems. Twenty-four hours ago, she felt like things had been going perfectly. She'd managed to warn the arms dealer she'd been using to prop up the Ukrainian resistance about the renewed push, then she'd organized a meeting with Jack Emery to discuss the nuclear proposal through back channels. She'd gone to bed thinking everything was under control.

Then Sokolov had sent a car to her house in the early hours of the morning. Two armed agents had escorted her to the airport with no explanation of where she was going. That was the first alarm bell. In Russia, politicians often disappeared in the darkness of night, and Sokolov was the sort who would continue that long tradition. The second alarm started ringing when Veronika's request to contact her own secretary was denied. The third was Sokolov's good mood, because when he was happy, Veronika generally wasn't. She had to regain the initiative and Sokolov's trust.

"Prime Minister"—Veronika spoke slowly, trying to get Sokolov's attention amid the color and movement of his victory parade—"may I discuss a matter with you?"

Sokolov frowned. He was in a good mood, but her words had clearly put up his guard. "Of course, Veronika. You don't need to ask."

She could have laughed at his statement, but to do so would have wasted the small window she had to extract herself from whatever mess she was in. "I wanted to tell you I've changed my mind about our Ukrainian adventure. I wanted to apologize for doubting you and offer my assistance moving forward."

As another bottle pounded into the window of the car, Sokolov's face clouded over and he sat back and crossed his arms. He knew Veronika had opposed the push into Eastern Europe, but he had enough allies in cabinet that her opposition didn't matter. Though Russia had enjoyed success, the capture of Kharkov had galvanized the international community against Sokolov. While the US had been measured, other countries had reacted strongly.

Sokolov spoke after a few moments, softly and slowly. "I find it amusing that you've had a change of heart now, Veronika. I could have used your help when the dogs in London and Berlin and Paris were barking, when they threatened sanctions if we didn't halt our efforts to reclaim what is ours."

Veronika frowned. She didn't feel like their conversation was going well. "Prime Minister Nikolai... I—"

He held up a hand. "Now that those sanctions have become reality and NATO troops are on our doorstep, it's too late. We approach an inevitable confrontation in which I do not see a use for you. In fact, only the Americans are showing any sort of restraint, which at first, I found amazing, given their usual bluster..."

Veronika kept her face impassive, unsure about where he was going with his story. If he hadn't expected the international community to react to Russia annexing a city of 1.5 million people, his delusion had finally overcome reality. It was also clear why the Americans were exercising restraint. They were holding off to see if Russia would play ball on the nuclear talks, which the McGhinnist administration had clearly deemed the highest priority.

He sighed. "I found it amazing, at first, then I found it troubling, so I had the intelligence services look into the situation..."

Veronika's eyes widened as the agent sitting opposite her produced a pistol and pointed it at her. "I—"

Sokolov didn't let her speak. "My men found evidence of your collusion with the Americans. You called Jack Emery, and now he's in Moscow. That's all the evidence of treason I need."

"Sir, please!" Veronika swallowed hard and forced her eyes to move from the barrel of the pistol to Sokolov's eyes.

"Meeting with Emery was a way to buy time. If we convince the Americans we're serious about their nuclear proposal, they'll continue to accommodate our push into Eastern Europe. If we refuse to talk, they have no reason to show restraint."

Sokolov didn't look impressed by her words. He locked eyes with her and snarled, "That was not your decision to make!"

"I—"

Sokolov held up a hand to forestall her response. "I have ordered Emery dealt with, and now I must decide what to do with you, Veronika. I made your career, but in return for this amazing opportunity, you committed the foulest deceit. You may as well have just knifed me in the back..."

Veronika kept quiet as Sokolov's voice trailed off. He crossed his arms and brooded, which usually meant he was about to take a dangerous new decision. She considered talking more, but with the agent aiming the pistol at her, she decided to keep her mouth shut. Sokolov had used the word *treason*, which meant her fate had been decided. If it hadn't, she doubted speaking in the next few minutes would improve her chances of survival.

She'd gambled everything to keep her dream for Russia alive and lost everything.

5

There have been several days of violent protests on the streets of Kharkov, Ukraine, after Russian Prime Minister Nikolai Sokolov visited the city. The tour was a huge show of support for the pro-Russian partisans that have taken political control of the city, while also being an unmistakable show of defiance to other world leaders. Russia has been the target of intense criticism in recent weeks, after opening several new fronts in a conflict that had been largely stagnant for some months. Sokolov appears set to continue his push beyond Russia's borders and into Eastern Europe, no matter the resistance or the cost to Russia's standing on the world stage.

—New York Standard

JACK LEANED against the wall of a nondescript townhouse, with his hands in his pockets and his patience growing thin. He was waiting for Veronika Oreshkin, who'd insisted on meeting him out front of the Russian Ministry of Foreign Affairs. It was a strange place to meet, rather than her office or the United States embassy or a neutral space—like a hotel lobby—but her conditions had been strict. Now she was late.

HE'D NEVER KNOWN the protocol for how long to wait when someone was late for a meeting, but he decided to cut his losses if she didn't show in the next five minutes. As the minutes bled away, it felt like any chance at a nuclear deal bled away along with it. He'd flown halfway around the world for a clandestine meeting about the nuclear deal, only to be stood up. He'd been played for a fool.

WITH THE FINAL seconds of his self-imposed deadline ticking down, Jack glared at the nearby Ministry of Foreign Affairs building and wondered which of the hundreds of windows was Oreshkin's office. He pictured her sitting at her desk, enjoying a laugh at his expense. He even briefly considered going into the lobby and asking to see her. If she wouldn't come to him, he would go to her. But he doubted that was a smart move.

AFTER THE TIME WAS UP, Jack sighed and pushed himself off the wall. "What a goddamn waste of time."

HE STARTED to walk south along Smolensky Boulevard, which had five lanes running each way. He had his eyes peeled for a cab, keen to get back to his hotel then to the airport as soon as possible. Within a minute, he caught the attention of a taxi driver who'd stopped at a set of traffic lights just down the street, so Jack stopped on the sidewalk and waited.

EXHALING SLOWLY, Jack turned his head to the left, trying to work out the kinks in his muscles as he waited for the cab to get through the lights and the heavy traffic. His eyes narrowed then widened. Two men wearing black business suits and white shirts were approaching, their eyes locked on him. The second he spotted them, one of the men reached inside his coat. They'd been watching him and started to follow him once he'd started to move.

JACK'S STOMACH SANK. He clenched his fists and ran onto the road. A glance over his shoulder confirmed the men had drawn their pistols and started to give chase. His gut had been right, and he needed to get out of there. He ran as fast as he could toward the cab, hoping to take it to the US embassy, which was two miles north. There, he would find some Marines who would take issue with any Russians trying to nab someone with an American diplomatic passport.

WHEN JACK WAS ONLY a few yards from the cab, the lights changed. Horns blared, and a dozen drivers shouted curses at Jack as they passed him, but his focus was on the cab. As it drew closer, Jack reached out to grip the door handle on the passenger side. It was locked. The driver looked straight ahead and accelerated, clearly not wanting to get involved. Jack stumbled along with the car as it increased speed, until he was forced to let go of the handle.

JACK FLINCHED and kept moving when he heard the crack of a pistol shot. The shot had missed, but the next one might not. Things had just become deadly. He kept low and ran as fast as he could through traffic and across the road. More shots popped off, and pistol rounds slammed into the bodywork of cars, causing drivers to swerve and vehicles to collide. Luckily, none of the hot lead found its way into his body, and Jack made it across Smolensky Boulevard intact.

WITH THE CAB A DISTANT MEMORY, Jack's next hope was to lose them in the tangle of back streets between Smolensky Boulevard and the Moskva River. Jack didn't know the streets and risked getting lost or stuck, but he had no other option. Although he didn't know who was after him or why, they'd already popped off and would take him down if they had the chance. He had to lose them in the maze.

JACK RAN down a side street then an alley. On either side of him were the rear of apartment buildings, their fire escapes clinging to the walls like creeping vines. He heard shouts behind him, so he kept running until he reached a fork in the alley. Looking left and right, Jack felt fear rise in the pit of his stomach—in both directions, the alley ended in a dead end.

JACK'S EYES darted all around, looking for a solution, but there was nothing that could help him escape armed pursuers. He saw only dumpsters and the normal detritus that could be found in any back alley the world over. He turned back around and started to run back down the alley, hoping he could get back to the entrance before his pursuers arrived, but he was too slow. The two Russians had beaten him to the mouth of the alley. He was trapped.

JACK PULLED up short and held his hands wide as the Russians aimed their pistols at him. He shouted as loud as he could, "I'm an American diplomat. Killing me will start a war!"

"THE PRIME MINISTER SENDS HIS REGARDS," one of the gunmen said in broken English. "You shouldn't have come to Moscow."

THIS WAS IT. After escaping dozens of near-death situations over the past decade, he'd reached the end. Jack closed his eyes and waited for the inevitable. He heard the crack of a pistol... but he felt nothing.

JACK OPENED his eyes and stared in confusion as one Russian slumped to the ground. The other turned to aim his pistol at whatever new threat had arrived, out of Jack's line of sight. The Russian was too slow. Another pistol shot boomed. Blood and brain matter sprayed from the side of the Russian's head, and he slumped to the ground next to his downed colleague.

SILENCE FILLED THE ALLEYWAY, and Anna Fowler entered his sight.

JACK STARED AT HER. "What the fuck are you doing here?"

"HELLO TO YOU TOO!" Fowler sported a grim expression as she put two shots into each Russian's head. "I thought we were past this point in our relationship."

"WHICH POINT?"

"THE POINT where I had to shoot people to save your ass." She flashed a small smile. "I stuck around in case the Russians tried to pull something."

"THEY DID..." Jack walked to where Anna was standing over the bodies of the dead Russians. He'd seen more dead bodies than he would have liked in the last few years, but the trauma of seeing them was lessened when they were trying to kill. He bent down and picked up one of their pistols. He wasn't familiar with the weapon, but a pistol was a pistol in circumstances like this. Jack locked eyes with Anna. "What now?"

~

"Now?" Anna's grin disappeared as she ejected her magazine and slammed a fresh one home. "We run."

SHE BROKE into a jog and led Emery away from the dead Russians. They'd been the first to eat a bullet today, but she doubted they would be the last. If Sokolov had decided to bring down the hammer on one of the American president's top advisors, his goons would keep trying until the job was done. Though Anna had saved Emery by a split second, she'd played her hand, leaving them both vulnerable. She had to get them out of Moscow.

THEY RAN through more back streets and headed for Anna's car, which was parked on the banks of the Moskva River. Around each corner, she expected to run into more Russian goons, but they made it to the car without issue. An hour earlier, the vehicle had felt like a poorly performing family sedan. It suddenly seemed like a mighty chariot that would carry them to safety. It was amazing how circumstances could change a person's perspective on such things.

ANNA DUG INTO HER POCKET, found her car keys, and unlocked the vehicle. "Time to get out of here."

EMERY WAS BENT OVER, breathing heavily, his hands on his knees. He glanced at the car then at her. "You're driving a Lada?"

"Get in the car." Anna rounded to the driver's side and got in, while Emery took the passenger seat. She rested her pistol on her lap, started the car, and got them on the road.

Despite his quip about their ride, Anna could tell Emery was already more relaxed. He was slowly catching his breath and calming down. She knew she needed to get him to safety soon, because when his adrenaline levels dropped, he would crash hard.

"You told me you were flying out this morning." Emery was looking to her for answers. "How did you find me?"

"A little bit of James Bond trickery..." She glanced at him and flashed a wide smile. "I put a tracker in your food at dinner the other day."

Emery blinked a few times. "I *swallowed* it?"

"Relax, it'll pass in a few days, easier than the steak will." She turned back to the road. "I wanted to keep an eye on you."

"Well, thanks..."

They settled into silence for a few minutes, and Anna

focused on driving. She headed north, looking for a bridge that would get them across the river, out of the city center, and onto the highway out of town. With each mile they drove, their chances of survival increased exponentially. The Russians had planned on killing Emery on their turf, but he was on the loose in a huge country that had lots of places to hide.

"WHERE ARE WE GOING?" Emery had a hint of concern in his voice. "I need to get to the United States Embassy."

"YOU COULD DO THAT..." Anna shifted gears and overtook a slow-moving dump truck. "But it'd be the last mistake you ever make."

"WHY?"

"YOU GOT the attention of Sokolov's personal hit team. They cut their teeth taking down stupid people. They'll expect you to go there, so we're... Damn."

"WHAT?"

"COMPANY."

ANNA HAD JUST CAUGHT sight of a black BMW in her rearview

mirror, weaving through traffic and driving well above the speed limit. She wasn't sure they were bad guys, but she would be damned if she gave up her lead on the other car to find out, given she would have enough trouble outrunning the BMW in the Lada as it was. She gripped the wheel tighter and prepared for a dogfight.

SHE TOOK a sharp left onto a bridge over the Moskva River and hit the E-30 about twenty yards ahead of the BMW. Free of the prison of central Moscow, she needed to get them to Belarus—the closest country where British and American assets could extract them. It was a seven-hour drive, but if she could get them out of the city and switch cars a few times, she was confident it could be done.

ANNA TRIED to lose the BMW in the traffic that was on the E-30, but she failed miserably. The BMW driver had her in range and was driving a far more capable vehicle. He inched closer with every passing second. Finally, the black BMW was so tight on her tail, it was like the Lada's shadow. Knowing she was running out of time, she kept the chase going in hopes another opportunity would come along.

"SHIT!" Anna cursed when the BMW nudged them for the first time. "These guys clearly got some tips from American highway cops!"

EMERY WAS PANICKING, craning around to look at their pursuers. "What can I do to help, Anna?"

ANNA CLENCHED HER TEETH TOGETHER. "PRAY."

ANNA GRUNTED as the BMW slammed into the rear of the Lada once again. This time, the driver didn't back off. She fought the steering as the more powerful car pushed into her vehicle, but she lost control, and the Lada veered off course. A second later, they slammed into a highway sign. Anna's teeth smashed together as she was thrown forward in her seat, only to have her momentum violently arrested by the seatbelt.

THEN IT WAS OVER. Anna groaned and coughed as she fumbled for the button to unbuckle the seatbelt. She felt like she'd been punched in the chest, but she was alive. Once clear of the seatbelt, she focused on finding her pistol. The Russians would be on them in a second, and she needed to be ready. The weapon was no longer in her lap, so she reached down and searched in the footwell of the vehicle.

"ANNA?" Emery's voice had an edge of concern, though he also sounded groggy from the crash. "We've got company."

ANNA KEPT SEARCHING for the pistol as she looked out the smashed driver's-side window. As she'd expected, two Russian agents were pointing pistols at her, shouting something she couldn't understand. The message was clear, though. She gave up on her search for the pistol and slowly raised her hands. The game was up.

ONE OF THE Russians kept his pistol trained on Anna while the other one moved around to Jack's side. Anna locked eyes with her assailant, watching and waiting for an opportunity as he reached for the door handle. The door popped and squealed open, clearly damaged from the crash. The Russian grabbed Anna by the arm, dragged her out of the car, and tossed her onto the ground.

"ON YOUR KNEES." The Russian spoke in terrible English.

ANNA SNEERED at him as she did as he'd instructed. Although she was trained to find an advantage in any situation, the slightest edge that would let her prevail, this one felt hopeless. She glanced at the highway, where motorists were speeding past and minding their own business. She glanced at Emery, who was still in the car and had a gun trained on him, a man likely in the final moments of his life.

THEN SHE LOOKED BACK to the Russian and heard the boom of a pistol.

JACK SQUEEZED on the trigger again and again, his pistol

booming in the close confines of the car. Each round punched through the Lada's door. Red patches blossomed on the Russian man's white shirt, and he dropped out of sight. Jack cried out with relief when the other man didn't fire the pistol he'd had trained on Jack, but he knew it wasn't over yet. Fowler had saved him earlier, and now he owed it to her to—

ANOTHER SHOT BOOMED, and Jack's head snapped to the other side, expecting to see Fowler dead on the ground. Instead, she was wrestling with the Russian who'd been standing over her. Although she was holding her own for now, forcing the bigger man to focus on her instead of Jack, her opponent looked equally skilled at hand-to-hand combat. Jack tried to line up a shot, but he couldn't get a clear aim.

"GO, ANNA!" Jack whooped when she twisted the Russian's wrist, forcing her assailant to let go of the gun. Then the Russian landed a blow to her temple, and she staggered back. "Fuck!"

JACK WANTED TO HELP HER, but he wasn't achieving anything from inside the car. He turned his attention back to the door, pulling on the handle and pushing on the door. The crash had warped the door frame so badly that the passenger-side door may as well have been welded shut. After trying a few firm shoves, he gave up on the door and started to climb over to the driver's side, where Fowler had exited from.

FOWLER AND THE RUSSIAN, two highly trained combatants, were duking it out. Despite the Russian's size advantage, Fowler was putting her edge in speed to good use. She moved like a gazelle, landing multiple blows for each of the Russian's, but he was bigger and seemed to hit like a truck. It seemed like both of them had a chance to land a killer blow at any time.

UNWILLING TO RISK Fowler's life on a coin-flip, Jack climbed out of the vehicle, raised the pistol, and approached the Russian. The other man's eyes narrowed, and Jack fired, but the Russian darted behind Fowler. The shot missed. With a friend in between him and the Russian, Jack was powerless. He winced when the Russian landed a punch on Fowler's chin that staggered her and made her legs go weak.

JACK CURSED as the Russian caught Fowler before she fell and used her as a human shield. He couldn't chance any more shots as the Russian kept her upright by wrapping her in a headlock using his forearm. Both the Russian and Fowler were facing Jack. Blood oozed from the Russian's nose, and Fowler looked like shit. The situation wasn't ideal. They were elite operatives, and he was an amateur who'd barely ever fired a gun.

"LET HER GO!" Jack knew they were running out of time, but he couldn't get a good shot at the Russian.

"FUCKING AMERICANS." The Russian spat blood and grinned.

His teeth were bloody. "I have help on the way, and you are a long way from home."

"TAKE THE SHOT, JACK!" Fowler's cry came out in a sort of muffled whisper, as the Russian pressed his forearm into her throat. "Take the *fucking* shot!"

JACK TOOK THE SHOT. The Russian's head popped back a little, then he fell, dragging Fowler halfway to the ground before she managed to detach herself from his dead weight. She fell to one knee, coughing and gripping her throat but never taking her eyes off Jack. They were filled with curiosity and surprise, which was understandable, since Jack had nailed the Russian square between the eyes.

FROZEN ON THE SPOT, Jack exhaled heavily, unable to believe he'd taken one life to save another. He'd killed before, but he'd never taken down two elite killers in less than a minute. After a few seconds, he gathered his senses and lowered the pistol. Although Fowler had stopped coughing, she still looked a little stunned. He walked over to her and held out a hand to help her to her feet.

"THANKS, JACK." Fowler's voice was raspy, but she seemed okay as she took his hand and stood up to her full height. "When did you learn to shoot like that?"

"I've been going to a range a few times per week since I got back from the UK last year. I didn't ever want to feel helpless again."

"My head thanks you for it." She smiled and reached down to take the Russian's gun. "We need to get out of here."

"You said that before. It didn't go so well..."

Fowler snorted and walked to the BMW, which had only minor damage to the front bumper caused by ramming the Lada. Jack glanced from the dead Russian to the trashed Lada. On the other side of the car, another man was probably dead. He wanted to check, but they didn't have time. He followed Fowler to the BMW and climbed inside. The second he closed the door, she floored the vehicle.

"What now?" Jack was gripping the pistol like it was a life raft. "I doubt they'll give up."

"They won't." Fowler shrugged. "We'll need to figure something else out to be extracted."

"Okay." Jack nodded. He wasn't sure what Fowler had in mind, but he trusted her.

THEY SETTLED into silence and drove for about half an hour, heading farther out of Moscow. It was the first time he'd had to think since running from the Russian Foreign Ministry Building. The last hour had been one of the most intense experiences of his life. He'd gone from hoping to meet with Oreshkin about the nuclear deal to wondering if he would even escape Russia. Any chance of a deal had turned to ash. That almost upset him more than the close call prior to Fowler's arrival.

JACK TURNED to face Fowler as she pulled the car into a gas station and killed the engine. "Thanks for getting me out of there earlier, Anna. I'd be dead if you hadn't shown up."

"AND I'D BE a dead woman if you hadn't put one between the eyes of the big guy." She shrugged. "Let's call it even."

SHE DUG into her pocket and pulled out her cell phone. "Call McGhinnist. Tell him you're okay. Tell him we're headed for Belarus. The Russians can't locate this phone, but they'll listen in."

JACK NODDED, dialed the White House switchboard, and put the phone to his ear. The call connected quickly. "This is Jack Emery. I need to speak with the president immediately."

THE CALL WAS CONNECTED in under five seconds. "Jack? What

the hell is going on in Moscow? Davidson just told me that the communication intercepts have gone crazy."

JACK HAD to choose his words carefully, in case the Russians were listening in, but there was one thing he could be blunt about. "Sokolov tried to take me out."

"WHAT?" McGhinnist sounded incredulous. There was a long pause as the president took a second to digest the information. "Does he want to start a war?"

"I WAS WAITING to meet with Oreshkin when two of his goons shot at me and chased me." Jack paused, not wanting to mention Fowler. "I got away. They chased me in a car, but I got away."

"JACK?" Caleb Davidson, the national security advisor, chimed in. "Tell us where you are. We'll get you out of there as soon as we can."

"I'M GOING to take care of that myself, Caleb. I'm in a car and driving to Belarus." Jack looked at Fowler, who nodded. "Bill, find out what happened to Oreshkin. I'll call you when I'm safe."

6

Ms. Oreshkin has not been seen in public since joining Russian Prime Minister Sokolov on a tour of occupied Kharkov. Although the Kremlin has been tight-lipped about her disappearance, saying only that Minister Oreshkin is battling an illness, the Standard *can confirm that key members of Ms. Oreshkin's staff have not spoken to the Minister in several days. With Russia's adventures in Ukraine and tense global negotiations about nuclear weapons ongoing, the timing for the disappearance of such a key Russian moderate could not be worse. Several leading experts on Russian politics have speculated that without Oreshkin to shackle his worst instincts, Prime Minister Sokolov has the potential to become more dangerous than ever.*

—*New York Standard*

Yuri crouched on his haunches and looked to his left, where Arsen was keeping low, as well. The two men shared a look of concern, just like they had five minutes ago when the deadline had come and gone without Stepan's return. Their friend had volunteered to scout the town of Merefa, to see if any Ukrainian Army troops were posted there, while Yuri and others who'd liberated Kharkov waited safely on the outskirts of town. Stepan hadn't returned at the time he was supposed to.

"We need to decide what to do, Yuri." Arsen glanced at the town. "The others are waiting for our instructions."

Yuri nodded. His shoulder muscles were knotted, and his head was pounding from the stress of waiting for Stepan. He'd hoped his friend would return to tell them the coast was clear and that they only had a few cops to worry about. Instead, for all he knew, the cops were waiting for them, or there could be a platoon of Ukrainian Army troops camped in the town.

Yuri had a decision to make, but there was only one choice. He and his comrades hadn't won Kharkov by being timid. He flashed a smile at Arsen. "It's time. Text the others."

It was time to take the town for Russia. Yuri stood to his full height and started to walk toward the town. As Arsen's text went out, more men and women from Kharkov followed him toward their latest conquest. Every patriot carried a different weapon, but they were all united in purpose. No matter what had happened to Stepan, Yuri knew there was no way a town of barely twenty thousand people could stop them... until a rifle report boomed out.

Yuri ducked instinctively, not sure who'd fired the shot. Either way, the element of surprise had been lost. When no other shots followed and with none of his comrades seemingly hurt, Yuri broke into a run. Time was of the essence. Like in Kharkov, the plan was to secure the large public spaces and key buildings first before moving to quell any armed resistance.

Yuri and some of his comrades were responsible for the school. They headed off down a short boulevard lined with trees. Yuri flicked off the safety of his sawed-off shotgun as his eyes scanned the front of the school, looking for trouble. It seemed quiet, which wasn't surprising in the middle of the night, though he could see something hanging from the flagpole out front of the school in the pale moonlight.

Yuri frowned. "What's that?"

"It looks like..." Arsen gasped. "It looks like a person!"

Yuri's eyes widened and closed on the flagpole. Ignoring the shouts of his comrades to stay back, Yuri got closer to the school. Stepan hung from the flagpole. Even though there was only a little light to see by, Yuri could tell it was his friend. Stepan wasn't moving, and his blood was dripping onto the ground. That one of the heroes who'd taken Kharkov could be treated so brutally ignited a fire in Yuri's core.

Yuri took a few steps closer to the flagpole. He untied the rope keeping Stepan suspended in midair then slowly lowered his friend. The others grabbed Stepan's body, eased him to the ground. Arsen checked for a pulse then looked up at Yuri, shaking his head. Yuri closed his eyes. He'd agreed to send Stepan into town alone, and the consequences of that decision would haunt him forever.

"Yuri, something is wrong..." Arsen said. "We should get out of here and link up with the others."

"No!" Yuri turned and shoved Arsen in the chest. "Whoever did this is going to answer to me. I... Ambush!"

Yuri dived to the dirt as gunfire roared around him. The shooter he'd seen in the window of the school out of the corner of his eye was firing at his comrades, joined by several others with pistols and rifles. A second later, Yuri's comrades returned fire, turning the situation into a confusing mess—

shots from all sorts of weapons, shattering glass, screams of agony, shouts of anger, and sprays of blood.

Yuri screamed as he raised the sawed-off shotgun and fired at one of the windows. The weapon boomed, glass shattered, and the window frame exploded. The shooter who'd been sheltering behind it dropped. Yuri knew he had one shot left, so he aimed at the next window and fired again. A woman went down in a shower of wood, glass, and blood.

Without ammunition, the shotgun was useless, so Yuri tossed it and reached for the pistol that was stuffed down the back of his jeans. Gripping the pistol, he climbed to his feet, leveled it at the school, and started to fire again. Yuri and his comrades were gaining the upper hand, and resistance from inside the school was starting to ease. The ambush had taken a toll, but the locals didn't seem to have the numbers or the firepower to win a decisive battle.

The gunfire slowed then stopped. The furious exchange of fire had lasted less than a minute, but half a dozen people on his side were dead or wounded on the school grounds. Yuri couldn't see anyone else left standing in the school, but he guessed the same number of local townspeople had been taken down. They'd fought bravely, armed with shotguns and hunting rifles, but it was over.

"Inside, now!" Yuri started to walk to the door of the school, keen to maintain the upper hand over any defenders who might be left inside. "Arsen, get the door."

Yuri waited while Arsen shot the lock on the school door, then he leveled his pistol and led his team inside. The school had one long hallway with four rooms on either side. Yuri gestured for a couple of his men to take the first room on the right, then he moved into the one on the left—the room the shooters had been inside.

He rounded the corner with his pistol raised. Three men and two women were inside the classroom. All were dead except one woman, who was huddled against the wall. She had a gunshot wound in her right shoulder and was clearly in a great amount of pain, grimacing as she pressed against the wound. Though it took her a second to notice Yuri and the others entering the room, she reached for her pistol when she did.

"Leave that where it is." Yuri stepped toward her and kicked the pistol away from her. "Stop resisting, and we will get you medical care."

"I'll kill you before I let you threaten my children." She looked up at him, her lips curled back into a sneer. "Like I killed your friend."

Yuri felt his anger spike, and a haze overcame him. Stepan had been his friend. More importantly, he'd been a patriot, one of the men and women prepared to give their life to carve out a better future for their countrymen. He took a step closer to the woman and pressed his pistol against her temple, but she continued to curse and spit more threats at him.

"You need to shut up!" Yuri's hand was shaking as he held the pistol against her head. "You know nothing!"

"I know of the atrocities you and your allies have committed." She snarled. "Is that what you wanted to become? An icon of fear? My husband will make you pay for every drop of blood."

Yuri was as tense as steel. The woman was shouting abuse at him, his comrades were telling him to end her, and his own mind was working overtime. He couldn't believe someone who'd helped to brutalize his friend and taken up arms to defend the corrupt despots in Kiev would dare speak to him of fear and atrocities. What did she know of sacrifice?

What had she done to make the lives of her countrymen better?

He felt something snap, and he pulled the trigger. Yuri tossed the pistol onto the ground, closed his eyes, and took several deep breaths. He felt his heart rate and his emotions return to normal. He didn't like losing control, but the woman had brutalized his friend and tried to undermine everything he was fighting to achieve. She was a human carcinogen, infecting the body of her country with her poison. She'd reaped what she'd sowed.

Yuri opened his eyes again, looked down at the dead woman, then locked eyes with Arsen. "Burn the school. Burn it to the ground."

KHARLOV'S HEART was pounding as his vehicle got close enough to Merefa to see a half-dozen tendrils of smoke rising from different parts of the town. He wasn't sure what kind of smoke was worse—the white or the greasy brown—but both were chilling portents of the destruction that had visited the town.

Kharlov felt an awful, crippling sickness in the pit of his stomach at the thought of it. His family was somewhere in that town.

The man Kharlov had put at the wheel turned to face him. "I wonder how much is left?"

Kharlov stared at the driver. If the other man made another sound, Kharlov would put a bullet in the man's head and put someone else at the wheel. He took the hint and returned his attention to driving the SUV, which was at the front of a convoy of five vehicles filled with Kharlov's men.

They were headed to Merefa, to find his family and reap terrible violence on whoever was responsible for the situation.

His outrage at his family being threatened was matched by his fury that he hadn't been warned about it. His Russian contact hadn't said anything about the town being in the crosshairs. The second his wife had called, saying she was hiding out in a school, he'd mustered as many men as he could and made for the town. That had been ten hours ago. He didn't know the fate of his wife and children, and their safety should never have been in question.

The driver broke the silence twenty minutes later. "They've blocked the road up ahead. This is our last chance to turn back."

Kharlov's eyes narrowed. Up ahead, a civilian truck had blocked the road, and armed men were standing around a forty-four-gallon drum with a fire burning inside. "Keep driving."

Kharlov opened the glove compartment and reached for his pistol. He rested the weapon in his lap and covered it with a scarf. As they approached the checkpoint, one of the partisans walked slowly to the middle of the road and held up a hand, his other holding a sawed-off shotgun. Kharlov's driver stopped the SUV only inches from the man on the road, wound down his window, and started to converse with him.

Kharlov gripped the pistol hidden under the scarf in his right hand, resting it against the door as he pointed outside. He faced the man. "My family lives in town."

"My name is Yuri." The man smiled. "Your family are fine, but the town is closed until the Russian Army secure it. You need to turn around."

"I don't think I'll be doing that." Kharlov spoke slowly. "I'm not going to be delayed by fools playing soldier."

"Is that so?"

Kharlov smiled as Yuri walked around the front of the SUV, headed for the passenger-side door. Kharlov waited until the partisan was just outside his door then squeezed the trigger five times. The pistol shots were deafening inside the car, but the impact on the man was far more severe. He reached down to clutch his stomach, his eyes went wide, and he stumbled to one knee.

Kharlov pushed open the door, put one more round in the partisan's head, then dived for the dirt. He landed next to the man then scrambled to put the engine block of the SUV between himself and the other partisans who'd been huddled around the drum. Only a second later, the gunfire started. The bursts of death were punctuated by the screams of men who'd brought violence to the feet of Kharlov's family.

Kharlov popped up from behind the car with his pistol extended in both hands. He aimed at one of the two partisans who'd survived the initial exchange, and he fired twice. The partisan went down. A split second later, Kharlov dropped the final partisan. The gunfire stopped and was replaced by the screams of wounded men. Though two of the four partisans near the drum had managed to reach their own weapons, the fight had been one-sided.

Kharlov walked around to the driver's side of the SUV and sighed when he saw that his driver was wounded. He opened the door, reached over to unbuckle the driver's belt, and pulled him out of the vehicle. He screamed, but Kharlov didn't care. Nothing would delay him reaching his family. He told another one of his men to help the driver then climbed into the driver's seat of the SUV.

He drove around the truck and got back on the road, speeding away from the checkpoint and into the town proper.

A few minutes into the drive, he thought to check his mirrors and saw two of the other SUVs were on his tail. The men in the other one must have stayed behind to care for the wounded driver. Looking back to the road, he saw a dozen burning buildings up ahead and the occasional body littering the road. The partisans had brought death to town.

As he reached the school where his children attended and his wife had called him from, unbridled fear filled the pit of Kharlov's stomach. The destruction in the town prepared him for the worst. When he made one final turn, his terrors manifested—the school was a burnt-out shell. Its brick frame remained at the end of the street, but it was a blackened shell and the roof had collapsed. Nothing inside could have survived; he just hoped that his family was safe

Kharlov drove the SUV onto the sidewalk and right up to the front door of the school. He climbed out and ran into the carcass of the burned-out building. Though it was hopeless, he still searched frantically. He found nothing in the first room he checked, but in the second, there were five charred bodies. Though the smell was unmistakeable, he walked inside and checked each body.

Kharlov inspected the first two bodies then slowed when he reached the third corpse. It was sprawled out on the floor, and he could tell it was a woman because of the wedding ring she wore. Though the ring was charred, Kharlov had no doubt it was the ring he'd slipped onto his wife's finger on their wedding day. He let out a wail of sorrow, bent over, and vomited onto the floor.

He couldn't think straight. His wife had been attacked by Russian-backed partisans. He hadn't been there to protect the most important woman in his world... but was his failure complete?

Kharlov shook his head, trying to clear it. There would be time to grieve later. He needed to keep going. He had to know if his children had survived. He climbed to his feet and walked back to the hallway. When his wife had called him, he'd told her to bunker in at the school and to lock their children in one of the classrooms. It had seemed the best way to help keep them safe until Kharlov could muster the cavalry.

He staggered down the hallway to the third doorway in the row. Its door was nothing but charred wood. He kicked it, and it collapsed. Kharlov's heart, which had been pounding since he'd seen the smoke rising from town, exploded with pain. He fell to his knees in the doorway, his eyes locked onto the six bodies huddled together. Two of them were almost certainly his children.

He wasn't sure how long he knelt there, stunned and crying. The children had suffered the most terrifying and terrible death imaginable. They'd died hugging one another while they burned. It was like the entire world around him disappeared into a black hole, except the small bodies his eyes were locked onto. He couldn't look away. He felt pain, failure, shame, anger, and sorrow.

Kharlov crawled forward and touched the bodies tenderly. He didn't even know which of the bodies belonged to his two children. They were all about the same size and were unrecognizable. His amazing son and daughter, so full of life, had been stolen from him. Their mother, his partner in life, had died trying to protect them. He cried until he ran out of tears and his throat became raspy.

Blood and death were part of his business, but this was the first time it had reached his home with such devastating consequences. After a while, he became aware of the other people standing behind him, keeping at a respectful distance while watching over their boss. Kharlov turned to face them and simply stared for a long few moments. They spoke, but he couldn't hear them.

Kharlov looked back to the remains of his children. His business was conflict, but he'd put precautions in place to make sure the tools of his trade never struck so close to home. Those had failed. He hadn't received the warning from his Russian contact. He'd kept up his end of the bargain, but Veronika Oreshkin hadn't. For that, she would pay a terrible price.

JACK LEFT one hand on the steering wheel as he reached down and took his coffee from the cup holder. He lifted the cup to his mouth and drained the last of the gas station coffee. It was terrible, but he drank it anyway. He needed every ounce of sustenance and stimulus he could get his hands on to keep him going. When he was done, he tossed the cup in the back seat of the car and gripped the wheel with both hands.

He flared his eyes and blinked a few times, trying to stay awake. Anna was dozing next to him in the passenger seat, days of exhaustion having finally caught up with her. She'd been out of it for a couple of hours. The car's lights were piercing the darkness up ahead, but he hadn't seen another vehicle for miles. That was exactly how Jack wanted it to be.

It had been a long few days. After escaping Sokolov's hit team, Anna and Jack had made it seem like they were headed for Belarus. They'd stolen and dumped a few cars on their way, deliberately revealing themselves on security cameras and leaving Jack's fingerprints all over the vehicles. Jack had questioned Anna's plan at first, thinking it was a recipe to get them killed, but as each hour passed, he'd grown more confident.

After leaving a trail of breadcrumbs that any idiot could follow, they'd changed tack. They'd shot north in the direction of Saint Petersburg and become ghosts. What should have been a nine-hour drive had taken several days. Switching vehicles every few hours, they'd stayed off the highways where possible and doubled back several times. He wasn't sure it had been enough, but there'd been no sign of the authorities on their drive north. And they were only ten minutes away from the end of it all.

Jack drove for five of those minutes in near silence, with only Anna's soft breathing to keep him company. Finally, he came to an intersection and turned right, onto the road he hoped would be the last he would ever drive on in Russia. Off to his left, in the darkness, the Koporye Bay of the Gulf of Finland waited like a friend to whisk him away. Ahead, he saw a few lights from Sosnovy Bor—a town of sixty-five thousand he had no intention of visiting. Somewhere between his current location and the town was his ticket out of Russia.

Jack reached over and squeezed Anna's arm gently. "Showtime, Anna. The GPS says we're coming up on Sosnovy Bor."

She inhaled sharply and was awake in an instant, sitting up in her seat and checking the load in her pistol in what he'd come to learn was a habit. "Drive slow. We're looking for a signal."

Jack glanced at her for only a second. "What kind of signal?"

"I don't know." She shrugged. "We'll know it when we see it."

Jack nodded and eased off the gas, until the car was

crawling along at fifteen miles per hour. Neither of them spoke as they searched for the signal, hoping they saw it before they reached town. There was no backup if Anna's plan didn't work, and he knew that sooner or later, the Russian authorities would catch up with them. They needed to get the hell out of Russia before that happened.

"Was that it?" Jack hit the brakes and stopped the car. Then he tried to spot the signal again, hoping his tired eyes weren't playing tricks on him. "Did you see it?"

They sat in silence for a couple of moments, the car's engine idling and their breath fogging up the windshield, then Jack saw it again—a brief flash of flame, like a struck match or a Zippo lighter. By her sharp intake of breath, he knew Anna had, as well. In no doubt they'd seen the signal, Jack stepped on the gas enough to pull the car over, then he killed the engine.

"What now?" Jack kept his hands on the wheel. "Do we get out?"

"Stay very still."

As they waited in total darkness and complete silence, each moment felt like an hour. Jack knew Anna had received very precise instructions and a warning that there would be trouble if anyone had followed them to the meeting place. As the seconds ticked by, Jack started to wonder if they'd been wrong. Then there was a knock on the driver's side window. He flinched. He hadn't heard or seen a thing outside the car. Whoever was outside moved as quietly as a ghost. Jack wound down the window.

"Aussies are shit at cricket." A British male voice broke the silence.

Anna's voice was next. "What do you expect from a pack of convicts?"

After the code phrase was exchanged, the British man spoke again. "Get out of the car."

Jack complied. He pulled on the door handle, and the car's interior light pierced the darkness. He paused for a moment, shocked by the six men surrounding the car, dressed totally in black. They were sporting balaclavas and night-vision gear, aiming assault rifles at the vehicle. These guys weren't ghosts. They were ninjas. And he was glad they were friendly ones.

Jack glanced over at Anna and saw she'd already exited the vehicle. He did likewise, and the minute his feet were on the road, the British man who'd spoken the code phrase gripped his arm and led him away from the car. With each step, the light from the car lessened, and the sound of the waves increased as they got closer to the coast. After less than a minute, the British operative stopped.

"My name is Daniel Sawyer. We're with the Special Air Service, and we're going to get you out of here, sir." Sawyer's voice was barely above a whisper. "We're about to take a small boat out to the edge of Russian territorial waters, where a British submarine will pick us up and take us to safety."

"Okay." Jack didn't know what else to say. His fate was totally in the hands of these British SAS operatives. "Is Anna coming with us?"

"She'll be with us in a second, sir." Sawyer led Jack toward the boat. "Watch your step and take a seat once you're inside."

Jack used his hand to feel out in front of him. The boat was right there. He climbed inside the boat, fumbled around until he found the bench seat, then sat on it. Sawyer sat next to him, and a few moments later, Anna and another operative joined them. Once everyone was seated, they were pushed off the beach by some of the other operatives until their boat was floating freely in the water.

"Time to get out of here." Anna spoke over the sound of the engine. "You did brilliantly these last few days, Jack."

Jack smiled. "You didn't do so badly yourself. McGhinnist will probably want to pin a medal on your chest for this one."

"Call it even. You stopped terrorists from using my country to start a war, so getting you out of here is the least I could do."

Jack laughed softly as the boat increased speed and took them farther from the coast. The zodiac boat's engine was quiet, and Jack hoped nobody along the coast would hear, either. As they settled into silence, Jack knew that with each passing second, the chances of being discovered lessened. He still couldn't figure out why Oreshkin had shirked the meeting or why Sokolov had tried to take him down, but he was happy to wait for answers to those questions. For the moment, he just wanted to get to safety.

Jack smiled, some hours later, when the boat got them safely out of Russian waters and the two SAS troops aboard the boat turned on small lights so they could see. "We made it?"

"We made it." Sawyer smiled. He'd removed his balaclava and night-vision goggles. "Not even the Russians will try anything in international waters."

"Nothing they do would surprise me." Jack held out his pistol to Anna. He'd been gripping it since leaving the car. "Take it."

She eyed the pistol with suspicion. "You don't want to keep it as a souvenir?"

"No. I plan to use other weapons to get one back on Sokolov."

ACT II

7

The already-bleak conflict between Russia and Ukraine has been darkened by another atrocity after hundreds of innocent people in the town of Marefa were gunned down. A number of civilians were killed as the town was taken over by pro-Russian partisans, with the school, the hospital, and other public buildings razed. A second assault by unknown gunmen added to the damage, although that group withdrew after only a brief time in the town. Despite the conflict, Ukrainian Army troops have regained control of the town.

—New York Standard

Jack disembarked from the helicopter and kept low as he walked across the White House lawn. The noise of the helicopter's rotors, though defeating, was music to Jack's ears. Once he was safely clear, he turned and waved as the Navy helicopter lifted off again. He watched it until it was a speck in the distance. Then he smiled. He was home again.

After escaping from Russia, he'd been picked up by the British submarine in international waters and ferried to the middle of the Atlantic Ocean. There, he'd transferred from a submarine to the U.S.S. *Ramage*, an Arleigh Burke class destroyer that had taken him to Naval Station Norfolk in Virginia. From there, he'd taken the Navy helicopter to the lawn of the White House.

Two members of the Secret Service escorted him to the Oval Office, and he couldn't hide his smile as he opened the door and stepped inside. His smile widened when he saw the president and Caleb Davidson waiting for him on the sofas in the middle of the office with a six-pack of beer on the table. Grins on their faces, both men stood to meet him. Jack crossed the room and shook Davidson's outstretched hand, then he faced the president.

"It's a miracle to have you back, Jack." McGhinnist held his arms out wide. "I thought we'd lost you over there."

"A miracle named Anna Fowler." Jack hugged McGhinnist, and the president slapped him on the back. "I'm just glad I made it back."

McGhinnist stepped out of the hug and sat. "There are some things to catch you up on. While you were gone, we continued working the phones with the other nuclear powers."

Jack took a seat and a beer. Since leaving Moscow, Jack had been convinced any chance at deeper negotiations and a deal on nuclear weapons was dead. "And?"

"Everyone except Russia has agreed to attend a conference in Barcelona about our proposal, on the condition that *all* the other powers are there."

"And let me guess... the one who hasn't agreed to attend is

the guy who just tried to take me out?" Jack scoffed. "There's no way Sokolov will agree to it."

"He might not get a choice." Davidson spoke for the first time. "We haven't responded to the situation in Kharkov yet, and their encroachment hasn't stopped. Either Sokolov plays ball, or we hit him with everything we've got: crippling sanctions, arms sales to the Ukrainians, more troop deployments into the surrounding NATO member states..."

Jack nodded and kept quiet. He was one of McGhinnist's most trusted advisors, but he was horribly compromised. He found it impossible to separate his pet project and the fact Sokolov had tried to take him out from the realities of international diplomacy. If McGhinnist was going to take one more step closer to war with Russia, he had to do it on his own terms, based on advice that wasn't biased.

McGhinnist watched Jack for a long few seconds. "You know, anyone else who'd just gone through what you went through would tell me to drop the bomb on him and sort it out later."

"You need to do what you think is right in this instance, sir." Jack shrugged. "You know the stakes."

McGhinnist sighed. "These are the moments that the textbooks and armchair experts miss. The moments when you must sacrifice one policy agenda for another. I'm either going to look soft on Russian expansion or look like a fool for giving up on nuclear disarmament so soon after my State of the Union address made it a priority."

The president seemed weighed down by the historical gravity of the decision about how to handle Sokolov, who really led Russia because of a weak president. McGhinnist stood up from the sofa, walked over to his desk, rounded it, and sat in his office chair. Jack watched in silence the whole time, but he failed to stifle a laugh when McGhinnist reached for the phone on his desk.

McGhinnist froze and raised an eyebrow. "What's so funny?"

Jack snorted. "I thought the red phone was meant to be red?"

"This isn't the red phone, Jack." McGhinnist laughed. "We do that by email these days."

Jack laughed again as McGhinnist picked up the phone, asked to be connected to the Russian prime minister, pressed the button to put the call to speaker, then placed the handset in its cradle. McGhinnist liked his advisors to be able to hear what was being said. They waited in silence for several moments, until Clara announced that she had Prime Minister Sokolov for them.

"Hello, Mr. President." Sokolov spoke English well enough to communicate without a translator. "I trust you're well?"

"Indeed." McGhinnist frowned. He'd clearly expected a discussion with more fire and brimstone from the outset. "I have Caleb Davidson and Jack Emery with me."

"*Jack* Emery?" Sokolov's voice dripped with false sincerity. "I hope he's able to visit Russia, someday."

McGhinnist tensed, but he didn't bite. "I thought it was worth us discussing several serious matters, Mr. Prime Minister, the first being your troops pushing into Kharkov. I—"

"You are mistaken. Russia respects Ukraine's sovereignty. Russian troops were invited into Kharkov to protect the rights of ethnic Russians living there, just like they have in several other towns and cities. The troops are helping to keep peace in the region."

McGhinnist sighed. "Mr. Prime Minister, I—"

Sokolov continued speaking. "In fact, the only country that does not currently respect national sovereignty is your own, Mr. President. While your nuclear disarmament proposal excited your Congress and your media, I saw it for what it really is—a campaign to remove Russia's teeth when it is growing strong again."

Jack's eyes widened. While he hadn't expected his work on the nuclear deal to survive the phone call, to hear Sokolov speak so poorly of McGhinnist was a surprise. He'd delivered the diplomatic middle finger to McGhinnist, and the president's hands seemed to be tied. With Sokolov refusing to budge at all, America would have to start punishing him for his actions and for his words.

"Since you're not mincing words, neither will I." McGhinnist's voice had an edge it had lacked a moment ago. "You face a choice. Option one, halt your advance in Ukraine and attend the Barcelona summit on nuclear disarmament. Option two, continue to refuse to talk and keep pushing into Ukraine and watch your economy melt, and your advance be checked."

"I would have thought my response to Mr. Emery when he traveled to Moscow would have showed you my feelings on the matter." Sokolov's voice was chilling. "You want to talk more?"

McGhinnist's voice boomed in response. "Either you or your foreign minister *will* attend the conference we're organizing for next week, or—"

Jack was surprised a moment later when Clara's voice came over the line, saying the Russian had killed the call. He laughed. "Guess he didn't like the choice."

"Sokolov is a bully, but he's a bigger bully if you're weak." McGhinnist spoke through gritted teeth. "Caleb, tell the JCS to make our force posture more aggressive in Eastern Europe."

Davidson nodded. "Will do."

"What a mess." Jack rubbed his face with both hands. "You mentioned Oreshkin. Has she surfaced?"

"Not exactly..."

Jack let out a long sigh and closed his eyes. McGhinnist's tone of voice said it all. Sokolov had continued the long tradition of Russian autocrats seeing off their political foes in the most terrible ways possible. He doubted Veronika Oreshkin would ever be seen again. Though he didn't know her and the aborted meeting with her had almost cost him his life, Jack mourned her loss. She'd been the one person in Russia willing to listen.

The dream had been good while it lasted.

VERONIKA'S EYES WERE CLOSED, and her head was bowed, her chin resting against her chest. It would be far too much effort to raise her head, requiring energy she didn't have and a spirit that had been beaten out of her. She knew she was counting down her final minutes, and there was nothing in the ten-foot square concrete box worth looking at anyway. She was ready for the end.

"I've told you everything I know." She whispered the words, barely louder than a breath. "Let me go, please."

Her torturer, the Russian intelligence agent in the cell with her, laughed. She'd nicknamed him the Coyote, because of the high-pitched cackling he emitted when he was amused. "I love it when traitorous pimples on the ass of Russia admit that I've squeezed all the puss out of them. It is the great pleasure of my job."

"Please, let me go." Veronika sobbed loudly. She didn't

want to feel any more pain or rot in the cell any longer. "Or kill me."

In response to her plea, he laughed again and stepped closer to her. Veronika could sense his presence. She opened her eyes and saw his boots, splotched with her blood. A second later, Veronika cried out and her head jerked hard to the right as he slapped her with all his strength. His laughter grew louder as her head settled back to its original position, her cheek on fire and blood dribbling from her mouth and down her chin.

"You'd like that, wouldn't you?" His shrill laughter died away and was replaced with a cold, menacing voice. "You're not going to die any time soon. You'll be my guest here until you renounce your loyalty to the Americans. Then you'll be taken to a prison in Siberia, where you'll work until you freeze to death."

Veronika stayed silent. She'd known her fate since being confronted by Sokolov in the limousine. He'd brought back the finest traditions of Stalin to deal with his internal enemies. She'd been tortured in a cell in Kharkov by agents totally loyal to him. She'd told them about her attempt to meet with Emery, her enthusiasm for the nuclear deal, her reservations about the Ukrainian incursions, and her efforts to contain it with Kharlov. The only thing they'd been surprised about was her contact with the arms dealer Dmitry Kharlov.

"I never had any loyalty to the Americans." Veronika's whisper barely escaped her mouth. "I just wanted to stop the madman you take your orders from. You're supposed to care about Russia's internal security, but you're blind to the biggest threat of all. Nikolai Sokolov is going to destroy us all."

"You still speak ill of the prime minister?" The Coyote snarled at her. "Maybe I *will* just kill you now. Or maybe I'll kill your husband, as well, to make sure the taint is expunged..."

Veronika was unmoved by the threats against her ex-husband. He was a brutish Russian general who'd beaten Veronika and her daughter, until the last time, when Veronika had smashed a bottle of wine over his head and held a corkscrew to his throat. Their relationship had never recovered, and when Veronika had become a minister, she'd organized to have him posted to a missile silo east of the Urals.

"Or your daughter."

Veronika's head shot up. Her nostrils flared, and her eyes locked onto the Coyote. He'd managed to get her to care again. She shot forward, trying to get at him with her teeth because her wrists and ankles were tethered to the chair. She got close, but the Coyote took a step back. The chair toppled over, and she fell face-first onto the floor. The Coyote simply laughed.

Veronika grunted as she landed, unable to brace her fall. The force of the impact rattled her teeth, but the pain was just the whipped cream on top of the giant sundae of abuse she'd suffered. It didn't matter. The Coyote could threaten her husband all she liked, but the second he'd threatened her daughter, Veronika had gained a purpose again. The fact she'd missed him hurt more than slamming on the floor.

"Nice try." His laughter continued as he kicked Veronika in the midsection, driving all the wind from her. "Maybe there's more fight left in you after all. I—"

Veronika heard a bang from outside the cell at the same time as he did, though she didn't know what it was. Though tied to the heavy chair, she managed to roll away from him and get onto her side. She looked up at his face, and his earlier laughter was nowhere to be seen. He was as stiff as a board, his eyes locked onto the cell door.

Veronika didn't have to wait long to find out what had bothered him. There was more noise, the chatter of automatic weaponry, outside the cell, closer this time. Veronika knew many of the former political leaders of the city were being held just a few cells away from her. Perhaps loyalists had attacked the prison, or the Ukrainian Army was retaking Kharkov. Russia's hold on the city could be slipping.

The Coyote clearly had the same questions running through his head, because he looked down cold eyes, dark and determined. Veronika knew Sokolov's fanatics would die before failing to complete their mission, so the Coyote was probably keen to finish his work before whoever was shooting the place up came calling.

The Coyote dropped to his knees next to her, and she gasped as he wrapped his hands around her throat. Whatever fight she'd gained when he'd mentioned her daughter increased infinitely when her survival instincts kicked in. She thrashed and fought as hard as she could to keep him from strangling her, but his thumbs pressed into her throat, cutting off her airway.

Then her senses exploded with brilliant color and deafening noise.

Veronika gasped and inhaled sharply as the pressure on her throat eased, then she started to cough uncontrollably. She couldn't see or hear, but she could breathe. The air she managed to suck down in between coughs was by far the sweetest thing she'd ever tasted. Something had forced the Coyote off her and had helped her to live for a few more moments.

Her senses still ruined, she cried out in surprise as she was gripped under each arm and hauled upright. A second later, someone cut the restraints around her wrists. Then the restraints around her ankles were cut, as well. She was free. She blinked repeatedly, trying to see her mysterious benefactors, but her vision was still affected by the flashbang grenade.

"Who..." Veronika's voice croaked. "What..."

"The cavalry has arrived."

Her hearing having recovered a little faster than her eyesight, Veronika recognized the American Southern accent, which was probably the least common accent to be found in eastern Ukraine. As she was pulled to her feet, she could finally see if she squinted. Four shapes—all men—stood in the cell with her. The Coyote was huddled on the floor in the corner.

The American who'd spoken earlier put a hand on Veronika's shoulder. "We're getting you out of here."

Veronika nodded. Her eyes flared as she tried to regain her senses. She glanced at the Coyote, who was under American guard. "Him?"

"He's yours if you want him, but we need to move quickly." The American pulled his combat knife out of its sheath and held it out to her. "Your countrymen will be here in a few minutes."

Veronika nodded and gripped the knife. She had no intention of taking her time with the Coyote. If he'd just beaten and tortured her, she would probably have been willing to leave him alone in return for her freedom. But threatening her daughter was unacceptable. She took several steps toward her former captor, who cowered away from her.

She smiled as he cried out and pleaded with her. Ignoring him, she pressed the blade against his throat. Her hands shook, and fury burned inside her, but with each passing second it become more obvious that she couldn't do it. She couldn't kill a man, no matter how much she wanted to or how much he deserved it. With a sigh, she handed the knife back to the soldier and left the cell. Behind her, she heard another single gunshot and knew the American had taken care of the Coyote.

JACK WATCHED the C-17 Globemaster touch down on the runway and start to slow. "Something that big shouldn't be able to get in the air."

Jack couldn't hear the response from McGhinnist or Davidson over the squeal of the jet engines. They were waiting on the tarmac at the Shepherd Field Air National Guard base in Virginia with a half-dozen Secret Service agents and a few military officers to mind them. McGhinnist had wanted no public attention on the flight of this aircraft, though only the president knew what was aboard the C-17 to warrant the secrecy.

Jack couldn't begin to guess what all the fuss was about. Since arriving back in Washington, DC, earlier that morning, he'd been locked in briefings for hours with dozens of his colleagues, intelligence officials, and military personnel. They'd brought him up to speed on everything he'd missed while he'd been on the run in Russia and asked him a hundred questions about everything he'd heard, seen, and done. Jack had given them everything he could, and he just wanted to go home.

Instead, he was watching a military plane deliver a mystery cargo. When the plane stopped and its engines finished spooling down, the most senior military man present, Admiral Tim Cesare, started to approach the aircraft. Jack followed

McGhinnist, Davidson, and Cesare across the tarmac to the rear of the C-17. By the time they reached it, the giant plane's engines had gone quiet as the cargo ramp descended with a whir.

"Sir, what's going on?" Jack looked at McGhinnist, his curiosity struggling to overcome his exhaustion. "Why are we here?"

"Earlier today, a Navy SEAL team hit the prison in Kharkov where the city's political prisoners are being held." McGhinnist smiled, seemingly enjoying the confusion as he fixed his eyes on the ramp. "I didn't tell either of you because I knew you'd try to talk me out of the idea. Admiral Cesare was one of the few people who know of the operation."

"The raid went flawlessly." Cesare seemed to take his cue. "SEAL Team 6 parachuted into the outskirts of Kharkov and made their way to the prison. The operation commenced at 2:07 AM local time. Resistance was light, and the mission was completed in eight minutes. The team rendezvoused with this aircraft at a Ukrainian Air Force base and then flew home."

"Sir, that makes no sense." Davidson looked from the admiral to the president. "Even if we've liberated all the political prisoners in Kharkov, the city is firmly in the hands of the Russians. You put the life of those men at risk for nothing. You almost *started a war* for nothing. There was nothing to be achieved by making this move except giving Sokolov the middle finger."

The smile vanished from McGhinnist's face, and his head turned like a gun turret to face Davidson. "I think you forget I used to run the FBI, Caleb. I know what I'm doing."

Jack looked back at the plane as Davidson received his dressing-down from the president. Once the cargo ramp was down, four Navy SEALs walked down the ramp and stood at the bottom. Then two more SEALs emerged from inside the plane, walking down the ramp on either side of a middle-aged woman wearing poorly fitting Air Force fatigues.

"It can't be..." Jack squinted at the woman as his mind went into overdrive, then his eyes widened. "Is that..."

"Veronika Oreshkin." McGhinnist seemed quite pleased with himself. "She decided she'd prefer our hospitality to a cell in Kharkov."

Jack couldn't take his eyes off the former Russian foreign minister. Although her face appeared fine, he could see dark bruising around her throat. He couldn't imagine the damage hidden under her clothing. She'd clearly had a tough time since they'd been scheduled to meet. Sokolov had apparently taken his displeasure out on Oreshkin in addition to trying to kill Jack. Their lives and their fates now seemed strangely intertwined.

"Mr. President." Oreshkin greeted McGhinnist first then turned her attention to Jack. "Mr. Emery, I—"

"Please, call me Jack." He held out his hand. It was clear to him that the aborted meeting had not been Oreshkin's fault. "It's wonderful to finally meet you."

"Likewise." She smiled with relief and shook his hand. "You must know that it wasn't me who ordered the attempt on your life."

Jack nodded. Though he'd initially thought Oreshkin had set him up, he'd known the truth as soon as he saw the news of her disappearance. The Russian state media had said she was unwell, and Sokolov hadn't appointed a replacement, but the veneer was wafer thin. He'd assumed she was lying in a shallow grave somewhere, yet another victim in Sokolov's reign of terror.

Jack let go of her hand. "I was looking forward to our

meeting in Moscow, but knowing we both survived makes meeting you here sweeter."

"Quite." She took a step back. "Now, if you gentlemen would be so kind as to allow it, I really do need to rest and get cleaned up before we talk about more substantial matters."

"Of course." McGhinnist waved for one of the Secret Service agents to step closer. "Agent McKissick will escort you to the White House, where you'll be our guest of honor."

"Thank you." Oreshkin smiled, then her face clouded over. "My daughter... she's under threat from..."

"Taken care of." McGhinnist smiled. "We've got a CIA agent stationed in Berlin watching over her. I'm told he's excellent. No harm will come to your daughter."

"Wonderful." Oreshkin sighed with relief, bid them farewell, and let herself be taken away by the Secret Service agent.

Jack was over his initial surprise at seeing Oreshkin, and his exhaustion was long forgotten. He turned to face the president and waited for some answers. Of all the people he'd expected to see come off that aircraft, the former Russian foreign minister hadn't been one of them. McGhinnist had risked a lot to extract her, but it wasn't yet clear what reward the president hoped to secure by doing so.

"Sokolov tried to checkmate the nuclear negotiations by taking you out, Jack." McGhinnist placed a hand on Jack's shoulder. "This is my countermove. I now have something *he* wants."

"Will he care that we've got Oreshkin?" Davidson chimed in. "He was torturing her, so surely he knows everything he needs to by now. She's no longer useful."

"You bet she is." Jack shook his head. "He locked her up, tortured her, and probably would have killed her. A man like

Sokolov doesn't like having his vengeance interrupted. He'll take it as a personal affront. He'll do anything to get Oreshkin back and keep his role in her disappearance quiet."

McGhinnist nodded. "Oreshkin has a small power base among the moderates in Russia. He knows she's a trophy for us and a threat to him if she reveals what he's done. He'll play ball."

Jack laughed. Ordering the SEALs in had required balls the size of watermelons, but the move had worked. America now had the most valuable currency of all in international relations—leverage. Sokolov was dangerous, but it was possible that he could be made to play nicely if McGhinnist could hold Oreshkin over his head. McGhinnist could dangle her like a carrot, threatening to go public if Sokolov refused to cooperate.

"Caleb, send a message to Sokolov via the Ambassador." McGhinnist's voice was cold. "Tell him to attend the nuclear conference in Barcelona, or we'll let Oreshkin tell the world."

Jack smiled. The game had changed again.

8

Though President McGhinnist has been working to open negotiations on a potential nuclear deal since his State of the Union address, until now Russia has shown few signs that it would participate. That changed on Monday morning, when Russian Prime Minister Nikolai Sokolov told Russian state media outlets that he had accepted an invitation to a conference of all nuclear powers in Barcelona, Spain. Prime Minister Sokolov denied he was playing to America's tune, instead saying, "It is imperative Russia is around the table when great international discussions are taking place, no matter how unlikely the outcome." Despite Prime Minister Sokolov's reservations, simply getting all of the world's nuclear powers in the same place to discuss disarmament is an achievement of note for the president.

—New York Standard

Jack lifted a forkful of paella to his mouth and ate a bite of the delicious Spanish dish, even though he was already full to bursting. Since landing in Barcelona the previous evening, he'd alternated between eating and sitting in meetings with officials, laying the groundwork for the arrival of their national leaders in a few days. He suspected he would be going home a few pounds heavier.

"This is perfect." He placed his hand on top of Celeste's hand. "You have a nose for finding the best restaurants..."

"That and the bangin' good looks and the red hair, right?" She laughed and squeezed his hand. "How's McGhinnist feeling about the conference?"

Jack rolled his eyes at her attempt to change the topic. He was experienced enough to know when she was trying to dig exclusives out of him. Sometimes she tried charming him, sometimes she tried tricking him, and sometimes she tried seducing him. He couldn't blame her, because when he was a journalist, he would have done exactly the same, and every now and then, it worked.

"Getting Sokolov into the room was a big step." Jack grinned and paused for one last forkful of paella. "You can quote an anonymous White House source."

She nodded. "How did you guys manage to do that?"

"We offered a very compelling incentive." Jack looked her right in the eyes. "He saw merit in our offer."

He wouldn't tell her the truth about that one in a million years. She knew he'd been to Moscow, but that was the sum of it. She didn't know he'd been shot at or that he'd shot someone else. She didn't know he'd barely made it out at all or that he was linked to the disappearance of the Russian foreign minister. And she *definitely* didn't know that Oreshkin was in America's possession and that she was the key to Sokolov's attendance at the summit. Some things had to be kept confidential, even from his fiancée.

Jack put his fork on his plate, although there was still plenty of paella left. "Had enough?"

"Yeah." She put her fork down as well. "Nobody could say we're going hungry."

.

Jack nodded, signaled for the check, and took care of it when it arrived. After thanking the waiter, Jack and Celeste left the restaurant and walked hand in hand along La Rambla. The main tourist thoroughfare in Barcelona was pulsing with the lunchtime crowd. A hundred restaurants lined the thoroughfare, and down the middle, stallholders sold all manner of stuff. In between all the tourist traps, locals headed for the large fresh food markets.

Jack had never been to Barcelona before, but it was rising up his list of favorite places in the world. Best of all had been the chance to see some of it with Celeste. He'd barely spent any time with her since the State of the Union address, so she'd arranged to cover the summit for the *New York Standard* so they could spend some time together. He was looking forward to more time together in Barcelona when their schedules allowed.

At the end of La Rambla, they stopped beneath the Mirador de Colom, the monument which featured Christopher Columbus pointing out past the Barcelona Marina to the Mediterranean Sea. It was one of the most beautiful parts of the city they'd seen so far, and Jack couldn't help but wonder if Columbus had felt as committed to achieving the impossible as Jack felt now. Had it ever felt hopeless or too damn hard?

Celeste seemed to sense his unease. She kissed him gently on the lips. "It's going to be okay."

His phone rang before he could respond. He pulled out his phone and answered it. "Hello?"

"It's me." Caleb Davidson's voice filled his ear. "I just wanted to let you know that our British friends have intelligence about a possible terrorist attack on the summit. McGhinnist wants to press ahead and trust the British and the Spaniards to clean up the mess. They'll be kicking in some doors later today to see what they can find."

"Thanks for letting me know." Jack paused, and his mind processed the news. "Do we have any assets we can deploy to lend a hand?"

"Some, but McGhinnist discussed it with his Spanish counterpart, and they agreed it was best to keep our powder dry. Even though we hold Oreshkin, if Russia were to find out our operatives were buzzing about, not even that would be enough to keep Sokolov in check. The paranoid motherfucker would walk away or do something stupid. It's too much of a risk."

Jack knew Davidson was right. Sokolov had only agreed to come to Barcelona because Oreshkin had information that could greatly damage him. His commitment to the conference was as perilous as a candle flame in a hurricane, so America couldn't risk anything that would cause him to pull out of the event. If Sokolov bailed, the other powers would too, and everything would collapse.

Jack glanced at Celeste, making sure to keep his words general enough that nothing important reached her ears. "Let's hope our European friends can keep things under control."

"We'll have CIA and Secret Service assets at the summit itself, but we're leaving the rest of the city to others..."

Davidson trailed off, as if he'd been interrupted. "Gotta go, Jack."

Jack didn't respond. He killed the call and stared down at it, processing the news that made an already-difficult situation worse. He didn't know the motivation of the terrorists who were targeting the conference, but it didn't matter. Any time world leaders and television cameras gathered, there was the risk of attack. Jack just had to trust the intelligence assets of America's friends and allies.

Celeste took a step closer, drawing Jack's attention back to the present. "Are you okay?"

"Fine." He forced a smile. "It's going to be an interesting few days, though."

Anna smiled as she took a drag of the cigarette then slowly exhaled the smoke out the window of the sedan they were sitting in. "This sure beats Ukraine."

Dalton shrugged from the driver's seat beside her. "If I'd known you were a fellow degenerate, we could have bonded in Kharkov."

Anna laughed, and they settled back into silence. Kharkov was still a sore point, and she wanted to focus on her current job in Barcelona. Against all odds, Emery had managed to get all the nuclear powers into one place to discuss disarmament. The British government was giving the conference some clandestine security support, which was why Anna and her team were in the city.

Anna wasn't surprised she'd been sent. She'd become the point woman for MI6 when it came to anything the American president's influential advisor was involved in. MI6 wanted security at the summit to be airtight, given tensions between Russia and the West were at the breaking point. The Spanish government had been all too happy to have Britain's elite spy service riding shotgun to help keep the conference secure. The Spanish authorities had been less pleased when MI6 told them they had intelligence that a terrorist cell was preparing to hit the summit.

"They're pulling out of the house, Anna." Dalton's voice was laced with excitement.

"Showtime." Anna picked up her cell phone from the console, dialed the lead operative in the other car, and put the phone to her ear "Patricia, they're on the move. Get ready."

Anna switched the call to speaker and put the phone back where it'd been. She resisted the urge to crane her head to look at the terrorism suspects, trusting Dalton to pull out behind the van the suspects were driving. Seconds later, they were on the road, driving two cars back from the van on the single-lane road. Anna leaned down to grip the silenced submachine gun in the footwell, its barrel pointing down.

"How aggressive do you want me to be?" Dalton briefly turned his head to face her.

Anna picked up the gun and rested it on her lap. "Don't lose them."

He laughed. "This one will be easy."

Anna didn't like the overconfidence. He was right that it should be an easy job, but she'd seen people die on so-called easy jobs. MI6 had intercepted a ton of traffic about a plan by the guys in the van to hit the summit within the next twenty-four hours. The timing didn't make any sense to her, given world leaders weren't arriving for several days, but she'd chalked it up to the fact the guys were amateurs. In a difficult business, she was happy to take an easy job, but she didn't want her people getting cocky.

They kept a reasonable distance from the van, already knowing the route their suspects were taking thanks to an intercepted text message. The traffic was light, and Dalton had no trouble keeping pace with the van as they closed in on the interception point. When they were less than two blocks away, Anna unbuckled her seatbelt and flicked the safety off her submachine gun.

As the terrorists' van approached the intersection where they'd planned to intercept it, Anna felt the familiar rush of imminent violence. "We've got them. Hit them!"

Within a second, Patricia Evans's sedan stopped in the middle of the intersection. The van's brakes screeched, and its horn blared. The driver managed to stop the vehicle only inches away from Evans's vehicle. When it was clear Evans wasn't going to move her car, the van tried to reverse, but Dalton had stopped their vehicle only inches from the van's bumper. The trap had been sprung.

Anna and Dalton burst from the tail car at the same time as Evans and another operative emerged from the lead car, all pointing submachine guns at the van. Shouts filled the suburban street, and civilians made themselves scarce as Anna and her team surrounded the vehicle like the four points of a cross, with Anna taking up position next to the driver-side door.

"Do not move!" Anna shouted at the driver, who was gripping the wheel like a vise and looked frozen in fear. His companion wasn't so smart.

"Target moving!" Anna warned the others as the passenger opened the door, exited the van, and became a live target. She didn't take her weapon off the driver—he still needed to be contained, and she was the closest agent. She trusted her team to take care of the other man, and they delivered. She heard shots then confirmation in her earpiece that the second suspect was down.

Anna processed the information on autopilot as she waited for the driver to make his move. His hands were still on the wheel, and his eyes were locked on to her. He seemed to be considering how much time he had before she put a bullet in him. The death of his partner seemed to jolt him into action. His hands disappeared from the wheel, and Anna opened fire. Bullets pounded into the van, and the driver slumped forward.

"Target down!" Anna shouted over the screams of the civilians in the area. "Moving in to confirm!"

Her submachine gun aimed at the driver, she moved in closer. Although he was slumped forward and not moving, being careful had kept her alive in plenty of situations. She reached out, pulled on the door handle, and gave the door a yank. She heard a groan, and the driver muttered something in a language she didn't understand. She couldn't believe he was alive, but she wouldn't waste the opportunity.

"Hey, shit stain, do not move." Anna poked the wounded man with the end of the barrel. "Who put you up to this attack?"

The terrorist kept his head resting on the wheel as he turned to face her. His eyes were big, and he looked confused. He was in shock. "What?"

Anna looked down for a split second. Her shots had ripped into his chest, stomach, and shoulder. He was bleeding all over the cabin of the van. "Who planned the attack?"

"The same man who made the bomb in the back of my van." The terrorist gave a dumb, evil grin as his hands dropped to his lap. "And all the other bombs."

Anna fired as she spotted the small remote trigger resting in his lap, then she turned and ran. "Bomb!"

Her voice was shrill as she ran from the van, shouting repeatedly and hoping everyone in the area heeded her cry. Only a few seconds later, the van exploded behind her, and she stumbled to the ground. Anna grunted as she landed hard, losing her grip on the submachine gun and grazing her hands bloody. On all fours, she sucked in a deep breath and turned to look at the van. It was a blackened, burning wreck belching smoke into the sky.

After pushing herself up to her knees then climbing to her feet, Anna reclaimed her weapon. She surveyed her surroundings. Near the totaled van, civilians were down on the ground. She ran around to the other side of the van to confirm the other terrorist was still dead, but when she spotted another body next to him, she gasped and raised a hand to her mouth. Tom Dalton was also down.

"Fuck!" Anna got back to business. "We have an operative and several civilians down at the intercept point. Get us some support over here."

"We're on it." There was a slight pause as the operational commander digested the information, then his voice filled her ear. "Please confirm the targets are down."

"Yes, they're fucking down." Anna's voice was visceral. "The driver mentioned something about more bombs."

"You're to bring him in for questioning and—"

"He's atomized, you idiot. One of my people has a piece of metal the size of a cricket ball in his chest, so would you get off your ass and send me some help?" Anna slid on her knees next to Dalton, but she saw right away she was too late.

∾

KHARLOV PUSHED the door open and stepped inside the bar. Immediately, he was assaulted by sounds and smells that were foreign to him: blaring music played by instruments he'd never heard before and accompanied by lyrics in a language he couldn't understand, food packed with fragrant spices that promised heat and flavor in equal portions, and alcohol he didn't recognize. It was all accompanied by a vibe that he wasn't welcome.

He took a few seconds to scan the interior. A bar ran the length of the far wall, while patrons sat at a dozen tables or stood in groups. Within a few seconds, Kharlov felt every pair of eyes in the place lock on to him. It didn't matter if people were halfway through a conversation, ordering a drink, or staring into one—the entire mass of humanity packed inside the bar was suddenly only interested in him.

The bar was in one of the seedier parts of Barcelona. The place, which he knew well, was packed to bursting with Eastern European migrants, men and women who'd taken advantage of the opportunity to move west inside the European Union, to find higher paying jobs and more stable societies. Fortunately, that same migration had also planted some of Kharlov's former associates in Barcelona, giving him a supply of labor to get a job done. They just didn't know it yet.

Kharlov walked all the way across the room to the bar on the far wall, past people throwing down cheap drinks. The customers were packed in tightly and showed little appetite to move out of his way, eyeing him with suspicion and muttering to themselves. Kharlov eventually managed to force his way through to the bar. He leaned an elbow on the bar and ordered a beer.

As the barman poured, Kharlov pulled out his wallet and put a five-hundred-euro note on the bar. He smiled when the barman gasped and stared at the note, clearly not used to his customers flashing such large amounts of money. The barman scooped up the note and went to the register, muttering to himself and clearly annoyed about the amount of change he was going to have to give back.

Kharlov waited for his change, pocketed it, then turned to face the room. Taking a sip from his beer, he simply waited. He was a stranger with a wallet packed full of euros in a bar where he wasn't welcome, so he knew with absolute certainty what was coming next. When it happened, he would have to unleash more violence to get what he wanted. He relished the thought of it. That seemed a good way to get the loss of his family out of his head for a moment.

Since his wife and children had been murdered, he'd focused on nothing except exacting terrible revenge. He and his men had taken out every pro-Russian partisan they could find. That was merely an entrée, though. Since retreating from Ukraine, Kharlov had planned the main course, a far more substantial payback than shooting peasants who'd bitten off more than they could chew.

It took less time than he'd expected for someone to build up the courage to approach him. Sauntering over with two of his friends keeping a half step back, the kid looked young and stupid, filled with booze and bitterness. He stopped only a yard from Kharlov, easily within arm's reach. Sporting a sneer, he looked Kharlov up and down. The man waited in silence, clearly expecting Kharlov to speak. Kharlov simply lifted his glass into the air and drank.

The young man's sneer got nastier, and he tried to converse with Kharlov in several different Eastern European languages. Kharlov stared back at him with a blank expression, although he understood the kid perfectly well when he tried Russian and Ukrainian. Even when the kid spoke in English, Kharlov kept quiet. He was enjoying seeing the kid's blood pressure rise and his friends goading him on even more.

Kharlov waited for a minute, watching the kid get angrier with each passing second, then he put down his beer and smiled. "Can I help you?"

"You understand me, motherfucker?" The tough guy switched to English and leaned in closer to Kharlov. "You're not welcome here."

"I've heard that all of my life." Kharlov's smile vanished. "I'm looking for the Duke."

Kharlov smiled when the kid suddenly looked unsure, glancing around at his friends. Kharlov wasn't surprised, and he waited patiently. Kharlov had worked with the Duke in the past. The well-known mercenary would accept any job if the price was right. Luckily, Kharlov had a job in mind, and he was willing to pay whatever the cost. He didn't want to get his own men killed—he had that much loyalty to them—but he would pay for different ones.

Finally, the kid turned back to Kharlov, having decided his course of action after conferencing with his friends. "What do you want with the Duke? You should get out of here..."

Kharlov sighed. He'd hoped to talk to these men and find the Duke without violence, but the currency of power was the same the world over. He'd deliberately shown he had money by dropping the large banknote from a wallet full of them. Now he had to get their undivided attention. It now seemed that statement wasn't bold enough. The punk standing in front of him was going to be the exclamation mark.

Kharlov pushed himself off the bar and exploded forward, aiming the crown of his head and striking the other man on the chin with incredible power. As the force moved through the kid's jaw bones, and they shattered like balsawood struck by a sledgehammer. The loudmouth dropped to the ground and struck his head on the floor. Either the headbutt or the landing had knocked him out cold.

Kharlov looked down at his fallen foe with pity. The kid really hadn't known what he was dealing with, so Kharlov saw no reason to maim him further. He'd made his point and had gained the attention of the others, whom he hoped would lead him to the Duke. He crouched and rolled the kid gently onto his side, to make sure he wouldn't choke to death on his tongue or any dislodged teeth before some medical professionals saw to him.

Only when he was sure the kid wasn't going to die did Kharlov return his attention to the thug's friends. For a pack of animals, they'd sure become shy. The age-old truth of bar fights had proven itself once again. The punk and his friends had been full of courage when they'd thought they were a pack of hyenas descending on a water buffalo, but when the water buffalo put the leader of their pack on his ass with a broken jaw, they melted back into the crowd.

Kharlov walked to the table in the middle of the bar and glared at the woman seated at it. Taking the hint, she picked up her drink and found somewhere else to be. Kharlov stepped up onto the table, which felt sturdy enough to hold his weight. He looked out at the crowd. Until a minute ago, the bar had been filled with music and the hum of human activity. After the fight, there was silence and stillness. All eyes were locked on him.

"I know the Duke and his associates frequent this bar." He paused as others whispered translation of his English in their own tongues. "Whoever leads me to him will be rich."

He waited as the conversation spread through the room.

He knew someone here would know the Duke, and the Duke could give him the men to achieve the impossible—storming a conference of world leaders and gunning them down. It only took a few seconds for a woman to step forward and whisper to him. She claimed she knew the Duke and that she could arrange a meeting with him.

Kharlov smiled. "Deal."

9

The leaders of the United States, Russia, Israel, and Great Britain landed in Barcelona this morning, joining representatives of China, France, India, Pakistan, and North Korea—all of whom arrived yesterday. Starting tonight, they'll attempt to make progress toward nuclear disarmament. The summit is going ahead despite some controversy, with a foiled terrorist attack in the city that killed four people and incendiary comments by Russian Prime Minister Nikolai Sokolov about the chances of success at the summit. "I travel to Barcelona only to face the Americans, who threaten to ruin my country and my people if their demands about nuclear weapons and Ukrainian self-determination are not met," Sokolov said. "It is time someone stood up to the bullies of the past half century."

—New York Standard

Jack lifted a glass of red wine off a tray carried by a passing waiter, who continued to move among the VIPs assembled in the large central courtyard of Castle Montjuic, an ancient fortress that dominated the mountains around Barcelona. The surrounds were almost as impressive as the wine, Rioja Gran Reserva, a famous Spanish red wine that a small army of waiters was distributing to the guests.

Jack turned back to Caleb Davidson and raised his glass. "Hard to believe we made it this far, Caleb."

"The end of the beginning." Davidson raised his glass and clinked it gently against Jack's glass. "Well done."

Jack lowered his glass and took a sip. The wine tasted extra sweet, because he'd achieved the impossible—getting the leaders of all nuclear powers together to discuss disarmament. Jack wasn't sure whether the summit would produce a solid disarmament outcome or not, but for one evening, he was content to enjoy the wine and the progress made so far.

Already, several of the powers had ruled out complete disarmament, but there appeared to be some potential for a drastic reduction in global nuclear stockpiles. Jack would be content with that outcome, which would be a wonderful first step for a journey he knew might take decades.

In the talks between officials, Russia had given nothing. France, the United Kingdom, and Israel had walked in lockstep with the United States. China had been cooperative but reserved. Jack wasn't sure what to expect from them once the leaders' talks kicked off, although he suspected North Korea would follow the Chinese line, given the bulk of their food and oil supplies came from Beijing.

Perhaps the biggest surprises had been India and Pakistan. Both countries had expressed a willingness to disarm if the other did. When prodded for explanation, officials from both countries had revealed a near miss on the border of contested Kashmir only a few months ago, which had taken them close to war and spooked the leaders of both countries. It was further confirmation that nukes needed to go.

"There's the boss." Davidson's voice snapped Jack out of his thoughts. "I hope he dunks it."

Jack put his wineglass on a nearby table and applauded as President McGhinnist made his way onto the stage, which had been set up directly opposite the entrance to the castle. McGhinnist smiled as a dozen cameras flashed, and the applause continued for a number of seconds. Only when the cameras had eased and the applause had gone silent did the president begin.

McGhinnist's deep voice boomed across the courtyard. "Although the world has eighteen thousand five hundred nuclear warheads, we know even a small conflict could spell disaster. Only one hundred nuclear detonations would create enough black soot to block sunlight, drop global temperatures, critically damage Earth's ozone layer, increase UV radiation by eighty percent, and wipe out fragile ecosystems. This would lead to unprecedented global catastrophe. The rich would use their resources to flee and find safety. The poor would be beset by famine. Intense conflict within and between countries would occur. Economies would collapse, governments would fall, and the world as we know it would cease to exist."

Jack was surprised that McGhinnist had started his speech with so much gloom, but it worked. Every other person at the reception was silent. Even the waiters had stopped moving and were listening to the president speak. Jack didn't know what was coming next, because McGhinnist had refused to share the speech with anyone. The president had wanted to make the statement to the world on his own.

McGhinnist continued, "We have long known the stakes. In 1961, John F. Kennedy said that every inhabitant of this planet must contemplate the day when this planet may no longer be habitable. Every man, woman, and child lives under a nuclear sword of Damocles, hanging by the slenderest of threads, capable of being cut at any moment by accident or miscalculation or madness. Who would ever consider unleashing such destructive power? Why do we consider these weapons a tool of statecraft at all?" McGhinnist eyed each of the eight national leaders one by one. "That *any* nation could have this capability is unthinkable. That *all* of our nations *do* have this capability is insane."

He saw several nods—enough people to give him hope that something could be achieved in Barcelona. Smiling, he turned his head and caught sight of Celeste amid the media pack near the stage. He'd organized to get her an exclusive interview with McGhinnist right after the speech, a perk he didn't mind providing to the woman he loved. When she saw him looking, she flashed a smile of her own.

McGhinnist's speech seemed to be reaching a crescendo. He gripped the lectern. "We have these weapons so our foes can't use theirs without retaliation. It is a false logic, given all that would be left is the charred bones of dead people on a ruined planet. A better means of ensuring our collective safety is to do away with them entirely. Welcome to Barcelona. Welcome to the most important nuclear disarmament summit in fifty years. Welcome to the place where we might achieve something all of us here will be remembered for."

Jack applauded loudly as McGhinnist concluded his speech, waved, then left the stage. The entire crowd applauded for what felt like an eternity, a rousing validation of everything McGhinnist had said and a shared commitment to the task that'd brought them to Barcelona. Jack knew talk was cheap, but the summit couldn't have started on a stronger note.

Jack waited until he was the last person still applauding then turned to Davidson. "He nailed it."

"Even Sokolov was giving him a half-assed clap." Davidson snorted then gestured behind Jack with his chin. "Looks like someone is looking for you."

Jack turned. Celeste was waiting for him with a hand on her hip and a smile on her face. After a speech like that, she was in a hurry to get her exclusive. Jack patted Davidson on the back then fought his way through the crowd to Celeste. She looked radiant, wearing an emerald-green gown that hugged her figure and sat off-the-shoulder, the perfect contrast for her flame-red hair.

When he reached Celeste, he gave her a small kiss then pulled away. "You look incredible."

"You're not too shabby yourself." She made a show of looking him up and down. "Are we still good for the interview?"

"Yep." He placed a hand on her back then gently led her to where McGhinnist was scheduled to meet them. "Then I hope I can interrogate you a little."

"FUCK IT!" Veronika threw her glass of vodka and soda across the hotel room and watched it smash against the wall, scattering ice and splashing liquid all over the carpet.

She collapsed onto the bed and exhaled loudly, frustrated that the Spanish cable television network had cut the feed from the summit immediately after the president's speech. She'd been cooped up inside the hotel room for almost an entire day since flying to Barcelona with President McGhinnist on Air Force One. Now, without even the feed from the summit to keep her informed, she felt like a prisoner again.

At least McGhinnist had set the scene perfectly. It was a shame it would all be for nothing. Though the Americans had used Veronika as bait to lure Sokolov to the summit, not even that would be enough to secure a deal with him. He hadn't even appointed another foreign minister. Technically, she still held the job, and he'd explained away her absence as a result of illness. It was only a matter of time before Sokolov torpedoed the summit entirely.

Veronika should be there, but she'd been sidelined. Since being rescued by the American special forces soldiers, she'd been little more than a prisoner. The only difference between being locked up in prison and her current situation was that the Americans generally kept her in five-star hotels. She was rotting while her peers attended the summit.

Veronika heard a knock on the door. She stood, crossed the hotel room, and opened the door. When she saw who was outside, she forced a smile. "Agent Grayson. What can I do for you?"

Grayson gave her a real smile. What the Secret Service agent might lack in personality, he made up for in cheer. "Hourly check-in, ma'am."

"I would like to go for a walk in the park." Veronika repeated the same request she'd made every hour since her arrival. "I can see it from my window."

"You know that's not possible, Minister. You're safe here, but we can't guarantee your safety outside the hotel."

"I won't do anything to compromise my *safety*." Veronika placed a hand on the agent's shoulder, hoping to sway him. "I want to breathe fresh air. I promise I won't talk to anyone."

Grayson's cheerful smile changed to a sympathetic one.

"My orders are straight from the president—nobody goes in or out of your hotel room."

Veronika sighed. The hotel had been reserved exclusively for the American delegation and had been locked down so tightly by the Secret Service and the Guardia Urbana de Barcelona that only members of the delegation and hotel staff were allowed to enter or leave. Veronika, however, had not even been allowed to leave.

She looked Grayson in the eyes. The agent was trying to be kind, but he wouldn't give her what she wanted. "I'll see you in an hour, Agent Grayson."

Veronika closed the door before he had a chance to reply. She put her back to the door and slid down it until she was sitting on the floor. With her teeth clenched and her fists balled, she closed her eyes and took a deep breath. While she was thankful the Americans had rescued her, she was reaching the end of her patience with being locked up. Being a prisoner for another government wasn't what she had in mind.

She stayed on the floor until she heard another knock on the door, five minutes later. She sighed, opened her eyes, pushed herself off the floor, and looked through the peephole. She frowned. There was no sign of Grayson—or anyone else— on the other side. With a shrug, she unlocked the door and pressed down on the handle to see what the Secret Service agent wanted.

Veronika grunted as her face exploded in pain. She stumbled back and fell to the ground. She gasped when she saw who'd forced his way inside the door and struck her—the same Russian agent who'd first pulled the gun on her in the car with Sokolov. He was one of Sokolov's personal cleanup men.

She was in a fight to the death. Veronika used her hands to

scramble away from him, pushing herself across the floor and deeper into the hotel room. The agent laughed, closed the door, and gripped his silenced pistol menacingly. Nobody else in the hotel would have heard the discharge when he shot Grayson. Suddenly, giving her an entire floor of the hotel to herself seemed like a miscalculation by the Americans.

"You should have died in Kharkov." He stared down at her as he followed her across the room, his eyes cold. "It's time to fix that mistake."

His laugh burned her like acid. He had her cold. Attacking her at the fortified hotel of the American delegation was genius, really. The Americans had never admitted to having Oreshkin in their care, so they couldn't publicly take issue with Russia eliminating her. They probably wouldn't even want to admit the hotel had been hit at all. The world would never know her fate or that of Agent Grayson, who'd bled out in the hall.

"Fuck you!" Veronika hissed, scrambling away from him. Then her back was against the wall, and there was nowhere else to go. Feeling the shard of the glass she'd broken against the wall at her fingertips, she locked eyes on neck. "You serve a madman."

The agent shrugged. "He wanted me to pass on a message before you died, though. He said to tell you that—"

With a guttural scream, Veronika lunged up and away from the wall, directing all her anger into the single act of plunging the shard into his throat. There would be no rescue this time, and she had no hope of overcoming an elite killer, but she wouldn't go passively.

"Crazy bitch." He laughed and fired his pistol, the silenced weapon delivering a round into Veronika's left shoulder.

Veronika was so full of adrenaline, she didn't even feel the shot hit her. She snarled as she saw his eyes widen a split second before she buried the jagged glass into the soft skin around his throat. Her body hit him a moment later, and it felt like she'd run into a concrete building. She fell to the floor as his blood showered down on her, and he let out an animalistic gurgling sound.

She felt fire in her shoulder and grunted as he kicked her in the midriff once then twice. He'd dropped the pistol and was trying to stem the bleeding from the gash in his throat, while at the same time trying to finish her off with his boots. Veronika dived at his ankle to stop him from kicking her. Hugging his leg, she felt something metallic through his black pants—a knife in a sheath strapped to his shin.

Even as he tried to shake her loose, Veronika grabbed the knife and used all her remaining strength to slice into his Achilles tendon. He crumpled to the ground and landed on top of her. Veronika grunted as his weight pinned her on her side, but her hand holding the knife was still free. She stabbed him again and again, burying the blade deep each time and not caring where.

Finally, he stopped moving, and sheer exhaustion overwhelmed her. With her attacker dead, her hand slumped to the ground, and the knife fell from her fingers. Panting like a caged animal, she attempted to push him off her, but her shoulder burned with indescribable pain. She failed to move him even an inch. He was too big, too heavy—a dead weight on top of a dying woman. After a few tries, she gave up. It was hopeless. Her head slumped to the side, her eyes glazed over, and her mind reconciled with the fact that she'd reached the end. She closed her eyes and smiled. At least she'd fought back.

Jack stared out into the night, enjoying the breeze on his face and the moment of quiet away from the other summit guests. He was standing on the battlements of Castle Montjuic, looking down the mountain. He could see every light in Barcelona. Below him, the city lights contrasted with the inky blackness of the Mediterranean Sea in the middle of the evening. It was an amazing sight that countless Spanish leaders had no doubt taken in over the centuries.

It wasn't hard to understand why the castle had been built atop the mountain four centuries ago. It allowed dominance of the city and the sea around it. Throughout that time, the castle's guns had been fired at invading forces and also at the city itself, when the citizens of Barcelona rebelled or refused to pay their taxes. For a time, the castle had been a symbol of power and might, much like nuclear weapons in the modern day. Except a castle couldn't annihilate the Earth.

The first evening of the leaders' summit couldn't have gone better. McGhinnist's speech had been a gauntlet thrown down to history. It had been the talk of the reception, and Jack felt a buzz of promise and hope. He'd never expected to get so far when he first proposed his plan to McGhinnist, but he increasingly felt there was a real chance to secure a deal.

He was done with official proceedings for the night. After he'd escorted Celeste to the president for the interview, he'd done one more lap of the room then gone upstairs to the battlements. He was surprised that no other guests had made their way up there, but that suited him just fine. He did his best thinking when he was alone, and he needed to mentally prepare for the next few days.

"Impressive view, isn't it?" A Russian voice broke Jack's train of thought. "I hope you don't mind me joining you."

Jack turned to face the new arrival and inhaled sharply. Nikolai Sokolov was standing six feet away from him. Jack's eyes darted around, looking for an escape, but Sokolov was standing right in his path. He was trapped, although at least Jack couldn't see any of Sokolov's goons.

"Relax, Mr. Emery." Sokolov chuckled. "If I still wanted you dead, I'd have one of my men walk up behind you and push you off the wall. You have survived a lot, like a cockroach, but a fall down a cliff and into the ocean would ruin your day. Luckily for you, my men are busy elsewhere."

Jack swallowed hard and finally managed to spit out some words. "What do you want, Prime Minister?"

"To take in the view." Sokolov stood beside Jack and looked down at the city. "And to meet the power behind the throne."

"Okay," Jack deadpanned. He was content to let Sokolov lead the conversation, because he had no idea what was in the mind of the Russian leader.

"You have achieved remarkable things for your president." Sokolov gave a small laugh. "I wish you worked for me."

Jack was unable to stay diplomatic after that comment. "You had your men ambush me on the street a few weeks ago."

"That was just business." Sokolov shrugged. "Ms. Oreshkin made a move. I made a countermove. It's how the chess game has worked in Russia for centuries. Your president clearly understands it. He now uses Veronika to hold me in check, though I'm yet to make my own countermove."

Jack turned to face Sokolov, his curiosity getting the better of him. "Why do you hate America so much?"

Sokolov's jaw clenched; he was clearly restraining himself. No matter how psychotic he was or how much he was used to having his way, he was in a foreign country, where he didn't set the rules. He seemed to consider Jack's question for a long while, then he turned his head and locked his eyes on Jack.

"Why do I hate America?" Sokolov raised an eyebrow. "Perhaps it's because my father and twenty million of my countrymen died fighting the Nazis, yet all the world hears about is the victories and sacrifices of the West. America lost thirty-seven thousand men on D-Day, and Russia lost over a million men at Stalingrad, yet history values the American life far more than the Russian. When it was my turn, in Afghanistan, I watched mujahideen armed with American machine guns and American rocket launchers mow down my comrades."

Sokolov's eyes glazed over, as if he had been taken back to that bitter time he spoke about. "I watched my entire company return home in body bags. I was the only survivor out of one hundred men."

"I—" Jack had barely spoken one word before Sokolov cut him off.

"All of those men were lost for nothing. Thousands. Tens of thousands. History regards their sacrifice as a footnote. It was a bitter lesson, and I was determined that my country would never again be a loser. I wanted to ensure that it was *we* who were feared and it was *we* who set the global agenda. But then it all fell apart. The Soviet Union ceased to exist. My country flirted with liberalism and instead found catastrophe. Our power was leeched away, our economy was ruined, and our allies turned coat." Sokolov gave a cold smile. "And instead of helping, America continued to move its pieces across the chess board, squeezing and isolating Russia."

Sokolov clamped a hand down on Jack's shoulder. "That's why I am pushing Russia's borders outwards. That's why I will never agree to surrender my nuclear weapons. That's why my country will remain on a collision course with America. The only choice will be whether your boss decides to stand in the way or move aside when the time comes."

It took all of Jack's willpower not to flinch away from Sokolov's grip. The Russian prime minister terrified him. His eyes were crazy, and his voice was ice-cold, but Jack refused to take a backward step. "Good thing we've got Veronika Oreshkin to keep you honest. If she spills your secrets, your people will be baying for blood."

Sokolov laughed long and hard, in a way that suggested he knew something that Jack didn't. He let go of Jack's shoulder. "Well, I need to get back to the reception. There's a photo scheduled for all the leaders. It may be the only thing that emerges from this event. I'm sorry that all of this effort will result in nothing, but I admire your tenacity, Mr. Emery."

Jack watched as Sokolov turned around and walked toward the stairs. Once the Russian prime minister was out of sight, he gasped and sucked in a deep breath. It wasn't every day he came face-to-face with the man who'd ordered his death, much less one who would admit to deliberately leading his own country on a path to war with the most powerful nation on Earth. Jack couldn't wait to hear what McGhinnist had to say about his encounter with Sokolov.

He exhaled loudly through his nose and shook his head. The reception would be starting to wind down, with officials and other guests retiring for the evening so they could get some sleep before a full day of meetings tomorrow. The leaders would still be awake, both for the photo and for long discussions with their advisors after the reception, but Jack would catch up with McGhinnist in the morning.

He cast one last glance at the city then started to turn. He froze in place when an explosion erupted in the middle of Barcelona, followed by a deep rumble and a fireball that lit the night sky. Jack cursed. MI6 had foiled a terrorist attack a few days ago, but another had apparently manifested.

A few seconds later, a second explosion boomed, closer than the first. Then there was another and another and another—each one closer to the castle. It was like missiles were striking the city, though he didn't know the city well enough to figure out what was being targeted. As each explosion got closer, Jack's stomach sank, then the explosions stopped. They had been a warning shot for something much more significant.

Jack shivered. A chill that had nothing to do with the cold ran up his spine.

10

The fiery speech delivered by President McGhinnist to open the Barcelona summit has been overshadowed by a number of explosions across the city. Though the situation is still unfolding, the Standard believes Sagrada Familia, Park Guell, and La Rambla have all been bombed, with high numbers of civilian casualties suspected. Although there are no reports of attacks on Castle Montjuic itself, where the summit's opening reception is being held, the wave of bombings has put the city on edge. It is not yet clear whether the first day of talks between world leaders will go ahead, but given the scale of the bombings, it is difficult to see the summit being unaffected by tonight's events.

—New York Standard

Kharlov aimed his silenced submachine gun at the Spanish soldier standing on the battlements of Castle Montjuic and fired a short single shot. The weapon popped, and the soldier fell off the wall of the castle, disappearing into the darkness. Kharlov couldn't help but grin. The eastern side of the battlements was now totally unguarded.

Kharlov kept his men back for another twenty seconds, waiting for the signal. The entire castle wall was shrouded in an inky blackness, and even the top was only dimly lit. For such a significant structure hosting nine world leaders, the security really was poor. There *had* been more armed men on the battlements, but the explosions in the city had drawn them toward the entrance, leaving only the single sentry, who was now dead.

It had gone exactly as planned. After hiring local mercenaries from the Duke, Kharlov had put in place a layered series of attacks designed to disrupt security at the summit and stall the arrival of first responders. That was the only way he would be able to get at Nikolai Sokolov and exact his revenge, which had fueled every action he'd taken since the death of his family.

Several days ago, he'd paid the least capable mercenaries to plot an attack in Barcelona using a bomb he'd supplied through one of his contacts. Those men had been as dumb as a bag full of hammers, and as he'd expected, the Western intelligence services had found out and crushed the plot—but not before the suitably explosive outcome on the streets of the city had killed several people.

He'd paid a group of better-skilled mercenaries to attack half a dozen locations in downtown Barcelona only minutes after the American president concluded his speech to open the conference. They hadn't let him down, lighting up the night with fireballs that had stolen the attention of the police and soldiers posted around the city.

Lastly, he'd bribed a local catering company to let the finest of his mercenaries onto the staff providing food and drinks to the summit delegates. The thought of his mercenaries carrying trays full of champagne made him smile, because when the time came, they would join in on the slaughter. Kharlov didn't particularly care if his men survived, as long as he got his shot at Sokolov.

"Time to go!" Kharlov whispered to the pick of the mercenaries he'd recruited from the Duke and brought with him to the castle.

Kharlov led them to the base of the wall, where the benefit of getting a few men on the inside was waiting for him. One of the mercenaries posing as a caterer was waiting at the top of the battlements with a rope, which he threw down the moment he saw Kharlov and his comrades. Kharlov urged his soldiers of fortune toward the rope and waited as they climbed one after another.

Kharlov waited until all but two of his men had scaled the rope, then he hung his submachine gun by its strap over his shoulder and scaled the wall. His muscles strained as he climbed, his legs pressing against the wall and helping to balance him. When he reached the top, two of his mercenaries reached down and pulled him up onto the battlements by the shoulders. Kharlov smiled as the last of his impromptu army reached the top of the wall.

Kharlov's men split into two groups. One group headed left, and Kharlov led the other group to the right. Their first task was to clear the battlements, then they could head downstairs to where the leaders were gathered. That was where Kharlov would find the Russian prime minister and reap the vengeance for the loss of his beautiful wife and amazing children.

Kharlov handed his submachine gun to one of the mercenaries and walked down the stairs to the reception. As he descended, he smiled at the thought of his men doing the heavy lifting above him, taking down any soldiers and police manning the battlements. Sooner or later, they would mop up all the resistance and make their way downstairs. Kharlov put them to the back of his mind, because they were as much a decoy as the bombs outside the castle had been.

Kharlov walked among the world leaders and officials, looking every bit the part. He reached out to grab a glass of wine from the tray of a passing waiter, took a sip, then froze. Across the room he could see Sokolov in the middle of a conversation with a woman, under the watchful eye of two armed men Kharlov assumed were his security detail. Kharlov's lips peeled back into a smile as he lowered the glass and placed it onto a table.

Knowing he needed only a second to kill the Russian prime minister, Kharlov tried to approach Sokolov, but he was instantly the focus of the security detail's attention. Sokolov's two goons looked like grizzled veterans. Their eyes were always moving, scanning the crowd for potential threats. Even though their boss was among his peers in a fortress swarming with security, they weren't relaxing. Kharlov knew he wouldn't get near Sokolov with those guys watching.

Luckily, that wouldn't be a problem for long.

Kharlov leaned against a wall and waited. Within a minute, his impromptu army stormed down the stairs and into the courtyard like a ravaging horde, shouting and shooting into the crowd. The soft, pampered officials turned into a herd of buffalo running headlong into a lion. The security forces guarding the guests kicked into action, drawing their weapons. Some returned fire, dropping a few of Kharlov's men, while others moved to protect their charges. Confusion reigned, as panicked people, already on edge after the bombings, ran in every direction. Kharlov stayed against the wall and watched his mercenaries unleash chaos. As people fell and his impromptu army ran wild, he simply waited.

The Secret Service shepherded the US president away, surrounding him with a mass of bodies and guns. The agents were more interested in getting their man to safety than in taking down the attackers. Other world leaders were similarly forced to run toward the castle entrance. Suddenly, one of the main security features of the castle—only one entrance and exit—was causing havoc for those inside.

Kharlov smiled as Sokolov joined the race for the exit while his two thugs provided covering fire. With each step, Sokolov got farther from Kharlov, and more men and women dropped on either side. His mercenary army had caused maximum carnage—dozens of bodies lay on the ground—but the superior training and experience of the defenders was starting to show. The mercenaries were dropping like flies as Sokolov got farther away. It was time to go loud, before it was too late.

Kharlov reached into his pocket, wrapped his hand around a small plastic square, flipped the safety cap off with his thumb, and pressed down on the button it had revealed. Instantly, the ground beneath him shook, and another bomb went off, this one right at the entrance to the castle, creating an earsplitting explosion. The device had been planted by Kharlov's men on the inside, and it had plugged the only escape route from the castle.

The herd heading for the exit stopped then spilled in different directions. Kharlov reached inside his suit jacket and gripped his pistol in its shoulder holster. He had his eyes locked on Sokolov, who'd stopped on the spot and looked worried for the first time. His goons were on the ground, and he looked unsure about where to go.

Though Kharlov still had a reckoning scheduled with Veronika Oreshkin, who should have warned him about the attack on Merefa, she wasn't here. Instead, the man who'd ordered partisans into Merefa would face justice. Kharlov drew his pistol and aimed it at Sokolov, relishing the look in the Russian prime minister's eyes when he saw the weapon pointing at him.

Kharlov grinned and squeezed the trigger.

JACK GRUNTED as he tackled Sokolov to the ground, putting to use the skills from a childhood spent playing rugby. They landed hard, though the sound of their impact was drowned out by the boom and chatter of gunfire all around them. As he scrambled off Sokolov, he expected to be shot with each passing second, but somehow, the maelstrom surrounding them left him untouched.

Jack glanced at Sokolov to see if he'd been shot. He looked intact, so Jack turned his head to locate the man shooting at the Russian prime minister. The surge of people had momentarily blocked the shooter's line of fire, but Jack knew that would only last seconds. He needed to get Sokolov to safety, because he'd seen Sokolov's protective detail taken down moments earlier.

Jack climbed to his feet and held out a hand. When Sokolov took it, he pulled the Russian leader to his feet. "We need to get out of here."

"You... saved me?" Sokolov's face was twisted in confusion.

He shook his head then looked up at Jack. "My men... I... I don't understand."

"Your men are dead." Jack looked around, trying to figure out an escape route. "We need to get out of here."

When Sokolov nodded, Jack led him away from the attacking gunmen, who'd dug in behind tables and large potted plants. Acting purely on instinct and forcing down the dread, Jack headed for the small museum inside Castle Montjuic. Judging from his tour of the castle earlier in the day, it seemed to be as defensible a position as any. It had thick walls, only two entry points, and at least a little cover. Jack hoped help would arrive before the bad guys reached the museum.

As they crossed the courtyard, they moved among carnage. Dozens of bodies were splayed out in unnatural poses. Blood had pooled and made red ribbons all over the ground, and brass shell casings shined in the light. An orchestra of screams and gunfire provided the soundtrack to the insanity. Jack had been in firefights before, but never one so chaotic, with such poorly defined sides.

He'd returned to the reception after leaving the battlements, intending to look for Celeste before retiring for the night. Only a few minutes after he'd returned, armed men had stormed into the crowded courtyard and started spraying the crowd. The dams of sanity had burst, and confusion reigned.

He didn't know where Celeste was. He'd hit the deck as soon as the shooting had started and looked around the courtyard, but she'd been nowhere to be seen. He hoped she'd bolted at the first sign of the gunmen, and he hoped she'd escaped the castle before the bomb at the entrance had gone off. He'd already lost his former wife to terrorism, and he felt a lump of fear in the pit of his stomach at the thought Celeste might be gone, as well.

He didn't know where McGhinnist was, either, but the Secret Service agents would have surrounded him and ferried him to safety the second the shooting started, leaving the rest of the guests to fend for themselves. Jack was under no illusions that they would come back for him. The protocol in such situations was clear. There would be time to worry about the others later. He had to be alive to worry.

"This way, Prime Minister." Jack gripped Sokolov's jacket and pulled the Russian leader into the doorway of the museum. "I think we'll be safe in h—"

"Freeze!"

"Drop it!"

Jack pulled up short and blinked when he found three pistols aimed at his head and men shouting at him. The defenders already inside the castle museum were clearly taking no chances. Jack scanned the faces of the gunmen to see if he knew any of them. He didn't. Beside him, Sokolov tensed and started shouting abuse at one of the men in Russian.

"This *mudak is* one of my men!" Sokolov hissed the words. "And if he doesn't let us through, I'm going to club him to death with his own arm after I rip it off."

The effect was instant. The Russian vouched for Sokolov and raised his pistol. He and Sokolov were ushered inside the museum and told to join the rest of the civilians at the back. Jack glanced at Sokolov, let go of the prime minister's jacket, and nodded at him. Sokolov nodded back. Their alliance of convenience was over, but Jack had saved the chance of a nuclear deal.

Jack walked deeper into the museum, his attention shifting

from Sokolov to trying to find Celeste. About thirty people were huddled inside the museum, being watched over by three defenders, so he searched through scared faces one by one. His heart rate dropped a little at first, as the intensity of the gunfire from outside in the courtyard let up and the sound of the shots was muffled by the thick stone walls, but then his heart rate spiked all over again.

"Jack!" Celeste's wary smile was like the first ray of sunshine poking through a snowstorm as she raced across the room toward him. "I wasn't sure you'd made it."

"I couldn't find you anywhere." Jack held his arms out wide and wrapped her in a bear hug once she reached him. "I haven't seen McGhinnist, either."

"I'm sure he's fine, Jack." Celeste pulled away from Jack's hug a little and looked him in the eyes. "What's it like out there?"

"Chaos. There are bodies everywhere, and the summit is finished." Jack sighed. "But we can worry about all that later."

Suddenly, Jack didn't care about any of it. The world leaders, the nuclear deal, or whatever else happened in Barcelona. All that mattered was that he had found Celeste. The woman he loved was alive. There would be plenty of time to assess the rest of the damage and to find those responsible. Whoever had been bold enough to shoot up the Barcelona summit would pay dearly.

Jack and Celeste separated and held hands as they waited for the horror to end. The gunfire outside started to wane. Torrents of automatic fire reduced to a stream then a trickle as shooters on both sides were killed and wounded. With each shot, Celeste squeezed his hand tightly, but Jack felt the tension inside the museum drop as the gunfire slackened. Then the gunfire stopped entirely.

Jack exhaled slowly, still tense and expecting more craziness, but after a few seconds of silence, it seemed over. He turned to Celeste and smiled. She smiled back. After they'd been through so much together, this felt like a new extreme—an unprecedented massacre at a meeting of world leaders. Jack felt somewhat responsible for the carnage. He was the one who'd spearheaded calls for the summit, and now many who'd attended were dead or hurt.

"It's not your fault, Jack." Celeste seemed to read his mind. "These monsters—"

Celeste shrieked, and her eyes darted to the entrance. Frowning, Jack turned in time to see four men burst through the door. Three of them he didn't recognize, but one was the man who'd tried to kill Sokolov earlier. They were armed with a mix of pistols and submachine guns, outclassing the defenders inside the museum. A brief and bloody close-quarters firefight erupted inside the entrance to the museum.

As the two groups exchanged gunfire, Jack covered Celeste with his body. There was nothing else he could do. He was unarmed, and the only thing he could focus on was keeping her safe. The armed defenders inside the museum were down in seconds, and the attackers aimed their weapons at the civilians. The message was clear—give up the fight, or the civilians get sprayed with automatic gunfire. Nobody tried to resist.

"Smart." The man who'd tried to take down the Russian prime minister earlier spoke with an Eastern European accent. His voice was full of menace. "Where is Sokolov?"

"Here." Sokolov's voice boomed from the back of the museum as he stepped forward to meet his attackers. "Who are you cowards?"

"I am Dmitry Kharlov." The man shifted his aim to

Sokolov. "Your lackeys killed my family in Merefa. You are first to die. Veronika Oreshkin is next."

Jack frowned at the mention of Oreshkin, a reference that seemed to confuse Sokolov, as well. The Russian prime minister opened his mouth to speak, but Kharlov fired, and Sokolov fell to the ground. The survivors in the hall screamed and cowered away as Kharlov and the other shooter started to retreat from the museum, their target dead. Jack prepared to follow the architect of all this misery, until he felt a hand on his shoulder.

He turned his head to see Celeste. Tears running down her face, she shook her head, a clear message that she wanted him to stay.

He fought a brief internal battle then gave up on thoughts of taking down Kharlov. Instead, he wrapped an arm around Celeste and pulled her close. "It's over."

"Sir, I can't obey that order." Anna clenched her teeth, knowing she might regret her words later. "The attacks in the city are a sideshow. The real battle is at the castle."

Anna worked the clutch, shifted the Lexus into third gear, and planted her foot on the gas. The engine responded with a satisfying throaty roar that was accentuated by the sound of car horns as she ripped through an intersection. She was pleased to be through the final red light before hitting the winding roads that led up Montjuic and toward the castle.

"I won't tell you again, Ms. Fowler." The MI6 Barcelona station chief's voice was cold and serious. "If you ignore your duty and continue onto the castle, you'll be in violation of an order."

"Deal with me later, then." Anna braked into a corner then floored the high-performance vehicle out of it. "But I'm out here trying to do something while you get splinters in your ass!"

"Fowler, I warn you, I—"

Anna killed the call and tossed the phone into the console, glad to be able to devote all her attention to driving once again. She would deal with the ramifications of her disobedience later, but first, she had to make sure she and Patricia Evans weren't splattered against a tree. As she took them higher, she felt the tension in the car increase, as Evans seethed in the passenger seat next to her.

She sighed as she took another corner. "What's wrong?"

"You're a mad woman." Evans's voice sounded full of equal parts admiration and fear, as she gripped the passenger handle with knuckles that seemed to turn whiter with each corner. "Even if you don't take us off the road, you'll definitely get us put in front of the firing squad."

"You can get out if you'd prefer."

"I didn't say that..."

"Then shut up and let me get us there before it's too late—" Anna's eyes widened. "Fuck!"

Just when she thought she was through the most hair-raising moments of the drive, Anna was forced to swerve out of the way of a convoy of four jet-black SUVs that turned the corner ahead of her. She barely had time to slow, so the Lexus and the convoy passed each other at dangerous speeds, with barely a few inches between them.

"I bet that was McGhinnist." Anna exhaled deeply when the convoy was safely past. "At least he made it out."

"He might be the only one..."

Evans's words hung in the air as Anna focused on driving,

worried the convoy of another national leader might tear around every corner. They needed to make it to the top of the mountain, where terrorists had struck the castle. The reports out of the castle were scattered, but it sounded grave. A bomb had gone off, and multiple gunmen had opened fire. It had been the final target on a night when half of Barcelona seemed to be on fire.

Anna, Evans, and the other MI6 assets in Barcelona had been on duty when the first bomb had gone off at La Sagrada Familia. Only minutes after that bomb—probably made by the same guy as the one a few days back—she'd received a call from the station chief, ordering her to check it out. Anna and Evans had been on their way there when other bombs had exploded one after another, each one closer to the castle than the last. Her suspicion that the castle was next had been right, as only seconds after she'd turned the car around, a giant fireball had climbed into the sky from the top of the mountain.

They drove the rest of the way in silence, climbing the mountain and driving past the old Olympic Stadium on the way to the castle. Up ahead, the lights of emergency vehicles and the flames rising from the castle lit up the night, while sirens and the constant ringing of her cell phone provided the soundtrack. Anna was focused on nothing but the fate of her friends and putting a bullet in the skull of whoever was responsible for all of this mayhem.

"What the—" Anna was forced to slam on the brakes when a well-built man walked out onto the road in front of her.

He was wearing a black business suit, and he looked wounded, gripping his left bicep as he stumbled across the road. Anna couldn't see any signs that he was armed, so she slowed the car next to him and tapped on the horn. Only then did he turn his head to look at her.

Anna lowered the passenger-side window and leaned closer to Evans so she could see the wounded stranger. "Do you need some help? What happened up there?"

The man continued to stare at them for a few seconds, and Anna started to wonder if he spoke English. With so many officials from so many countries, it was possible he didn't. Any doubts she had were dispelled when he took his right hand away from his wound, reached into his coat, and produced a pistol. Anna and Evans both swore and reached for their own pieces, but they were a split second too slow.

The stranger fired. Anna winced as Evans's blood sprayed over her face, then she slumped forward against her seatbelt. Anna shouted a curse and gripped her pistol. The stranger had made his way around the back of the car and started to run away. She unbuckled her seatbelt, opened the door, and climbed out of the car. Taking a second to aim at the suited man, who was fifty yards away and approaching maximum visual range, she fired three shots.

"Got you."

Anna lowered her pistol a little as she saw him stumble, off the road and down the hill. Normally, she would have stopped to make sure he was dead, but he'd disappeared out of sight and she had more pressing matters to attend to. He'd likely been one of the men who'd shot up the summit, but he might not be the last. She returned to the car, glanced at Evans's lifeless body, and pounded the steering wheel with her fist. She was sick and tired of losing her people.

She put her foot to the floor, got back on the road, and arrived at the castle inside of a minute. The scene was carnage. Small fires were still burning at the entrance to the castle, where a bomb had exploded. Emergency vehicles were swarming into the parking lot. Anna parked and climbed out of her vehicle, gripping the pistol in case the shooting at the summit wasn't over.

She approached the entrance, but it quickly became clear to her the shooting was over. A fire was burning at the entrance to the castle, and nobody could enter or leave until it was put out. While she waited, she got a paramedic crew to take care of Evans's body. Rage filled the pit of her stomach, but she was unable to channel it in any helpful way. She'd disobeyed an order, Evans had been killed, and nothing useful had been achieved. Now she was left waiting to see if the British prime minister or anyone else had survived the attack inside the castle.

When the fire was out, several battered and bloody guards led the British prime minister out of the castle. Her eyes wide, Anna pushed herself off the Lexus and closed the distance to Graeme Egan, who looked up at her when she was a few yards away. Egan's eyes looked blank. He was shell-shocked. But he stopped walking and stared at Anna for a few moments.

"I know you." He waved off the police who were trying to keep him moving then frowned, as if trying to place Anna's face. "What's your name?"

"Anna Fowler, sir. I work for MI6." Anna stopped and kept a respectful distance. "Are you okay?"

Egan continued to stare at her, his expression changing from a look of shock to one of disgust. "I sent you here to stop this."

Anna felt the words like a punch to the gut. Anna and her team had done their best in Barcelona—like they had in Moscow and Kharkov before that—but they hadn't been able to interdict the enemies of Britain and the Western world before they'd struck. Now she was the only one left. She opened her mouth to speak, but no words came out. After another second, Egan shook his head and walked to a waiting vehicle.

Anna closed her eyes, stunned that her leader had called out her failure so bluntly. She felt lost. She didn't know what to do next. She wanted to put the people responsible for this atrocity into the ground and make sure they never had the chance to strike again, but after disobeying a direct order from the local station chief, the chances she'd be allowed to were low.

"Anna?"

She opened her eyes. She gave a slight smile when she saw a weary-looking Jack Emery approaching her, his arm around the waist of a stunning redhead. The man she'd gone through hell with and survived looked to have done it again. He had blood on his shirt, and he looked exhausted, but he was still standing. It seemed like there was nothing that could kill Jack Emery.

"Jack..." Anna smiled at him. "What a fucking mess..."

"You should see the other guy." Emery laughed. "At least it's over."

Anna doubted he was right.

11

In addition to the explosions across the city, there are reports that the summit at Castle Montjuic has also been attacked. The Standard *is still trying to confirm the situation, but there appears to have been an explosion outside the castle and armed gunmen on the loose inside of it. As the situation continues to develop, it seems like the attacks in Barcelona are the most synchronized and deadly terrorist attack since September 11.*

—*New York Standard*

"WHISKEY ALL ROUND." Jack collapsed into the booth and slid over to the wall, then he glanced at Celeste and Anna. "Do you guys want some food too?"

"I DON'T THINK I could keep it down." Celeste sat next to Jack.

"I will take the whiskey, though. And that's just to start."

JACK NODDED and wrapped his arm around Celeste as Anna slid into the seat opposite them. They sat in silence and waited for the waitress to return with their drinks, coming to terms with the fact they'd survived. As soon as they'd finished up talking to the police at the castle, Jack had asked one of the cops to drive them down the mountain and into the city. He'd taken Anna and Celeste to the bar inside the hotel where the American delegation was staying. Even though the president had flown out, the hotel was still one of the safest places in Barcelona.

THE FULL PICTURE of events at the castle was slowly becoming clear. The losses had been catastrophic. In addition to Nikolai Sokolov, the president of Pakistan was dead. Countless diplomats, national officials, and security personnel had also been killed or wounded. Everyone who'd been at the castle and survived was scarred by an atrocity they would never forget. It would take days for the entire cost to be tallied, but Jack was already devastated.

DMITRY KHARLOV HAD thrust a spear into the chest of Jack's pet project and pierced its heart. The Barcelona summit was in ruins. Those world leaders who hadn't been killed or injured were already in the air and on their way home, including McGhinnist. The officials who'd been in Barcelona for the summit would depart in the coming days. The shared purpose that had brought them all together had turned to ashes.

JACK SMILED at the waitress when she brought the drinks. He raised the glass to Celeste and Anna. "To those who didn't make it."

JACK CLINKED his glass against the others then took a sip of the whiskey, savoring the burn as it raced down his throat. He looked at Celeste. She still looked shaken. A few hours ago, she'd been covering the summit's opening reception, with significant progress on nuclear disarmament looking like a real possibility, and now, half the people she'd spoken to were dead. He placed a hand on top of her hand and squeezed it.

AFTER SMILING AT CELESTE, he shifted his gaze to Anna, whose face was as unreadable as ever. "Why the hell were you in Barcelona, anyway?"

"HELPING our Spanish friends keep the summit safe from terrorism." Anna shrugged. "Clearly didn't do so well, did I?"

"IT WASN'T YOUR FAULT—" Jack paused as his phone rang and broke the sentence. He dug the phone out of his pocket and answered. "Hello?"

"IT'S ME." Caleb Davidson's voice was grave. "I'm aboard Air

Force One with the president. Sorry we couldn't get you out, Jack."

"IT'S FINE, Caleb. I'm back at the hotel with Celeste and Anna Fowler." Jack glanced at each of the women as he spoke their names. "We made it out okay. A lot of people didn't."

"WE'VE GOT the CIA and the Bureau working the camera footage. They've confirmed the kill of every attacker, except one."

JACK SNORTED. "A man named Kharlov? Wearing a navy-blue business suit? The same guy who blew Sokolov away?"

JACK DIDN'T HEAR Davidson's response, because he saw Anna immediately stiffen at his description of Kharlov. Her expression had clouded over. He frowned at her. "What?"

ANNA'S EXPRESSION was impossible to read, until she opened her mouth to speak. "That description sounds like the guy I shot coming up the mountain—the guy who killed my partner."

"WHO'S THAT? Does she know something about Kharlov?" Davidson asked. "Put me on speaker."

"It's Anna Fowler." Jack removed the phone from his ear, switched the call to speaker, and put the phone on the table. "You're on speaker, Caleb."

"I want you to answer very carefully, Ms. Fowler." Davidson paused. "Are you saying you killed Dmitry Kharlov?"

"He shot my partner, and I shot him." Anna shrugged. "I couldn't confirm he was dead, though. He stumbled off the road and out of sight. Down the mountain. I kept on to the castle."

Jack disengaged from the conversation as he tried to process the strands of information—the things Dmitry Kharlov had said and what he'd learned since. When Kharlov killed Sokolov, it didn't seem like his crusade was over. Instead, it had sounded like the man who'd blown up half the attractions in Barcelona and orchestrated an assault on a fortress filled with world leaders was just getting started.

Jack's eyes widened. "He planned for it to be a one-way mission, but then Oreshkin wasn't there. He mentioned her before he blew Sokolov away. She was as much the target as he was."

"Did he say why?"

"No."

"HASN'T Oreshkin dropped off the radar?" Celeste leaned forward, her journalistic curiosity clearly piqued. "Do you guys know something about her?"

"WELL..." The taste filling Jack's mouth was far stronger than the burn of the whiskey. He looked at Anna, who wasn't about to reveal a thing about Jack's near miss in Moscow. Then he looked at his fiancée and saw that her piercing eyes were staring back at him. "Sokolov tried to kill her..."

"AND WE GOT her out and used her to get Sokolov here." Davidson bailed Jack out of trouble. "We had her safe here in Barcelona, until someone attacked her in her hotel room."

"WHAT?" Jack scoffed, surprised at Davidson's revelation. "When?"

"AT THE SAME time as the castle was being shot up. She's been rushed to hospital with a bullet in her..." Davidson's voice trailed off. "Now I think of it, it would be useful if a newspaper reported that she's in a hospital. It would smoke out Kharlov if he did make it off the mountain and also give Russia another option for prime minister now that Sokolov is dead..."

JACK SMILED and looked at Celeste. "I think I know a reporter who'd love that kind of scoop, especially one that might help put an end to all this."

CELESTE ROLLED HER EYES. "That reporter would need more than what you guys are giving me. She'd need a quote from the woman herself or a reason *why* Kharlov was after her."

DAVIDSON LAUGHED. "Get her down to Hospital de Barcelona. We've got people there watching over Oreshkin."

JACK OPENED his mouth to speak, but the line went dead. He pocketed the phone and drained the glass of whiskey. His two companions did likewise. They were all in a hurry to get to the hospital and get answers from Oreshkin. Much more than when he'd gone to meet her in Moscow or when she'd been sprung upon him when he'd returned to America, Jack felt a sudden connection with Veronika Oreshkin that went beyond the nuclear talks.

THE WORLD HAD CHANGED in the last twenty-four hours, but Veronika Oreshkin would be one of the people who dictated how it changed in the days and weeks to come.

VERONIKA'S EYES flickered open then immediately closed again, the searing light overwhelming her senses. A while later, she tried to open them again, with a similar result. More time passed—her mind couldn't process how much—and the process was repeated several times. Finally, she managed to hold her eyes open for more than a few seconds.

AFTER THAT SMALL victory and with her mind still cloudy, she shifted her focus to figuring out where she was. She couldn't hear anything except silence, and she couldn't see anything except halogen tube lighting interspersed with white ceiling tiles. No matter how hard she thought, the answer to her current location was always just an *inch* away. Her mind had the pieces to a simple jigsaw puzzle, but she was unable to put them all together.

WAS SHE IN HEAVEN? Hell? A hospital? Yes... a hospital. That was far more likely. The gears in Veronika's head continued to turn. She was alive and *probably* in a hospital. That was as much as she was going to learn in bed, so she tried to sit up and made it about an inch before an indescribable pain tore through her shoulder. Her groan for help was barely audible as she was forced to lie down again. She was confused and in pain. Her mouth felt like a desert. All she wanted was answers...

SOME TIME LATER, Veronika woke again, feeling more lucid. The drugs had started to wear off, and she was more aware of her surroundings. She opened her eyes and turned her head. She was clearly in a hospital room, surrounded by machines with digital displays that told passing medical professionals she was still ticking.

SHE TURNED her head a little more and was surprised to see two men standing just outside the door of her hospital room. They were wearing a uniform she didn't recognize and holding submachine guns. Though they were chatting casually, the fact they were there at all confused her. She was struggling to figure out why armed guards were outside her room, then her eyes widened.

SHE REMEMBERED. Nikolai Sokolov's killer had come to assassinate her in her hotel room. They'd fought and she'd been shot, moments before she'd sliced his throat open.

VERONIKA STARTED to hyperventilate as confusion catalyzed into panic. She didn't know if she was still in Barcelona or in a Russian hospital, guarded by her foes. She lifted her hand to feel for the gunshot wound in her shoulder, but the tangle of IV tubes in her wrist restricted her. She gripped the IV lines and yanked on them, wincing in pain as the tape holding them in place tore at her skin. Alarms started to wail, and the guards at the door turned to face her.

VERONIKA KEPT her eyes locked on the guards. One of them ran inside the room, his eyes shifting between her and the machines, which were blaring. He didn't seem to know what to do as blood dribbled from her wrist. His partner ran to get help. With her free hand, she reached up to where she'd been shot. She felt around her shoulder, gently at first, then more firmly as she realized the whole area was padded with gauze and bandages.

VERONIKA'S GAZE shifted to a female nurse who'd entered the room, followed by the second guard. In contrast to the armed men, the woman was calm as she reached the bed, gripped Veronika's hand, and gently placed it back in its original position. She spoke in Spanish, which immediately calmed Veronika. Although she didn't understand the language, it meant she was still in Barcelona.

VERONIKA LET the woman do her job, silencing the machines and reinserting the IV lines. She smiled at the nurse. "Do you speak English?"

"YES." The nurse didn't look away from her work, but she did give a shy smile. "You're going to be okay."

"WHERE AM I?" Veronika tried to lift her torso up on the bed, wanting to see where the guards had gone. "Who are those men?"

"MINISTER ORESHKIN, PLEASE STAY IN BED!" The nurse placed a hand on Veronika's shoulder and gently pushed her back down onto the bed. "You've lost a lot of blood."

Veronika closed her eyes, suddenly feeling light-headed as the nurse continued to fuss. A second later, her eyes shot open. "Where is the Russian prime minister?"

Veronika felt the nurse tense and saw the two guards look at each other. Something was wrong. Although she hadn't expected to survive the fight in the hotel room, she'd taken down Sokolov's lapdog and lived to tell the tale. She'd escaped death at the hands of his lackeys twice, but she didn't think for a second that Sokolov would quit. He was a vindictive man who eradicated his enemies no matter the cost.

"Minister Oreshkin..." The woman was clearly uncomfortable about revealing whatever she knew.

"Tell me!" Veronika snapped then instantly regretted it. The nurse had been nothing but nice to her. "I'm sorry. Please, tell me."

"Terrorists attacked Castle Montjuic last night." The nurse's lips pressed together. "Prime Minister Sokolov was gunned down at the opening reception for the Barcelona summit. So were other world leaders. We have dozens of wounded survivors here in this hospital, but a lot of people didn't make it. It was a catastrophe."

"HE'S... DEAD?"

"YES." The nurse nodded. "I need to continue my rounds now. We're very busy."

VERONIKA NODDED and looked up at the ceiling as the nurse left the room. She couldn't believe the news. Sokolov had been the tyrant in charge of Russia for a decade and a giant in the country's politics for longer than that. She'd tried to thwart his worst abuses and been locked up. When he'd put her in prison, she hadn't imagined a scenario where she might outlive her captor. But if the nurse was right, she'd done exactly that.

SHE NEEDED TO PLAN. Without Sokolov, there would be a power vacuum in Russia the likes of which the country hadn't seen in decades. It would make the bloodbath after Stalin's death look like a paper cut. The president would look for stability, Sokolov's lackeys around the cabinet table would vie for power, while others on the fringes of politics would see a chance to improve their positions. Violence and manipulation would be around every corner.

VERONIKA WAS NO DIFFERENT. A career she'd thought lost suddenly had enormous potential once again. Before her exile, she'd been the leading moderate and one of the most senior figures in Sokolov's inner circle. Now that he was out of the way, she had the chance to live and work again. She would have to move quickly, because Russian politics didn't reward the cautious or the tame.

VERONIKA TRIED to open her eyes again, but a fresh dose of drugs had made her sleepy.

~

"I NEED to speak with Minister Oreshkin." Jack's nostrils flared at the nurse as he tried to keep his cool. "It's a matter of national security."

THE NURSE'S face remained neutral, the same as when she'd told Jack he couldn't visit Oreshkin six hours ago and in the many hours since. "You're not in your country, sir."

"YOU DON'T KNOW the half of it." Jack sighed. He was an Australian, trying to see a Russian in a Spanish hospital room, on behalf of the American government. "When can I see her?"

"WHEN THE DOCTORS SAY SO." The nurse provided the same deadpan answer she had the last few times Jack asked. "Now, excuse me, I have work to do."

JACK CROSSED his arms as the nurse walked away. They were close to missing the print deadline for the *New York Standard*, which meant their plan to reveal Oreshkin was alive and flush out Kharlov might be scuttled. If the terrorist who'd hit the summit was still alive, Jack figured he would soon be long gone. If they didn't get Celeste in front of Oreshkin soon, they would blow their chance to catch the mastermind behind the attacks.

AFTER A SIGH, Jack returned to the waiting area, where Celeste and Anna were waiting. Celeste didn't even look up from the magazine she was flicking through. She was as tired as Jack had ever seen her, but at least she was still awake. Anna Fowler was a different story. The British agent was living up to the reputation of soldiers and spies getting sleep whenever and wherever they could. Her chin was against her chest, and she was out of it.

JACK SAT in the seat next to Celeste and exhaled slowly through his nose. "They're still not letting any visitors through."

"I'VE GOT fifteen minutes to file the story. It's written, but without me sighting her and getting a quote, I can't run it." Celeste shrugged. "It wouldn't be fair to leak it without telling her, either."

JACK NODDED. He agreed they couldn't put Oreshkin in danger without her agreement, and he knew the editorial policies of the *New York Standard* as well as anyone, given he'd worked there for years prior to joining McGhinnist's staff. No, unless they got to Oreshkin soon, their entire plan would be ruined. Kharlov would escape Barcelona, and their plan to put Oreshkin in the mix to become the Russian prime minister would be at risk.

JACK FELT an elbow to his ribs and opened his eyes. A doctor was standing in front of them, and the nurse from earlier waiting a few steps back. Jack stood. "What's up, Doc?"

THE DOCTOR ROLLED HIS EYES, clearly familiar enough with Bugs Bunny to get the reference. "I understand you wish to speak with Ms. Oreshkin. I've asked, and she is happy to see you. I will permit you to visit her for five minutes on the condition that you don't get her excited or upset. She's very fragile. Okay?"

"YEP!"

JACK FOLLOWED the medical staff to Oreshkin's room with Celeste and Anna in tow, both women now awake and alert. They'd waited hours for this moment, though it remained to be seen if their stakeout had been worthwhile. Once the huddle of people was outside Oreshkin's room, the doctor fixed them with another hard glare—another warning—and they entered the darkened room.

JACK KNEW Oreshkin had been shot, but seeing her was still a shock. She was very pale and hooked up to machines. He smiled at her when she turned her head to look at him. "Hi."

ORESHKIN GLARED at him for a few seconds then turned her attention to Anna and Celeste. "Who are you two?"

JACK PUT a hand on Celeste's back. "This is Celeste Adams, my fiancée and a reporter for the *New York Standard*—"

"AND I'M ANNA FOWLER. I work for MI6," Anna cut in. "My last job before I arrived in Barcelona was saving Jack in Moscow after you failed to meet with him."

ORESHKIN CRACKED A HINT OF A SMILE. "You have my thanks for that. Sokolov always had a certain way of expressing his feelings."

"YOU KNOW HE'S DEAD?" Jack watched Oreshkin carefully then continued when she nodded. "A man named Kharlov shot up the conference and killed Nikolai Sokolov."

"KHARLOV?" Oreshkin frowned, clearly confused and still fighting through the effects of the drugs pumping through her system. "*Dmitry* Kharlov?"

THE SIGNS of recognition in Oreshkin's eyes made alarm bells in Jack's head wail. She opened her mouth to speak more then closed it again, frowning. Though he didn't know why Kharlov had wanted her dead, it was clear Oreshkin had a history with the man. Jack suddenly wanted to know all about their past and see if it gave them some answers.

"TIME IS OF THE ESSENCE, MINISTER." Jack took a step closer to the bed. "Kharlov might already be gone, but if he's still in Barcelona, we hope to use your presence here to smoke him out."

"I'M in a hospital because your people failed to keep me safe, and now you want to dangle me like bait?" Oreshkin scoffed. "You have no idea how dangerous he is."

"SO TELL ME!"

"DMITRY KHARLOV IS the most prolific arms dealer on the planet." Oreshkin looked between Jack and the two women. "He's armed both sides of every conflict all over the world for the last two decades, but I bet nobody in your countries have ever even heard of him. He can find any weaponry that his buyers want, but he has other uses, as well."

"I DON'T like the sound of that..." Jack's voice trailed off, making it clear that Oreshkin should continue.

"FOR THE LAST THREE YEARS, I've been supplying information to Kharlov about Russia's movements in Ukraine." She paused to take a breath. "He'd arm the locals, and I'd tell him where to avoid."

"WHY?"

"BECAUSE I WANTED Sokolov's ambitions to be frustrated and curtailed. I wanted him to be mired so deep in Ukraine that his ambitions were limited elsewhere."

A GIANT PIECE of the puzzle fell into place in Jack's mind. "Before Sokolov locked you up, did you know Merefa was going to be hit by partisans? Did you warn Kharlov?"

"NO." Her face went ashen. "That's where Kharlov's family lived. I promised to keep the town safe, and in return, Kharlov flooded weapons into Ukraine to frustrate Sokolov's efforts."

"I THINK YOU FAILED. He blamed you and Sokolov for the town being razed and his family being killed, but only one of you is still alive."

"THEN HE'LL NEVER STOP HUNTING me." Oreshkin closed her

eyes. "He's relentless—a god of the criminal underworld. So do what you need to do to flush him out while we have the chance."

JACK NODDED and glanced at Celeste. She started talking to Oreshkin, getting the few quotes she needed to run the story in the *Standard*. He'd already worked with her to craft the story. It outlined how fortunate Oreshkin had been to get ill and miss the summit's opening reception, but its real purpose was to lure Dmitry Kharkov to the hospital. If he did blame Oreshkin for the death of his family, it was possible he would disregard his safety and try to attack her again. If that happened, there were assets in place to stop him.

"THAT'S ALL I NEED." Celeste smiled at Oreshkin after a minute then looked at Jack. "I'll get the story filed. It'll run online instantly, and it'll be on the front page the day after tomorrow."

JACK NODDED and waited until Celeste had left the room, then he looked back at Oreshkin. "If he comes here, we'll nab him."

"THAT'S FINE, but I won't be here." Oreshkin fixed Jack with a hard glare. "I'm no use as your pawn now that Sokolov is dead. I want to return to Russia to stake my claim."

JACK SMILED. "That's precisely what we had in mind."

12

Amid all the death and destruction in Barcelona, one amazing story of luck has emerged. The Standard *has confirmed that Russia's foreign minister, Veronika Oreshkin, who was not in attendance at the summit, is still alive. It is believed that Ms. Oreshkin has recently been suffering from an illness, which had been kept secret by the Russian prime minister and resulted in a lack of public appearances in recent weeks. Though she was in Barcelona to advise Nikolai Sokolov, Ms. Oreshkin's illness meant she was not in attendance at the summit's opening reception at Castle Montjuic. The minister is currently being treated at Hospital de Barcelona. With her leader dead and the summit in disarray, Ms. Oreshkin has some work ahead of her when she recovers.*

—New York Standard

Kharlov whistled as he strolled the boardwalk along the Barcelona foreshore, headed toward the city's marina a few hundred yards away. On one side of him was the ocean, quiet and dark, while on the other was a mixture of bars and restaurants. Despite it being close to midnight, the area would usually still be buzzing with locals and tourists out for a good time, but the bombings had clearly scared them off. That suited him just fine.

He was walking with a slight limp, but otherwise, he was in good enough shape and totally focused on escaping the city. With his description in circulation and security camera footage from the attack at the castle being shown in the media, he had to get the hell out of Barcelona before some cop got lucky and managed to corner him. He knew that the risk increased with every passing second. He'd come to Barcelona to wreak his vengeance, but his success was only partial.

Although he'd splattered Sokolov's brain over the walls and floor of Castle Montjuic, Veronika Oreshkin was still alive and breathing. He'd been tempted by the media reports that said Oreshkin was in the hospital, only a few miles away from where he was, but he knew he couldn't get within one hundred yards of her before he was taken down. It was time to get the hell out of Dodge. He had to get out of the city, develop a new plan, and strike at Veronika Oreshkin when the time was right. Only then would his vengeance finally be complete, the death of his family avenged.

After killing Sokolov and escaping the castle, he'd barely made it halfway down the mountain when a car pulled up alongside him. He'd seen the people inside were armed, so he'd used his last bullet on one of them then fled. The other woman in the car had shot him in the back, but the bullet had hit him in the Kevlar vest he'd been wearing. Although the bullet hadn't penetrated the vest, it had left him with a terrible bruise and a cracked rib.

Once he'd reached the bottom of the hill, he'd broken into an empty townhouse. After a shower, he'd turned on the television and watched the news, knowing he needed information to stay on top of the situation. The coverage had confirmed the noose was tightening on him. He'd faced a choice: lie low or try to break out of the city and escape the attention of the authorities. He'd chosen the latter option, leaving the townhouse and heading to the marina. He was starting to regret it, though.

He stopped one hundred yards away from the marina and cursed. He stood and watched for a long few seconds, staring at the police car up ahead with its light flashing. He knew any form of conventional transport was too risky. Air or rail travel was impossible with his description in circulation, and the roads would be swarming with cops. Stealing a boat from the marina had been his best option, but that possibility was being blocked by the cops. They had to be dealt with.

Kharlov entered the nearest bar—a small intimate wine bar—and sat. He ordered a vodka. While it was being poured, he looked at the other patrons. There was a group of three women sitting at the bar, a couple on one of the sofas, and a single man on a different sofa. He was the one who interested Kharlov the most, because he wouldn't be missed by any partner or friends. With a plan in his head and his drink ready, he sipped and waited for his moment.

Fifteen minutes later, the single man headed to the bathroom. After waiting for half a minute, Kharlov stood from his barstool and followed him into the bathroom. It had a urinal on one wall, a washbasin opposite, and a single cubicle past both of them. The Spaniard was already at the urinal, so Kharlov locked the door as quietly as he could then headed for the cubicle. As he passed the Spaniard, Kharlov bumped into him and muttered an apology.

"Puta madre!"

Kharlov smiled and turned around. The Spaniard had finished peeing and had turned to threaten Kharlov. Without hesitation, Kharlov hooked the man to the jaw with his right fist. Pain exploded through Kharlov's hand, and he muttered a curse, but it was nothing compared to the effect on the Spaniard. His eyes went glassy, his legs gave out, his head slammed into the urinal, and he flopped to the floor.

Kharlov reached down, gripped the man's belt, and dragged him into the cubicle, leaving a trail of blood from the man's destroyed jaw. Once inside the cubicle, Kharlov placed a hand under each arm and hefted the unconscious lump up onto the toilet. A quick search through his pockets produced the cell phone Kharlov had been hoping to find. He used the unconscious man's thumbprint to unlock the phone, pocketed it, and left the bathroom.

He returned to the bar long enough to settle the bill then left the bar. He sighed when he saw the cop car was still parked out front of the marina, its lights still flashing and showing no signs of moving on. After stealing a phone, he had a plan for that. He pulled the phone out of his pocket, dialed the local emergency number, and put the phone to his ear.

Kharlov ignored the operator, who answered the phone in Spanish. He raised his voice and asked, "Do you speak English?"

"Yes, sir." The operator switched seamlessly into English, her voice cool and calm. "What's your emergency?"

He smiled. "I have spotted the man on the television. The man wanted for the bombings. He's in a bar just near the marina. It's called Senorita Sangria."

"Thank you, sir." The operator's tone changed. There was a slight pause, and Kharlov could hear the sound of typing. "Don't approach him. We'll take care of it."

Kharlov killed the call and put the phone back in his pocket. Within a few seconds, the cop car out front of the marina blared its sirens and tore down the street. Kharlov smiled and resumed his walk to the marina, his head down and his hands in his pockets. He hoped the cops had tunnel vision, focused on the big bust and not on the man walking right past their speeding vehicle.

"Come on..." Kharlov whispered to himself as the cop car passed him, its sirens hurting his ears and its flashing lights illuminating his face against the darkness. "Come on..."

The cops didn't stop. Kharlov increased his pace and didn't look back. He reached the marina and walked out on the pier, selecting one of the smaller vessels at random. He looked left and right then boarded the vessel. A locked door guarded the bridge, so Kharlov put his boot through the window and reached through to unlock it. He stepped inside the bridge and smiled at the sight of his new ride.

"Hello, beautiful." Kharlov gripped the wheel for a second then pulled out the cell phone. He dialed a number he knew by heart and put the phone to his ear.

It took far longer for this call to be answered than when he'd called the emergency operator, but eventually, he heard someone breathing heavily. "What?"

Kharlov snorted. "It's me."

"Dmitry?" Natalya inhaled sharply in surprise, her voice suddenly clear and her tone changing dramatically. "Where are you?"

Kharlov had expected the question. He'd walked out on his people and traveled to Barcelona alone. They would never have let him go alone, so he'd simply not told them. He'd expected Barcelona to be a one-way trip, and for the most part, he'd been right. His mercenaries had been slaughtered. He would have happily died with them, except his vengeance wasn't complete. So now he needed to call upon his men once again. Or his woman, in any case.

"I'm in Barcelona... I've taken care of one of the men responsible for killing my family."

"I did wonder if it was you who put on such an impressive show..." Natalya paused. "How can I help, Dmitry?"

Kharlov smiled. She knew him well enough to know he wouldn't just be making a social call. Though he'd used none of his regular crew to hit the Barcelona summit, he would need their help with the next phase of his vengeance—his escape from the city and his move against Veronika Oreshkin. Thankfully, Natalya had a specific set of skills that would prove very helpful in solving his first problem.

"Natalya, I need your help to hot-wire a boat..."

ANNA PUT her hands in the pockets of her trench coat and walked down the hallway of the apartment complex. On either side of her were doors that led into apartments worth more than she would earn in a lifetime, residences that highlighted the opulence that Russia's elites lived in while the majority of its people fought over the scraps. As she walked, she briefly wondered what percentage of people who lived in the complex had made their money legally.

Not many, she guessed, but at least one of those elites was going to have a reckoning. That was what had brought her back to the Russian capital. This job was a personal one, because she'd been a rogue agent from the moment she disregarded an order from the MI6 Barcelona station chief. There was every chance she wouldn't have a job when she finally reported in, but first, she wanted to help Emery and get some vengeance for Graeme Tanner, the colleague she'd lost in Kharkov.

She reached the door to the apartment, knocked on the door, and waited with a fake smile plastered on. Normally, two burly men armed with submachine guns would have been standing out front of the apartment, ready to intervene in situations exactly like this one, but she'd timed her move perfectly. The apartment and the man inside it were as exposed as she felt, naked on the bottom except for some flimsy underwear.

Russian Defense Minister Sergey Popov was about to pay for his immorality. She'd come to Moscow to blackmail Popov out of Russian politics. She'd flown aboard Veronika Oreshkin's medical transport, an undocumented passenger who'd boarded in one city then melted away in another. Apart from Oreshkin and Jack Emery, nobody knew she was in Russia. Anna hoped to complete her mission and get out of the country without that fact changing.

Emery had provided some US intelligence that revealed Popov sent his security away and ordered prostitutes in each Sunday night, the evening before meetings of the Russian cabinet. The pattern was like clockwork. The pattern that had successfully fooled his wife had also created a vulnerability that Anna intended to exploit ruthlessly. Popov would stay in his apartment in central Moscow rather than the home he shared with his wife, ostensibly because it was closer to the meeting, but really so he could screw around.

When Anna heard the dead bolt disengage, she smiled a

little wider. The door opened, and Anna found herself face-to-face with Popov, who was wearing even less than she was under her trench coat. He was an older man, with some of the sagginess to show for it, but beneath his thin layer of flab, he still had the foundation of a formerly chiselled body. Popov had been a soldier before he was a politician, and he was still in pretty good shape.

Anna kept smiling as Popov grumbled at her in Russian and gestured for her to enter. She walked past him and stopped just inside the doorway. Her surroundings were opulent, with expensive furniture and a living room that was more than double the size of any apartment Anna had ever lived in. It made her feel like she should ask for a pay rise, if she still had a job at all.

Anna stayed anchored to the spot as Popov closed the door, locked it, then walked to the kitchen. Anna heard the pop of a champagne cork, the crunch of ice, and the clink of glasses. A second later, he reappeared, holding an ice bucket that had a bottle of champagne and two glasses inside. Without even looking at her, he carried the ice bucket down another hall to the bedroom. Popov was a real charmer, that was for sure.

Anna followed Popov to his bedroom, scanning her surroundings to make sure he had no cameras or other security she hadn't factored into her plan. Though Emery had been right about Popov dismissing the guards on the door, American intelligence hadn't known anything about the inside of his apartment. She needed to be sure that what happened in the next few minutes would stay a secret forever.

She reached the bedroom. Popov was already sprawled out on his back on the king-sized bed, his eyes locked on her. On the bedside table, the champagne bucket and glasses sat alongside a pistol, which was close enough that he could reach it in seconds. Suddenly, a job Anna hoped would be simple had become a whole lot more complicated.

Anna walked to the edge of the bed and started unbuttoning the trench coat. When she reached the last button, she shrugged the coat off and laid it out gently on the end of the bed. She felt his eyes feasting on her as she stood just inches away from his body, wearing only the tiniest bra and panties. She felt self-conscious in the tacky lingerie, a cheap set she'd purchased at an all-night sex shop in Moscow.

Anna walked around the bed to the side table, where she lifted the champagne bottle out of the ice and poured a glass. After taking a sip, she placed the glass back on the side table and smiled down at Popov. She reached out and gently placed a finger on each of his eyes. When he closed them, she brushed her hand gently over his face then down his chest and kept going. She could see the bulge in his underwear, but she avoided the area.

Anna kept her eyes locked on him as she reached inside the pocket of her coat at the end of the bed. She pulled out her silenced pistol and aimed it at him. A few seconds passed, and he opened his eyes. She enjoyed the split-second change in his facial expression, from lust to confusion to fear to anger. His lips curled back into a snarl, and he started to throw more Russian words at her.

Anna stepped forward and jammed the pistol into his exposed ribs. "I know you speak English, dickhead. If you move, I'm more than happy to put bullets in hard-to-reach places."

"You're... British?" He seemed confused again. "I'm assuming you're not a hooker who's come to rob me."

"Correct." Anna smiled. "But it's going to look like one did, right down to the building concierge who I flashed a little skin at."

To his credit, Popov didn't cry or beg for his life. He looked cold and calculating. He was a soldier, used to the transaction of life and death. He sighed. "So, which of my enemies decided it was time to make a move against me now Sokolov is dead? It was Mikhailov, wasn't it? That fat bastard could never do his own dirty work."

"I imagine there's quite a long line, but this one is all me." Anna spat the words, resisting the urge to pull the trigger and end the life of a certified human stain. "You've committed countless war crimes, most recently using poison to slaughter hundreds of cops and soldiers. You also killed my friend. You owe the world a great moral debt, and the bill has come due."

"Kharkov?" Popov laughed. "This is about Kharkov?"

Anna nodded. "Do you know what hollow-point rounds do to the human body?"

"Of course, I—"

"The sadists who designed them sound a little like you. They decided regular bullets weren't damaging enough, so they invented some that fracture into small micro-shards when they enter your body. They rip and tear all sorts of important squishy bits, turning your insides into pulp and making it near impossible to save your life. Best of all, they're painful."

Popov didn't show any hint of fear. "I hope you realize you'll never make it out of Moscow alive?"

"They said the same thing about Jack Emery, but I got him out." Anna enjoyed the flash of recognition and anger in the man's eyes. "I bet you know all about that."

"Emery was meddling in something that didn't concern him. I was following the orders of my prime minister and eliminating a feral animal." Popov shrugged. "It was the same story in Ukraine. I'm certain you work for the British government—MI6 probably—so you're used to following orders, as well. You and I are merely servants. I just get paid more than you do—"

"That excuse didn't stack up at Nuremburg." Anna cut off the conversation. "Now here's what's going to happen. I have evidence linking you to underage hookers. If it is released, either your enemies or your citizens will take you out. Although I want you dead, I'm happy enough if you just disappear. Resign from politics, withdraw from public life, get out of Oreshkin's way."

"You think my colleagues care about my sexual proclivities?" He scoffed, but his eyes showed fear for the first time.

"You bet I do." She smiled. "I think they'll eat you alive if they find out, especially now Sokolov isn't around to protect you. Now, it's time to choose."

Anna aimed the pistol at Popov's head as she waited. He would either comply with her instructions or try to make a move. Now that he knew the stakes, he faced a choice that would define the rest of his life. Anna gave it about an even chance that Popov would try to take her down. He wasn't the type of man who let himself be blackmailed, especially when it involved his professional ruin.

Anna half-squeezed on the trigger as Popov turned his head to glance at his pistol. He was on his back, so his chances of reaching his piece before she ended him were almost zero, but he might consider the odds better than succumbing to her blackmail. He looked back at Anna and stared into her eyes. His eyes, cold and calculating, showed no fear. He was a military veteran making a calculated choice.

The moment he moved, Anna pulled the trigger.

Anna sighed as she looked down at Popov's corpse. She hadn't wanted to kill him, but he'd gone for the gun. Now his brains were splattered over the bed. The silencer had dispersed most of the noise, and the hollow-point rounds had worked as advertised. All that was left was the cleanup. She lacked the time and the resources to remove his body completely, but there were a few steps she could take.

She dressed in the trench coat then put her pistol in the grip of his hand for only a second, getting his prints on the weapon. Satisfied, she tossed her pistol on the floor and pocketed the pistol he'd had on the bedside table. By leaving her pistol with both sets of prints on it for the cops to find, Anna hoped it might now look like a hooker had messed up Popov with one of his own guns. She wasn't worried about her prints. She was a ghost.

VERONIKA WINCED as the limousine she was riding in hit a pothole, causing her to bounce a little and hit her shoulder against the back of the seat. Pain immediately shot through her shoulder, feeling like someone was branding her, reminding her yet again that Nikolai Sokolov had failed to take her life. She leaned back against the seat, inhaling sharply through clenched teeth as the pain from her gunshot wound subsided.

When she was settled again, Veronika pressed a button on her armrest, which lowered the glass separating her from the driver. "Please be more careful."

"My apologies, Minister. The roads in Moscow..." The

driver shrugged. "You may as well ask me to fly a kite to the moon."

Veronika nodded, raised the window, and settled back into silence. She knew they were close to the Kremlin, where the president had asked the members of Sokolov's cabinet to meet to determine a new prime minister, and she needed all the time she could get to mentally prepare. She was about to walk into a room full of predators. Surviving the attempts of Sokolov and Kharlov to kill her might just be the entrée.

Veronika sat in silence for the next few minutes, readying her mind and trying to put thoughts of Sokolov and Kharlov out of her mind. One of them was dead, and she hoped the other was too, given the whole world now knew she was alive. The second Jack Emery's fiancée reported the news, she'd been transported to a different hospital in Barcelona, in case Kharlov came to attack her.

He hadn't, though. Although the Barcelona police had been stationed at her original hospital, ready to strike if Kharlov appeared, he hadn't shown up. Days had passed with no sign of him, and it appeared he was dead or had been smart enough to recognize the trap and fled. It was a bitter disappointment, because if Kharlov really blamed her for his family's death, then he would never stop coming for her.

At least she was back home, no matter how dangerous the meeting with her colleagues was going to be. She'd flown out of Barcelona several days after the attack, aboard a specialized medical aircraft where she was supervised at all times by medical staff. Anna Fowler had escorted her almost the whole way. The second they'd landed, Fowler skulked away into the shadows.

Veronika wasn't sure what work Fowler had planned, but Emery had told her that it would vastly increase the chances of her becoming prime minister. She was prepared to trust Emery and his British spy friend, because in the small amount of time she'd known him, he'd proven to be a man of honor. She was determined to confront her colleagues and stake her claim for leadership, but a little help would do her no harm.

The limousine entered the Kremlin and pulled up. Two uniformed soldiers were waiting, their assault rifles held at attention. The cabinet secretary was waiting in between the soldiers. He was the main official in charge of the cabinet, and he reached out to open Veronika's door once the vehicle had stopped. The look on his face when he saw Veronika step out was one for the ages.

Veronika smiled at him as she stepped out of the car. "It's been a while since I caused a man's jaw to drop."

"Minister Oreshkin..." The cabinet secretary recovered his composure quickly. "I'll call ahead to tell them not to start the meeting without you."

"Please don't. I'd like to make an entrance." Veronika waited until he'd nodded, then she walked away from the car and toward her destiny.

Minutes later, Veronika walked inside the cabinet meeting room and did exactly that. It took only a moment for all conversation to die and for her colleagues to lock their eyes on her. She enjoyed their stunned reactions. They clearly hadn't expected her to attend the meeting after being exiled by Sokolov then shot in Barcelona. She smiled and headed for the seat at the head of the table—Sokolov's seat.

"Shall we begin the meeting, gentlemen?" Veronika sat in the chair then looked down the table. "I see Popov hasn't seen fit to attend..."

Yevgeny Mikhailov was first to speak. He'd been Sokolov's

minister for agriculture and was also the sycophant who'd warned her. "We're not sure you have a place at this meeting."

She'd expected that. She had a lie ready. "I'm still the foreign minister. Sokolov sent me to Barcelona early, in preparation for the summit, where I was shot."

"Well, you see... Nikolai... Sergey..." Mikhailov stammered. He clearly knew Sokolov had banished her, but with Sokolov dead and Popov absent, the power dynamics had changed.

"Nikolai is dead, and Popov isn't here." Veronika shrugged. "The business of state will not wait indefinitely. We need a new prime minister."

She looked around the table, and none of her colleagues spoke out. They were stunned by Sokolov's death and the absence of the logical successor. Sokolov had been grooming Popov for years, and there was no clear third choice. It seemed Jack Emery and Anna Fowler had been good to their word, giving Veronika the opening she needed. The rest was completely up to her.

"There's no time to waste." She looked at the cabinet secretary. "Have you spoken to the president?"

The cabinet secretary looked around the table, surprised to have been called upon. "I... uh... my colleague in the president's office tells me the president trusts us to make the appropriate decision. He looks forward to meeting with the next prime minister of Russia at the appropriate time..."

First hurdle cleared, Veronika resisted the urge to smile. Veronika was about to speak again when there were two sharp knocks on the door. Veronika and her colleagues looked at each other in confusion, while the cabinet secretary moved to answer the door. He opened it only a crack, enough for whoever was outside to pass a note in. Veronika raised an eyebrow as she watched the man close the door, unfold the note, then go white.

"What is it?" Veronika sensed the tension in the room ratchet up a notch, though she suspected she knew what was written on the piece of paper. "What has happened?"

The cabinet secretary seemed to struggle with the words for a few moments, then he looked straight at Veronika. "It's Popov... he's... dead. He was found shot in his apartment."

Veronika sat back with her arms crossed as the room erupted into pandemonium. If the remaining ministers had been shocked by Sokolov's death, they were positively shattered by Popov's. They shouted across the table at one another, fighting to be heard, until Veronika pounded her fist down on the table over and over again. It took a few moments, but eventually, they calmed down.

"My friends, these are dire times." She paused and looked at each of them in turn. "We are under attack, and our most respected leaders have been murdered by terrorists. I was attacked myself and should also be dead. Our troops continue to fight in Ukraine, while the West continues to scheme against us..."

"Yes!" Mikhailov pounded the table. He'd sensed the prevailing winds, and it seemed he was getting aboard. "Under such attack, we need a leader with experience on the international stage. Nikolai made our nation strong again, and who better to continue his work than the woman he trusted to lead our efforts abroad?"

"I accept your nomination, Yevgeny." Veronika smiled. "Of course, if you all decide to grant me the honor of being your prime minister, I will be relying on all of your support and need a strong team around me. Now is not the time for upheaval. I would ask all of you to continue to serve in my cabinet."

Veronika looked around the table and saw more and more nods. With Sokolov and Popov dead, she knew none of the others had the strength to fill the power vacuum. Most of them were followers, not leaders. By promising that they'd keep their jobs, she hoped to tilt enough of the conservatives onto the side of the moderates, giving her the numbers she needed to win the job—and to reshape Russia.

13

The upheaval in Russian politics following the death of Prime Minister Nikolai Sokolov has continued, with the murder of Defense Minister Sergey Popov in his apartment and the appointment of Foreign Minister Veronika Oreshkin as prime minister. Oreshkin, a leading moderate in the cabinet, was considered an outside chance to take the top job given the prominent number of ultra-conservatives in the senior leadership group. Though it remains to be seen whether the direction of the country changes significantly under Oreshkin's leadership, there seems a chance that Russia's aggressive foreign adventures of recent years may begin to ease.

—*New York Standard*

"*I never thought we'd be saying this after the slaughter in Barcelona.*" The talking head on the television stared down the camera. "*But things just got a whole lot more interesting...*"

"No kidding." Jack scoffed as he pointed the remote at his

television and muted it, silencing the anchor's yammering about developments in Russia.

He sighed as he stood, tossed the remote onto the sofa, and walked to the kitchen. He'd been glued to the news for hours and was starting to get hungry. He opened the refrigerator and stared inside. He was struggling to focus. The news that something he'd orchestrated had occurred and changed the world had stunned him, filling his mind with fear and excitement in equal measure.

Veronika Oreshkin was the new prime minister of Russia. That part had gone to plan. Sergey Popov had been murdered. That part hadn't.

What had seemed impossible only days ago had been achieved. In Oreshkin's hospital room in Barcelona, he'd cooked up a plan to take Popov out of the picture and make Oreshkin the leader of Russia. He and Oreshkin had agreed that it seemed like the last hope to keep the chances of a nuclear deal alive, and they'd enlisted Anna Fowler to help them. He hadn't expected their gambit to work, but he'd been determined to try.

He'd given Fowler the intelligence she needed to blackmail Popov and take him out of the leadership race. Fowler had left him a message on a dummy internet account a few hours ago. Four words had told him all he needed to know: *He didn't play ball.* Popov hadn't responded to Fowler's attempts at blackmail how they'd thought he would. Now he was dead, but Fowler had covered her tracks. Though the chances of a nuclear deal might be back on the rails, it had come at a cost. Still, it was hard to feel much for the man responsible for the Kharkov massacre.

Jack sighed and reached inside the fridge for a tub of yogurt, which was about all he could stomach at the moment. He knew a call from McGhinnist was coming, and he was nervous about it. The president wasn't stupid. He must know Jack had visited Oreshkin in the hospital, and he would find out that Jack had accessed intelligence about Popov. That was all the former boss of the FBI would need to piece it together.

As if on cue, a police siren in front of his house let out a whoop. He opened his eyes, stood, and walked to the window. A convoy of police cars and several black Secret Service SUVs had pulled up outside. That could only mean one thing. He walked to the front door, opened it, and stood aside. Within seconds, four Secret Service agents had pushed inside, sweeping the house then radioing their colleagues that it was clear.

"You guys want a beer?" Jack cracked a grin at the Secret Service agents. He knew each of them by name, but they responded with stone-faced silence. "No?"

Jack shrugged and returned to his sofa. He waited with a neutral expression on his face until McGhinnist and Davidson entered through the front door. Jack could sense how tense they were, with stiff bodies and pursed lips. There was no hint of the comfort he usually felt around the president or the banter he usually shared with Davidson. They moved to join him on the sofa without asking to be invited and fixed him with a hard gaze.

"Thanks for seeing us, Jack." McGhinnist leaned forward on the sofa. "I need to hear it from your mouth."

Jack knew he'd crossed the red line with McGhinnist. When he'd told Veronika Oreshkin to go back to Russia to fight for the leadership and asked Anna Fowler to help her, he'd thought his actions were necessary to save the chance at a nuclear deal. He'd been mischievous, but he'd known

McGhinnist would forgive him when he saw the results. Popov's death had changed everything, though.

Jack shrugged. "I wanted Oreshkin to become prime minister of Russia and keep the chance of a nuclear deal alive."

"I don't have a problem with that." McGhinnist's voice turned cold and distant. "I *do* have a problem with you freelancing and taking steps to make sure it happened."

"Your actions led to the death of the leading candidate to replace Sokolov," Davidson cut in. "And you used *American intelligence* to help you."

"You put the idea of Oreshkin as PM into my head." Jack's head turned like a gun turret to face Davison. He wasn't going to hide Davidson's role. "You told me to get her in the paper..."

"To flush out Kharlov if he was still in Barcelona and *maybe* make the decision for replacement Russian prime minister more difficult." Davidson scoffed. "I didn't tell you to kill Popov."

"He wasn't supposed to end up dead, Bill." Jack looked back to McGhinnist. "Fowler was supposed to blackmail him to stay out of the race."

"Well, that's just dandy then!" McGhinnist's voice boomed like an exploding star. "What the *hell* were you thinking, Jack?"

"I did what I thought was necessary to salvage a nuclear deal." Jack shrugged. "Popov would have picked up where Sokolov left off."

"To prevent a nuclear war, you risked starting one! What do you think would have happened had Fowler been caught?" The fury on McGhinnist's face was clear. "Or if she still *gets* caught?"

Jack started to speak then hesitated. He looked at Davidson for support, but any friendship they'd previously shared had been extinguished. The national security advisor was sitting back with his arms crossed, letting this battle play out. Jack turned back to McGhinnist and realized there was nothing else to say. The president's face was devoid of warmth.

He and McGhinnist stared at each other for what felt like an eternity. Jack wouldn't back down on this one, and his boss knew it. On the other hand, Jack doubted McGhinnist had come simply to vent. If he'd wanted to do that, he could have just waited until Jack was next at the White House. No, McGhinnist had clearly come intending to do something bigger and was struggling with the emotion of it.

Then the president closed his eyes for a split second, and Jack knew it was over.

"You can't accuse me of not standing up for what I believe in, Mr. President." Jack gave a small smile and felt a tear well up in his eyes. "But I didn't mean it for end this way."

"I know, Jack. If you did, you'd be walking out of here in handcuffs." McGhinnist's rage seemed to cool, and he let out a long sigh. "You took it too far this time..."

Jack knew then he'd sacrificed everything for what he believed in. He prepared for the execution. "What happens now?"

"You get to work." McGhinnist's eyes were pits of emotion, showing no warmth. "I called the British prime minister earlier. We're planning a meeting in London in a few days with the Brits and the Russians. I spoke to Oreshkin earlier, also. She said she'd think about it. I think we'd have more luck getting her to attend if the invite comes from you."

Jack smiled. "I—"

"No, Jack. Time to listen." McGhinnist stood from the sofa. "Your job is to get Oreshkin there and get her to accept a nuclear reduction and a halt to Russian aggression in Eastern Europe."

KHARLOV CLOSED his eyes and dozed as the woman at the front of the university lecture theatre droned on in German, pausing only occasionally to change the slide of her presentation. Even though he couldn't understand the lecture, he was amazed that anyone could choose to study whatever the hell she was yammering on about. He was trying to sleep while he waited for her to finish, trusting Natalya to wake him when it was time to work.

He was a man who'd pushed himself to the physical limit, stopping to sleep for only a few hours at a time since stealing the yacht. He'd sailed to Nice, France, and disembarked. After a quick Google search and another phone call to Natalya, he'd stolen a car and driven to Berlin, taking advantage of the European Union's porous borders to cross the entire continent with no trouble.

He'd met up with Natalya outside Humboldt University— one of the finest schools in the city—where his vengeance against Veronika Oreshkin would commence. Natalya had brought the guns and more information about their target than a simple Google search could provide. She'd managed to procure the university's entire student database, including student class timetables.

That's why Kharlov was sitting in the class, listening to the professor drone on and waiting for his time to strike. He would have preferred to wait outside, but there were four exits from the lecture theatre, and he didn't have the manpower to cover them all. Instead, he and Natalya were seated five rows back from the daughter of his worst enemy.

Now that Oreshkin had been made prime minister of Russia, realizing his vengeance had become much more difficult. She would be buttoned up tight, particularly after Sokolov's brains had been splattered against a wall. Hitting the Barcelona summit had been one thing, but getting to Oreshkin in Moscow would be almost impossible.

Thankfully, in a globalized world, not everything Oreshkin treasured was so well protected. He could get to Oreshkin through her family, which was the only thing that had stopped him from aiming his pistol at Sasha Oreshkin and turning the back of her head into a mess of blood, bone, and sinew. It would be some sort of justice, but not the kind that would salve his outrage and avenge his family. Only the death of Veronika Oreshkin herself would do that.

A while later, Natalya elbowed him hard in the ribs, and his eyes shot open. The German professor had stopped droning on, and he realized he must have drifted off. When he turned his head to look at Natalya, she nodded. It was time. He smiled and nodded back. They both stood from their seats at the back of the lecture theatre and made their way to the end of the aisle.

Kharlov led the way down the stairs and to the front of the lecture theatre, where most of the few hundred students who'd been in the lecture were exiting, headed to their next class or to the bar. Only a few students had milled around the professor, forming a line and politely waiting their turn to ask a question. Sasha Oreshkin was third in line and looking down at her cell phone while she was waiting.

Kharlov and Natalya joined the line, ignoring the curious looks from a few of the other students, though Sasha Oreshkin didn't look back at them. It took a few minutes for the small handful of students to disperse, leaving only the professor and Sasha with Kharlov and Natalya inside the cavernous lecture theatre. Only then did Oreshkin's daughter step forward and start talking to the professor.

"Miss Oreshkin?" Kharlov's voice was enough to stop the conversation midsentence. "I need to speak with you a moment."

Sasha turned from her conversation with the professor, her eyes darting between Kharlov and Natalya. "And who are you?"

"I'm from the university's security office. You need to come with us. We have received information that there is a threat against your life."

Sasha forced a smile, but it was clear she regarded Kharlov about as highly as something she might scrape off her boot. "I have my own security. My mother organized it after she was shot."

"We really must insist." Natalya took her turn, stepping closer to Sasha and placing a hand on the woman's arm. "It is—"

"I'm *not* going with you!" Sasha took a step back from Natalya and swatted her hand away. "Who *are* you?"

The professor stepped in front of her student, her fists balled by her side. "That is an excellent question. You claim to work for the university, but you're not speaking German."

Kharlov sighed. He was tired of the charade. He glanced at Natalya and gave a barely perceptible nod. Immediately, both he and Natalya reached inside their coats and pulled out their pistols. Working in complete synchronisation, Kharlov aimed his pistol at Sasha, while Natalya leveled her weapon at the professor's head and fired. After the pop of Natalya's silenced pistol and a squirt of blood from the professor's head, the older woman dropped to the ground.

Kharlov smiled at Sasha Oreshkin as she squealed and stared down at the corpse of her teacher. "I'm not going to ask again. You come with me or you join *her.*"

Kharlov waited a moment, but Sasha was clearly in shock. Her eyes were flickering between the body on the floor and the pistols being aimed at her. It wasn't a surprise to see someone freeze at the sight of a body, but he had neither the time nor the patience to wait for her to snap out of it.

Instead, he took a step closer, grabbed a fistful of her blouse and jammed the pistol into her ribs. "You come with us or you die right here."

His words finally had the desired effect. She turned to face him and nodded. Kharlov stuffed his pistol into the waistband of his pants then reached down to grab her hand, interlocking his fingers with her. As he dragged Sasha to the exit, he let Natalya take the lead. Though she'd put her pistol back in her purse, his offsider was coiled like a rattlesnake and ready to strike again if needed.

He followed Natalya out of the exit. The second they were outside, Kharlov saw the security detail Sasha had referred to. A man was leaning against a brick wall, smoking a cigarette and looking like he couldn't care less. Only when he saw his charge being escorted by two complete strangers did his eyes narrow. He pushed himself off the wall and reached into his pocket.

Kharlov sounded his warning. "Natalya..."

Kharlov kept walking on the path as Natalya peeled off to deal with the threat. Surprisingly, the man had pulled out a cell phone instead of a weapon, but that was almost as dangerous. He had a number dialed and the phone halfway to his ear when Natalya shot him in the head. As other students screamed and ran, Kharlov felt Sasha's hand tense, and she shrieked as the bodyguard slumped to the ground.

"Watch her." Kharlov nodded at Natalya, then he let go of Sasha's hand and walked over to the dead man. He picked up the phone, put it to his ear and kept quiet.

"What do you want? I pay you to watch my daughter and solve problems, not call me every time with them."

Kharlov smiled as he realized he had Veronika Oreshkin on the line. He killed the call, looked down at the screen, and memorized Oreshkin's number. It would come in handy later. He wiped his prints off the device and tossed it on the ground next to the dead man. He didn't want to be tracked, and he could pick up a burner phone the next time he needed to call Oreshkin.

Kharlov led the way to the parking lot and let Natalya take care of the girl, dragging her along with a pistol jammed into her side. She alternated between sobbing and pleading for help, but when other students saw the pistols, they turned and ran the other way. In America, there might have been armed campus police to worry about, but not in Germany. They faced no resistance as they reached the parking lot and tossed Sasha into a van. As he slammed the doors closed, Kharlov smiled at the thought of Oreshkin's terror when she finally found out he had her daughter.

VERONIKA ORESHKIN SWEPT everything atop her desk onto the floor. Papers that had been neatly stacked toppled and fluttered to the floor, their landing as soft as a whisper. The crash of the telephone and laptop computer was much louder.

Her stationary and personal effects scattered across the floor. Not even her coffee cup was spared. The whole time, Veronika kept her eyes locked onto Yevgeny Mikhailov.

"I'm all ears, Yevgeny." Veronika spoke only when the carnage had stopped and the detritus she'd scattered had settled. "This office now has a blank desk and a new start."

The edge of Mikhailov's lips curled into the slightest smirk. "I look forward to helping ensure what crosses it is productive, Prime Minister."

Veronika gestured for Mikhailov to sit in the chair on the opposite side of the desk, then she put her elbows on the desk and clamped her hands together. "Let's get to it, then."

He nodded and took his seat. They made small talk for a few minutes, easing into what she knew would be a difficult conversation. Though Mikhailov had been one of Sokolov's henchmen, he was nothing but a follower. The second he'd sensed the balance of power tipping, he'd shifted his support to her and helped her into power. He now spoke for the hawks, and she didn't think for a second their support would come cheap.

Theirs was an alliance of political opposites, a combustible combination of complex interests and priorities. The slightest miscalculation by either of them—the smallest spark—would ignite all of Russia.

Once their talk of the weather and other trivialities was at an end, Mikhailov finally smiled and leaned forward. "Madam Prime Minister, we need to discuss terms."

"Of course." Veronika matched his smile. "I appreciated your support at the cabinet table and the continued support of you and your allies to keep the country under control."

Veronika meant it. Even though their alliance could explode at any moment, she would take a potential crisis over a real one. Already, parts of Russia were aflame in civil turmoil following Sokolov's death. He'd kept the country united under an iron fist and through ruthless application of power. His use of the military, intelligence, and law enforcement rivaled the vilest examples from Russia's history.

"Our support doesn't come for free, I'm afraid." Mikhailov looked genuinely pained. "I need your help to keep my colleagues happy."

Veronika nodded. She needed the hawks, but she couldn't control them. She knew she couldn't change the minds of those who wanted to push outward from Russia's borders, and she didn't have the power to stop them. She had to find a way to accommodate their demands and keep herself in power, while offering the Western leaders enough concessions to prevent a global war. She'd tried to convince Sokolov of the same delicate balancing trick, but he'd always been as subtle as an uppercut from a heavyweight boxer.

"I'm prepared to keep nibbling on Ukrainian territory and reasserting our traditional sphere of influence." Veronika watched Mikhailov closely, but his face remained completely impassive. "In return, I want your support to explore a deal with America and the other nuclear powers to reduce the number of nuclear weapons globally."

"This again?" He scoffed. "I thought we'd decided against pursuing that matter. It did result in Sokolov's death, after all."

"It's something I must insist on." Veronika kept her eyes locked on Mikhailov. "The Americans are pushing hard, and refusing them will risk a conflict we can't win. If we agree to some sort of deal, I'm confident we can continue to carve out a larger sphere of influence, keeping your colleagues content..."

Veronika let her words hang. Earlier in the day, she'd been contacted by the American president, inviting her to attend another conference about nuclear disarmament—this time in London. She'd read between the lines, knowing the meeting would cover the border disputes in Eastern Europe as much as it would nuclear weapons. She'd told the president she would consider his invitation then got off the line as quickly as possible. She had no appetite for continuing Sokolov's push into Ukraine and had actively colluded against it, but there were limits to her newfound power and fragile alliances to be maintained.

"Sokolov may be dead, but he wasn't the only voice advocating for a return to a more... balanced... international order." He chose his words carefully. "When the Soviet Union fell, NATO and the Americans didn't return to their corner. They kicked us while we were down. Insulting us. Degrading us. Pushing their influence right to our border."

Veronika nodded. She'd heard it all before and had some sympathy for the logic, but the world had moved on a decade ago. On its own, a few miles of territory in Ukraine wasn't worth the political and economic cost to secure it. But if she could leverage those gains into even more power and influence by satisfying the hawks and securing their support for more ambitious reforms, it was worth it.

"My colleagues and I can support you attending the conference." Mikhailov nodded. "We'll want to see the terms of a deal before we can sign off on it, though."

"In that case, I'll allow the operations in Ukraine to continue and let you know how the London meetings get on." Veronika stood and held out her hand. "I expect you'll hold up your end."

Mikhailov stood, shook Veronika's hand, then left her office. The minute the door was closed behind him, Veronika collapsed back into her chair and closed her eyes. It felt like she'd won a stay of execution and bought another day, but she knew every bargain she had to negotiate with the hawks pushed her closer to a line she wasn't willing to cross. Her tactics—balancing the hawks against the West—would work for the time being, but not forever.

She exhaled slowly and opened her eyes again. Her office looked like it'd been hit by an artillery shell, with the stuff from her desk scattered all over the floor. Though her theatrics had won her a moment of attention from Mikhailov, she felt a little guilty that her staff would have to clean everything up. The only thing Veronika retrieved off the floor immediately was her cell phone.

The moment she touched the phone, it started to ring. She stood to her full height and looked at the screen, frowning as she saw who was calling. It was almost as if the Americans had her office bugged and the man calling had known the moment Mikhailov had left her office. The deal she'd just cut with the hawk would mean nothing if she couldn't achieve a deal with the West.

She answered the call. "Hello, Jack."

"We need to talk." Emery sounded stressed. Her warning from earlier probably had something to do with it. "The president tells me you're reluctant to attend the meeting in London."

Veronika snorted at the timing of Emery's call. "I can't just dance to your president's beat. When Sokolov was killed, a thin ray of sunlight shined through the very dark clouds that have sat over my country for decades. But that first hint of sunshine doesn't turn into summer instantly."

"I understand how fragile the situation is, Veronika. It's the same here in America." Emery was talking slowly, as if choosing each word carefully. It was a formality she hadn't experienced before with the president's advisor. "That's why I'd like us to come together and try to find common ground—on the nuclear weapons and on the situation in Eastern Europe."

She didn't speak for a long few seconds, as if she were weighing some grave matter, when in reality, she'd already achieved exactly what she wanted. "As long as the president and his allies understand that the dark clouds could easily dominate Russia once more and that I'm trying to stop that from happening, we might be able to do so."

"The last thing we want is for another extremist to seize power. We understand you'll need concessions in return for making them."

Veronika smiled, pleased that she'd played the situation perfectly. "Then I'll see you in London, Jack."

14

The eyes of the world are on London today, as world leaders descend on the city for a second attempt at a conference on nuclear disarmament. After the carnage at the Barcelona summit, the London event has been planned with much less ceremony and much more security. The leaders will be in the British capital for an intense two-day program, after which they'll leave behind their officials to work through the finer points. Another hot topic on the lips of everyone in London is Russia's continued push into Ukraine, while Russia's new leader does nothing to stop the aggression in Eastern Europe.

—New York Standard

"You want to ride on *that*?" Jack frowned as he looked up at the London Eye then shifted his gaze back to Oreshkin. "Is that what a deal is going to cost me?"

"That and more, I'm afraid." Oreshkin laughed. "I want to talk somewhere where we won't be interrupted, and the inside of a glass bubble a few hundred feet in the air seems a good bet."

Jack made a show of exhaling loudly then nodded. They walked together to the entrance to the London Eye, one of London's premier tourist attractions. Located on the bank of the Thames River and in the heart of the city, the giant wheel let its passengers see many of the city's other highlights. It had been cleared of regular visitors and locked down by British police an hour ago, when Oreshkin had asked to visit it.

As they entered one of the pods, Oreshkin's security detail peeled off and joined the armed police waiting at the bottom of the Eye, facing outward and making sure no threat interrupted the two VIPs. The door closed, they sat on the bench in the middle of the pod. Moments later, they were rising slowly into the sky and looking down on London like a pair of birds.

They sat in silence on the way up, content to take in the view and relax for a few minutes after a tough day of meetings at the London summit. After getting down to business, with none of the ceremony of the Barcelona summit, the talks had focused on nuclear weapons and Russian annexation of chunks of Ukraine. Though all sides had talked tough and conceded little initially, once the leaders were behind closed doors, the meetings had gone a little better.

Having Oreshkin instead of Sokolov at the negotiation table had changed the tone. Oreshkin had put the first ace on the table, saying Russia was willing to be a constructive partner in any global effort to reduce nuclear stockpiles. That had been welcomed by the other leaders present, though they'd also made comments urging Russian restraint in Eastern Europe. It had fallen to Jack to issue the ultimatum.

"Veronika, I'm glad we made some progress today. I know it

wasn't easy for you, given the threats you have at home." Jack reached into his pocket, pulled out a piece of paper, and held it out to Oreshkin. "McGhinnist has concluded negotiations with the British, French, and other key NATO leaders. This is the deal we can offer you."

Oreshkin frowned, making no move to take the sheet of paper from him. "I don't like ultimatums, Jack. I'd prefer it if the president spoke to me himself."

"That's never going to happen." Jack shrugged. "I give the president deniability if this leaks to the media."

Jack waited for a response. Instead of speaking, she took the piece of paper from him and unfolded it. He kept quiet while she considered the map he'd given her. It showed the red line that McGhinnist had agreed to with the other NATO leaders, the limits of their tolerance with Russian expansion into Ukraine. Jack hoped it would be enough to let Oreshkin keep her foes on her side and also progress discussions on the nuclear deal.

They rode the Eye in silence for several minutes. Jack was unable to concede any more territory than McGhinnist and NATO leaders had agreed, and Oreshkin was clearly unwilling to accept their ultimatum right away. If they couldn't come to an understanding, then the entire London summit would be a waste of time. He felt his heart pounding as he waited for Oreshkin to speak.

Finally, she stood and walked to the edge of the bubble. She pointed at the ground, far below them. "Look down, Jack. Just take a moment to look at all of those people."

Jack shrugged, stood, and walked over to the window. Though he didn't like heights very much, he looked down anyway. As expected, a bunch of people were out for the evening, walking along the Thames River or enjoying one of the world's greatest cities in one of a million different ways. After watching them for a few moments, Jack turned to face Oreshkin and waited for her to make her point.

"They all look like insignificant tiny specks, but each has dreams, fears, loves, hates, strengths, and weaknesses." She held his gaze. "We have the opportunity to make the world a better place for billions of specks just like them, but to do so, a few million will suffer. That's the brutal arithmetic of this business."

"I know that." He glanced at the people walking along the river for one more moment then looked up at Big Ben. "I can't shift the red line, though."

She sighed and looked down at the list again. "There is territory on here that the hawks in Russia won't agree to leave untouched, Jack. Can I submit a counterproposal?"

"No." Jack shook his head. "McGhinnist pushed to get you as much freedom to move as possible, but France and the UK stood firm. That map is the best I can do."

Jack waited as Oreshkin's emotions played out on her face. Her glare was not a happy one, and she looked like she was barely containing her anger. Jack couldn't blame her. She was juggling razor-sharp knives, with more being added to the routine all the time. It would take only one slight mistake for her enemies to cut her down. It was a brutal reality that Western politicians simply didn't face.

Finally, she folded the piece of paper and put it into her purse. "If that's the line I have to work with, then I will try to stay within it. Forcing me to do so makes the world an infinitely more dangerous place, though. The hawks will not hesitate to move on me if I disappoint them. If that happens, the nuclear deal turns to ash in your mouth and you risk a war."

Jack nodded. He understood, but he couldn't offer anything else. Neither of them got what they'd wanted, but Jack and Oreshkin had been on the same page about the need to eliminate nuclear weapons the whole time, so they were both prepared to swallow one bad deal in return for that.

"We'll get the nuclear deal done, Jack. We'll save all the billions of specks across the planet." Oreshkin held out her hand. "It just requires that we sacrifice a few others to do so."

Jack didn't want to admit that handing her the piece of paper had sentenced several million people to a prison sentence. In coming weeks, their lives would face great upheaval, and they would find themselves under the jackboot of Russia. They would look back in the decades to come and wonder why the West had abandoned them, never knowing of the negotiations in London that had reduced their lives to little more than poker chips. It would all be worth it, though. It had to be.

He smiled and shook Oreshkin's hand, feeling like over a year of time had led him to this point. From the moment three backpack-sized devices had been stolen and deployed by terrorists trying to stop *another* deal—between Israel and Palestine—Jack had felt like the scourge of nuclear weapons defined his life. The nuclear deal would be his legacy, his peace offering to a dangerous world. Jack recognized the historical gravity of that moment. He savored it. Then the ringing of a cell phone pierced the glass bubble.

Oreshkin frowned as she dug through her purse to find her phone. "I told my staff that I wasn't to be disturbed. The only people who have this number are my daughter and..."

Jack raised an eyebrow. "Who?"

"My daughter's security guard." Oreshkin answered the call and put the phone to her ear. "What's going on?"

Jack's eyes widened when Oreshkin dropped the phone.

KHARLOV LAUGHED at the sound of the phone hitting the ground, a muffled rumble that was followed by the sound of a woman inhaling sharply and a man asking what was wrong. He kept his own phone tight to his ear, listening hard and savoring every moment as Veronika Oreshkin's world crumbled around her. The reaction had been better than he could have imagined.

As he waited for her to pick up the phone and get over the shock enough to talk again, he smiled and looked out the window of his motel. The view from the cheap roadside accommodation on the outskirts of Minsk was nothing special, but he was happy anyway. The sun was shining, and his vengeance was almost complete. All he'd told Oreshkin so far was his name and that he had her daughter. Given her reaction to that, he couldn't wait to get to the juicy stuff.

After another few moments, Oreshkin finally spoke again. "Please, don't harm my daughter. She's innocent."

Kharlov's smile disappeared, and his laugh sounded like something from the darkest pits of hell. "You didn't seem to care about my family when your partisans set fire to Merefa."

"I'm sorry about your family, but I didn't know about that!" Oreshkin's wail of anguish was almost enough to make Kharlov believe her. Almost.

Kharlov kept silent for a long few seconds, enjoying the pain in her voice. He was tightening his grip on her heart, crushing her happiness. He knew that no person could stay calm as their loved ones were threatened and harmed. It was a universal truth that Kharlov had often relied on in the conduct of his business. It was no longer just business. It was personal, and far more satisfying than simply shooting Oreshkin in the head.

"I don't care about your denials." Kharlov's voice was a snarl, his anger and hatred welling up to his mouth like bile. "You took everything from me."

She took a few deep breaths then finally spoke. "I need proof that you have my daughter and that she's alive."

Kharlov turned from the window and walked over to Sasha Oreshkin. She was curled up on the bed of the motel room, still wearing the pinafore dress she'd had on when he took her from the university. Although he lacked a change of clothing for the young woman, Kharlov hadn't harmed her at all. She was an innocent. She wouldn't be harmed at all if her mother played by his rules.

Though Kharlov hadn't physically harmed her, he was enjoying her terror. It was a proxy for her mother's fear. Her eyes went as wide as saucers when he approached. They were puffy and bloodshot, with tears moistening her cheeks. Her wrists were cuffed, her ankles were tied, and Natalya was watching over her. He wasn't taking any chances with his prize catch. She was too valuable.

He put the phone to Sasha's mouth, but she kept quiet. Earlier, he'd told her that he would cut out her tongue if she spoke a word while he was on the phone. "Say hello to your mother."

"Mama, help me." Sasha sobbed. "I—"

Kharlov pulled the phone from her mouth and put it to his ear. Oreshkin was crying and babbling to her daughter, but he spoke over her. "Satisfied?"

"Thank you..." Oreshkin sobbed again. "I'm sorry about

your family. Is there some way for me to put this right and get my daughter back?"

Kharlov scoffed. "We had an agreement. I supplied the Ukrainian resistance, and in return, you were supposed to tell me where Russia was turning up the heat. Those warnings were supposed to keep my business interests and my family safe. You failed to live up to the deal, and my family paid the price. You owe me a priceless debt, and the bill has come due."

"Please, I'll do anything." Oreshkin was breathless, her desperation palpable. "Just tell me what you want."

"You're about to walk through a minefield of my design." Kharlov smiled. "Can I trust you to take the first step?"

"Yes, of course, anything."

Since taking Sasha Oreshkin in Berlin, Kharlov and Natalya had stayed on the road. They'd changed cars regularly and driven several hundred miles per day, until they were in Minsk and within striking distance of the Russian border. Getting over that border was the next challenge, but he would never succeed while his name and face were all over the news.

"I'm currently near the Russian border, and I want to cross it. I'll have a gun against your daughter's head, and I'll pull the trigger if I'm stopped by the border guards."

"But, I..." Oreshkin seemed to struggle momentarily with the ramifications of his words. "You want me to open the *entire* border?"

"Yes." Kharlov smiled and looked back out the window at the sunshine. "I cross the border one hour from now."

"I—"

"I have contacts in Russian intelligence agencies and the military. You can try to use them to find me, but if I find out, your daughter will be killed immediately."

"If—"

"You better make some calls."

Kharlov killed the call and dropped the phone into the small sink, which he'd already filled with water. The cheap plastic cell would be as useless to anyone else as it was to him. He was buying burner phones from grocery stores as he needed them, making only one call with each device. It was a small precaution that would help to keep him safe until he reached his final destination.

Kharlov turned to face Natalya. "Get the car ready."

"On it." Natalya stashed her pistol down the back of her jeans then left the motel room.

Kharlov waited until Natalya had closed the door behind her, then he walked over to Sasha Oreshkin. She looked up at him with wide eyes. She'd heard one side of the conversation and knew the stakes. He smiled and gently caressed her cheek with his index finger. When she flinched and tried to move away from him, Kharlov brought his other hand close to her and jammed his pistol into her stomach.

"You and your mother are going to learn to cooperate." Kharlov resumed his caress, even though he was clearly making her skin crawl. "So is your father."

JACK PLACED a hand on Oreshkin's shoulder as she continued to stare down at her phone, the fragile link with her daughter severed. "We'll get her back, Veronika."

"He has my daughter..." Oreshkin crumpled onto the bench in the middle of the carriage as the Eye continued to turn. "This is a disaster..."

Jack listened in silence as Oreshkin relayed every detail she could remember from the phone call—her daughter speaking, Kharlov's threats, his demands that she stand-down the border guards, and his claim to have moles inside Russia's security agencies and armed forces. As she spoke, she gradually started to calm down, transforming from panicked mother to detached and calculating world leader before his very eyes.

"We'll get her back, Veronika," Jack repeated. "I'll do whatever I can to help."

She gave a sad smile. "I might need to hold you to that. I don't know if his claim to have infiltrated my agencies is true, but I can't take the risk..."

Jack nodded. He knew what she was asking. "Let me take care of that while you stand down the border guards."

Jack walked to the corner of the bubble and used his cell phone to dial McGhinnist. As he waited for the president to answer, he gazed out at the scenery. The number of people walking on the streets below had lessened as it got later in the evening, although none of them were aware that the tectonic plates of global politics were shifting inside the tourist attraction above them.

"What's up, Jack?" McGhinnist answered the phone and broke Jack's thoughts. "I'm just having dinner with the French and British leaders."

"We've got a problem." Jack kept his voice low to avoid upsetting Oreshkin further. "Kharlov has Oreshkin's daughter, and her hands are tied. He claims to have infiltrated her intelligence agencies and her military. He's threatened to shoot the girl if Oreshkin makes a move. We need to use our own assets to find Kharlov and the girl."

"Damn it." McGhinnist's voice was like a long rumble of thunder, then there was a long pause as the president digested the news and Jack's request. "We have some CIA and special forces assets watching over Ukraine. I'll ask Davidson to repurpose them. I'll see if the Brits will give us some support, as well. If we get the girl back, will Oreshkin be more likely to do a deal?"

Jack looked to Oreshkin. She was already on the phone to her people and not paying attention to his conversation. "I'm sure of it, sir. She'll do whatever we ask in return for our support."

McGhinnist grunted. "How did she take our proposal? I assume the news about her daughter has overtaken her mind a little?"

"She wasn't thrilled by it. She's worried it won't be enough for the hawks. But she's promised to do her best." Jack paused. "We should be able to get a nuke deal done."

"Is she going back to Russia?"

Jack watched Oreshkin for a long few moments before answering the question. She'd regained her composure, but he couldn't imagine how she felt. "I'm going to suggest she stay in London until the completion of the conference tomorrow. If she heads home before then, it just gives Kharlov another victory."

"Sounds smart." McGhinnist sighed. "Christ, what a mess. I can't imagine I'd be able to hold it together if my kids were taken. Is there anyone else at risk?"

Jack frowned. It was a good question. Jack did a quick mental stocktake but quickly realized that she'd never talked about any of her family or friends in the short time they'd known one another. He knew she had a daughter and an ex-husband, who was a general in the Russian military, but he didn't think there were any other vulnerable targets for Kharlov to take advantage of.

"I don't think so. Not unless Kharlov is ballsy enough to go

for her ex-husband, who's in the middle of a military base."
Jack sighed. "No, I think he's done."

"Oreshkin isn't the soft touch he thinks she is." McGhinnist
paused. "Get back to her, and I'll get things moving with
Davidson."

Jack killed the call and turned away from the window to
face Oreshkin. She'd finished up her call and was simply
staring into space. She was no longer crying and looked a little
more composed, but it was probably all for show. He'd felt
empty—destroyed—when his wife had been killed in a
terrorist attack, yet he couldn't imagine how Oreshkin felt.

Oreshkin turned to face him. "The Russian border will be
totally open within the next few minutes..."

"And McGhinnist is going to get American assets onto the
job immediately." Jack shrugged. "Then that's all we can do
for now."

"I agree." Her eyes were probing him, as if she were
assessing whether he could be trusted and relied upon. "My
people can't know that the monster who killed Sokolov has my
daughter, Jack. If the hawks find out I'm compromised, they'll
take me down faster than a bullet to the head."

Jack nodded. "I'll only share the knowledge with the
people who absolutely must have it—the president, his inner
circle, and the assets we deploy to find your daughter."

"Okay." She seemed satisfied with his promise. "I'm going
to stay for the meetings tomorrow, and after that, I'll fly back to
Moscow."

He nodded, and they settled into silence until they reached
the bottom. When the door of their pod opened, Jack placed
his hand on Oreshkin's back, and they walked out into the
night. She glanced sideways at him and smiled warily. Then,
just like that, she had her business face back on again, and all

the grief she'd shown moments earlier had disappeared. The only signs it'd been there at all were puffy cheeks and red eyes.

Jack waited as Oreshkin left with her security, walking along the Thames toward the vehicles they'd arrived in. Only when she was out of sight did Jack head in the opposite direction. He didn't know where he was going, just that he didn't want to return to his hotel right away. He was exhausted. Every time he thought he had things figured out, they changed again. The more he tried to make the world safer, the more dangerous it seemed to get.

15

The London summit has concluded with world leaders flying out of the city only two days after they arrived. Though participants were tight-lipped, leaders from the eight nuclear countries and other major NATO powers insist the talks have laid the groundwork for progress on nuclear arms reductions and resolving the conflict in Ukraine. Officials from each country will remain in London for another week to discuss matters further, ahead of another summit all leaders committed to attend in six months in Beijing.

—New York Standard

"It's great to hear your voice." Jack smiled at Celeste, whose face was on the screen of his laptop. "What's happening on the other side of the pond?"

"The usual debauchery." Celeste smiled back at him. She was Skyping from their home in New York. "I just ate a pizza."

"Live it up." Jack's laugh trailed off into a sigh. "I don't think I'm going to be back in the States anytime soon. Things have really gone to hell."

Jack settled in for the long Skype call with his fiancée, trading details about their days and catching up. It was the first time they'd spoken in days. Jack had been busy with meetings in London, and Celeste was always busy with her job at the paper. Finally, McGhinnist had flown out, and the schedule in London had shifted back a gear so that he had time to speak with her.

As they spoke, he found his mind drifting to the developments in London.

After the meetings, McGhinnist had boarded Air Force One and headed for home, while Jack remained in London to wrap up another week of meetings with officials from other countries. It also left him closer to Russia and the situation in Eastern Europe, ready to act if the situation developed and a senior American official was needed on the ground. Jack had become the president's man in Europe.

Meanwhile, the intelligence apparatus of the United States had roared into action. McGhinnist had made it the number-one priority and agreed to provide all the support the American intelligence community could to help find Oreshkin's daughter and remove the dagger from her throat. The agencies had started work immediately—reaching out to their contacts, analyzing all the information they had, and working to find more.

As the intelligence services got to work, a trickle of information about Dmitry Kharlov had turned into a stream then into a river. With each passing minute, more pieces of the puzzle fell into place, and it was only a matter of time before there was a breakthrough. Terrorists and enemies could survive in the shadows, but once America's intelligence spotlight started to search for one man, he would have nowhere to hide. Jack had been briefed a few hours ago, and he was due on a call with the president in...

"Jack?" Celeste's voice had an edge of annoyance. "If your mind is elsewhere, we can talk later."

He shook his head, forcing his mind to focus. "Sorry. There's just a lot going on at the moment."

Celeste sighed. "There's always a lot going on, Jack. I sometimes wonder if there's too much going on..."

Jack's face clouded over, her words feeling like an uppercut to the chin. He'd invested a lot in the nuclear deal, and it seemed like the bill might be coming due. McGhinnist was out of patience with him, and Celeste was saying the same thing. The two people at the core of his life were questioning his commitment to the nuclear disarmament cause.

"I need to land this deal, Celeste." Jack watched her expression change to a frown as he said the words. "I can't step away from it."

"I know." She gave a sad smile. "I just wonder if it's going to consume you, Jack. I'm worried about you. I'm worried about *us*. We've never struggled so much to find a balance."

"We'll get it back again." Jack tried to force a smile. He loved her, and he wanted to be with her, but he also needed to finish the job he'd set for himself. "I want to prove it to you."

"How?" Her eyes twinkled. She clearly wanted to believe in him and to hope for the future, but he was going to have to prove it.

"Let's make the wedding date six months from now." Jack's smile was real this time. They'd been engaged a while, but never confirmed a date. "And I'll resign from the president's staff."

Jack could see the shock in her eyes at his unexpected offer to walk away. In truth, it wasn't much of a concession. He felt like his time with McGhinnist was almost over. The president's patience with Jack was coming to an end. While Jack wanted to land the nuclear deal and secure it as his legacy to the world, he needed to secure what came after that, as well, and there was only one thing he wanted once he stepped away from the job.

"I'm serious, Celeste. In six months, we'll get married, and I'll find a less-demanding job." He spoke again when she didn't immediately respond. "I just want to close this out."

"Okay." She smiled, the relief clear on her face. "I'm sorry if that felt like an ultimatum, but I want us to work."

"Me too. We better get planning." Jack laughed then looked at his watch. "I've got a phone hookup with Caleb in a minute, Celeste. I have to go."

Jack and Celeste exchanged farewells, then he ended the Skype call. Once he was alone again, he lay on the bed of his hotel room and stared at the ceiling. He felt like his foundations were being tested under the load on his shoulders, but he wouldn't take the pressure off himself yet. He was too close to achieving the impossible, though he had just given himself a new deadline.

A few minutes later, his cell phone started to ring on the bed beside him. He answered it and put the call on speaker. "Hi, Caleb."

"Hi, Jack." The National Security Advisor sounded more formal than usual. "I'm here with the heads of the CIA, the FBI, and the NSA."

That explained the formality. It also suggested there was

something big to report. "Good to speak to you all. What have we got?"

"Mr. Emery, it's Stacey Carruthers here, from the FBI." A female voice filled Jack's hotel room. "Our forensic financial analysts have been working to find a money trail for Kharlov's arms trading. Though he deals in cash a lot of the time, we have found some accounts to sift through..."

"And?"

"We've found a woman in Ukraine who Kharlov has paid thirty thousand dollars per month for the last decade."

"That's millions of dollars." Jack frowned. "Is there anything else showing us this woman is significant?"

"Nothing." Davidson spoke next. "Which is why we think we should use our assets in Ukraine to investigate. There is some risk, though. If the operation goes poorly or Kharlov has people watching over this woman, we could be signing the hostage's death warrant. It's a calculated risk, but we have few other options."

"Is there any alternative?" Jack's words hung heavy, and he was answered by silence. "Nothing?"

"Nothing that will get us on the front foot," Davidson said. "We've workshopped all the options, and we think this is the best one, unless we're prepared to wait for more information. I've spoken to McGhinnist, and he's prepared to greenlight the operation if you're on board."

Jack hesitated for only a second. Then he decided that if he only had six months left in the job, he wouldn't leave anything on the table. "I agree. Let's do it."

"THERE'S two conscripts inside the front guardhouse." Kharlov spoke softly into his headset as he crouched low in the grass, his submachine gun pointed at the dirt. "Rear team, report?"

"Two guards." Natalya's voice was crisp and clear in his earpiece as she reported an identical situation at the other guardhouse. "We're ready to move on your order."

Everything was in place. His final act of his vengeance was close. Kharlov and his team were in the middle of Russia, a hundred miles from the nearest city and surrounded by nothing except farms. Kharlov and Natalya had driven straight there after crossing the Russian border several days ago with Sasha Oreshkin in the trunk. The girl's mother had been true to her word, and the Russian border guards hadn't attempted to stop them.

The only remarkable thing about their current location was that it hosted the Soviet-era missile base that Kharlov and his team were currently watching. For half a century, the facility had waited like a silent sentinel, ready to launch intercontinental ballistic missiles tipped with nuclear warheads into the sky and lay waste to the world. Though the world had moved on, the base remained staffed and equipped for doomsday.

It had seen better days, though. From Kharlov's limited reconnaissance from outside the base, he could see the facilities were falling apart. Buildings were decayed, metalwork was rusted, fences were in disrepair, and half the external security lights weren't working. It felt like a place that time had forgotten, yet it contained exactly what Kharlov needed to complete his terrible vengeance on Veronika Oreshkin.

Kharlov smiled. "Execute."

He rose to his full height and started to advance briskly toward the front gate. He kept his eyes locked on the men inside the guardhouse, but the two conscripts were chatting to one another, oblivious to the monster emerging from the darkness. He knew the same process would be playing out at the rear gate, as his forces attempted to secure both entrances to the base. At both entrances, well-equipped and well-trained men were carrying out a surprise attack on the base. They weren't two-bit mercenaries like he'd used at Castle Montjuic. Kharlov had brought his best crew.

Once they were close enough, Kharlov and his team opened fire on the guards with their silenced submachine guns. Rounds peppered the flimsy guardhouse, shattering glass windows and punching holes in the thin aluminum siding. The two conscripts inside each took multiple rounds to the upper body. They never stood a chance. One slumped forward in his chair, and the other fell to the floor.

When he reached the guardhouse, Kharlov ordered his men to form a perimeter while he entered the structure. He kicked away the conscripts' weapons then checked on the men. The man in the chair was stone-cold dead—shot through the head—while the other was sucking in short breaths and crying out. Blood had sprayed the walls and pooled on the floor, combining with the broken glass to paint a gruesome picture.

"Is the general inside the base?" Kharlov looked down at the soldier—a boy—and waited for an answer. The conscript focused his eyes on Kharlov then nodded, a pained expression on his face. Having heard the answer he wanted, Kharlov shot the young man in the head then keyed his headset to speak with his team. "Front gate secure, and the general is home."

Kharlov pressed a button on the console inside the guardhouse and watched as the gate started to open on its rails. He left the guardhouse and nodded at his two men who'd just dragged Sasha Oreshkin from their staging area. He hadn't wanted to put her at risk until he knew the general was inside the base, but she was a key part of his plans. She was terrified and cuffed at the wrists, with a gun pointed at her at all times.

Kharlov got close to her. "You're about to have a little reunion. If you cooperate, you'll probably live."

He gripped Sasha's arm and followed four of his men through the gate, pulling her behind him. Four more of his men brought up the rear, while another pair stayed at the gate. They penetrated deeper into the base, with the defenders still having no idea they were under attack. Kharlov made for the general's residence with Sasha and a quartet of his men, while the others peeled off to take care of their respective jobs. Kharlov had no doubt his people would take care of their responsibilities, and as he headed for his target, his men radioed in that they had other parts of the base under control.

"Main barracks doors barred and explosives planted."

"Officers' barracks barred and explosives planted."

"Base security post taken. One casualty. Three hostiles down."

"Silo exterior secure."

Kharlov smiled. He felt like an octopus whose tentacles were slowly squeezing key parts of the base, constricting its life and establishing his dominance. That he was doing so without its defenders having any clue was even more satisfying. Rarely did things go so flawlessly, but he'd been right in assuming the security at an ancient Russian military base in the middle of nowhere would be lax. The fact that base had nuclear weapons just made it even more astounding.

He reached the front of the general's residence, which was a much nicer building than the rest of the base. He waited while his four men fanned out to cover every direction. Then he released Sasha's arm, stepped behind her, grabbed her in a headlock using his forearm, and pressed the barrel of the submachine gun into her back. She immediately tensed, though she was smart enough to keep quiet.

"Stay smart, and you'll stay alive." Kharlov's whisper was loud enough that only she could hear it, but his next phrase was loud enough for the headset mic. "Execute phase two."

A second later, a series of loud explosions and rolling fireballs from different parts of the base broke the calm of the night. His men had taken care of the conscripts and their officers, placing explosives around their barracks and detonating them on cue. Kharlov didn't relish the slaughter, but he had business with the man inside the residence, and he didn't want to be interrupted.

Kharlov waited in silence for about ten seconds then smiled when the door to the general's residence opened. "Hello, General."

The older man who stepped out was dressed in his uniform pants and boots, with nothing on top. He had severe scarring interspersed with tattoos on his chest and arms. General Vladimir Oreshkin was a fighting man who'd risen through the ranks, rather than a political stooge. Kharlov could respect that. The general was carrying a standard-issue Russian service pistol, but the weapon clattered to the floor when he saw Kharlov's hostage.

"Leave my daughter alone," General Oreshkin thundered. He clearly knew he'd lost, but he wasn't a coward. "What are your terms?"

Kharlov was about to speak, but Sasha cried out to her father and broke free of his grip. He didn't fire his weapon. Instead, he grabbed her hair and pulled hard on it. She cried out in pain, reaching up to grip his hand as he flung her to the ground. As she landed hard on the concrete, Kharlov aimed his submachine gun down at her.

"Enough!" Kharlov shouted, causing her to freeze, then he glanced at General Oreshkin. "Your officers and soldiers are dead. I want you to order all civilians on base to assemble here."

The general nodded, slowly reached into his pocket for his cell phone, then made a call. As General Oreshkin barked orders down the phone in Russian, Kharlov kept a watchful eye on both General Oreshkin and his daughter, alert for the slightest hint that she might try to run or that her father might try to turn the tables. He needn't have bothered. They were both as compliant as baby lambs.

Kharlov grinned. He had gained control of a nuclear missile facility and the man who was able to launch the weapons.

ALEXEI STEPANOVICH CURSED LOUDLY as the hammer slammed into his thumb and pain shot through his hand. "Damn it!"

Alexei dropped the hammer, and it fell over the edge of the gantry he was standing on, disappearing from sight. He didn't give it a second thought as he held his thumb with his opposite hand, clenching his teeth together. Slowly, the sharp pain started to subside, replaced by a throbbing that would probably last for a long while. He knew from bitter experience that the thumb was going to bruise and that he would probably lose the nail. He'd fallen victim to one of the occupational hazards for men who worked on machinery for a living.

Alexei rubbed his face and leaned over the gantry, trying to spot where the hammer had gone. He was two levels up, working with his team to service the intercontinental ballistic missiles inside the silos of a Russian nuclear missile base. It was a reasonable posting for a Russian military engineer, far better than some of the alternatives, but it was still hard work.

The maintenance of hundreds of nuclear missiles all across Russia fell to hundreds of overworked and underpaid engineers like Alexei. Each day, they worked to keep the weapons that could end the world in top shape. The work was hard, because the technology was aging and budgets were always being cut, leading to maintenance backlogs that could never be overcome. Alexei alone had seen dozens of accidents and near misses, with aging military technology pushed to the brink of disaster. Luckily, the accident had only cost him a bruise.

With a sigh, he gave up on trying to spot the hammer. His hand still throbbing, he turned and walked to the stairs that would take him down to the bottom of the silo, where he could find the tool. But when he reached the stairwell and was halfway down the first flight of stairs, a klaxon started to wail, and lights affixed to the wall flashed red. Alexei stared at one of the lights for a full two seconds, not believing what he was seeing. For all the near misses he'd seen, he'd never before been ordered to evacuate the silo.

Protocol dictated he evacuate immediately, so he left the hammer and climbed back up the stairs. He reached the top of the gantry in less than a minute. The two engineers who'd been working inside the silo were waiting for him with toolboxes in their hands and panicked looks on their faces. They were new to the base and to the army, young men who were looking to him for guidance.

"What the hell are you fools waiting for?" Alexei screamed at them. "If you hear the alarm, you get the hell out of the silo!"

"We were waiting for you." Boris raised an eyebrow. "Where's your hammer, Alexei?"

Alexei looked down at his hand, which was already red and starting to bruise, then he looked at both of the other engineers. They stared back at him. They all knew that leaving a tool inside the silo was a mistake, and for Alexei to verbalize his mistake would make it real. In the Russian Army, real mistakes required reporting—and punishment.

Alexei smiled when both of the junior engineers turned and headed for the exit, overlooking his missing tool. He followed them out the door and into the night, expecting to find large groups of people streaming toward the emergency evacuation area, but when he made it out of the silo, all he could see were fires burning and men clad in black pointing submachine guns at him and shouting.

Alexei pulled up short and raised his hands, only seconds after his colleagues had done the same. The armed men weren't wearing the uniform of any army, so he wondered if they were American special forces soldiers who'd come to strike out at Russia's nuclear arsenal. Then he disregarded that option. The men didn't look American, and they weren't speaking English.

The armed men shouted at Alexei and gestured with their weapons for him to move. He complied. He was no hero. He was led past the main barracks, which were aflame, where more armed men stood outside. Whoever the attackers were, they'd taken care of the garrison and had complete control of the base. Alexei wondered if the Russian Army was already on the way to recapture the base, then he had another thought. Did Russia even know the base had been taken?

He was taken to the front of General Oreshkin's residence and pushed among a cluster of around fifty people out front of the house. Armed men and one woman formed a ring around them, while on the steps of the house, another man waited with his submachine gun aimed at two other people who were kneeling on the ground: General Oreshkin and a terrified-looking young woman in her early twenties.

Alexei joined the other captives and dropped to his knees, his two subordinates doing the same. They were clearly the last people to gather, because as soon as they were settled, the gunman on the stairs barked an order at his men. Two of the other gunmen climbed the stairs and took watch over the general, while the enemy leader started to walk down the stairs.

"I am Dmitry Kharlov. I have your general's daughter, and he's going to play nicely." He reached the bottom of the stairs. "Each time my men or I are disobeyed, one of you will die."

Though Alexei kept his mouth welded closed, he winced enough to catch Kharlov's attention. He knew a launch from these old Russian silos was theoretically possible with a commanding general's codes and a few engineering workarounds. The ancient facilities lacked the safety features of the newer ones. The knowledge made Kharlov far more dangerous, but he hadn't meant to show it on his face.

Kharlov walked over to Alexei and leaned in close. "I'm going to guess you're the chief engineer here?"

Alexei's stomach went weak. He felt like he was going to shit himself. He forced himself to nod. "Yes, I am."

"We're going to be the best of friends, then." Kharlov

waved his hand lazily in the direction of all the other captives. "If you cooperate, these men will live. Do you understand?"

"I'll cooperate." Alexei glanced at his colleagues and memorized their faces, trying to build up the courage to do whatever needed doing to keep them all alive. "Just don't hurt us."

ACT III

16

The progress at the London summit has seen the world take another tentative step toward a reduction in nuclear arms. Although the event was a much more modest affair than Barcelona, the London summit made ground in several important areas of negotiations. The parties agreed to a framework for future talks, a halt to all nuclear weapons testing and new arms development, and to reduce the standing deployment of nuclear arms by fifteen percent.

—*New York Standard*

"Thanks for the ride." Jack gave the driver of the car a thumbs-up then slammed the door closed.

He looked around. He was in front of a nondescript house in an unremarkable residential neighborhood, the perfect location for a CIA safehouse. Inside was the woman Kharlov had been paying. CIA assets had scooped her up and taken her to the safehouse, and Jack was about to meet her. He'd flown from the UK to Ukraine, landed at a Ukrainian Air Force base in Kiev, then driven in a convoy to the safehouse.

Steeling himself for what he would find inside, Jack crossed the sidewalk and walked up the driveway. Once he reached the front door, he pounded on it and waited. A few seconds later, there were several dull thuds from the other side, the sound of heavy bolts being unlocked. Then the door opened only a small crack and Jack found himself staring down the barrel of a pistol.

"I'm Jack Emery." Jack kept his hands by his sides. "I'm here to speak with the woman you have here."

Jack exhaled when the pistol disappeared, and the door opened, revealing the man on the other side for the first time. He had close-cropped hair and intense eyes. Still holding the pistol, the man stood aside and gestured with his head for Jack to enter the house. Jack walked past him then waited on the other side of the door while the other man closed and locked it again.

"I'm Dan Gilleslee. CIA." Gilleslee smiled at Jack, visibly more relaxed than when he'd answered the door. "It's good to have you here, sir."

"I doubt that, Agent Gilleslee." Jack laughed. In his experience, having the bosses around was a buzzkill. "It's good to be here, though."

"I'll introduce you to Anya Petrovich." Gilleslee started to walk down the hallway then paused, turning his head to face Jack. "She's pissed."

Jack nodded and followed the CIA agent through to the living room, where a pair of agents were standing around a middle-aged woman. Though she wasn't restrained, the agents were keeping a close eye on her. She responded to Jack's arrival by staring at him blankly. Whoever she was and whatever her connection to Kharlov, she wasn't showing any fear. She wasn't showing anything at all.

Jack took a few steps closer to her and smiled. "I'm a representative of the United States government. I want to ask you a few questions, Ms. Petrovich."

She didn't respond.

"I need to know about Dmitry Kharlov." Jack crouched so he was at her level. "We know he has paid you a lot of money. That's going to stop. We've frozen his accounts."

More silence.

"The United States government can replace the payments, but we need to know about your link to Kharlov and any information you have that might help us to locate him."

Nothing.

"We can crack her open if you want." Gilleslee's offer to torture their captive was as casual as he might offer Jack a cup of coffee. "We've got experience at it."

Jack bristled. One of McGhinnist's achievements as president had been stopping those practices by America's intelligence agencies. Jack turned and stared at Gilleslee. "No."

"Suit yourself." Gilleslee shrugged. "She's not going to tell you anything, though. She hasn't said a word since we took her into custody."

Jack thought for a second then smiled. "I'd like you all to leave the room and leave me alone with her."

Gilleslee scoffed. "You want us t—"

"Yes, I do." Jack stared at Gilleslee until he and his men left the room, then he turned back to the woman in the chair. "Sorry about the heavy-handed treatment, Ms. Petrovich…"

"I was married to a madman for five years. You think *that* was heavy-handed?" A hint of a smile cracked her face. "Please, call me Anya."

"Okay, Anya." Jack smiled. He felt like he'd made some progress. "I need answers from you. The safety of the world is at stake."

"Because of Dmitry?"

"Yes." Jack nodded. "He's taken a young, innocent woman hostage and is using her to blackmail a very powerful person. We need to stop him. You said you two were married?"

"A lifetime ago." Her eyes scanned his face, as if she were assessing whether he could be trusted. "Dmitry was the love of my life, but he terrified me. Although he never harmed me, when I got pregnant, I couldn't take the risk that he'd snap. I left. He resisted—at first—but eventually, he accepted my decision and promised I'd be taken care of."

Jack nodded. "That's what the money is for?"

"Yes." She shrugged. "I wasn't going to take it from him, but raising a child as a single mother in Ukraine isn't the easiest thing in the world..."

Jack didn't respond immediately. His mind was swimming. He hadn't expected to hear that Kharlov had another kid. All the possible scenarios he'd imagined for this woman and the money were trashed. He'd expected to find a terrorist or some other criminal, but instead, he'd found a woman who'd made a heartbreaking choice and a man who'd accepted it and done the right thing by her.

"Kharlov's new family—his second wife and his children—were killed in Ukraine." Jack finally got the words out. "Does he know he had another child with you?"

"No." Petrovich squeezed her eyes closed and shook her head. "I knew his business and his nature. He was a gentle lover and a wild lover. I used to call him my dormant volcano."

Jack understood. She'd kept Kharlov in the dark to protect her child. He suddenly saw a reason to hope. He'd hoped to squeeze her for information about Kharlov's location and business operations, but instead, she offered something of far more value. He needed to convince her to give it up.

Still crouched in front of the sofa, he stared into her eyes. "Kharlov has kidnapped the Russian prime minister's daughter and is holding the world hostage."

"Why would he do that?" She looked genuinely shocked. "I always thought he had the potential for violence, but nothing on that scale."

"Because he blames Veronika Oreshkin for the death of his family, and he thinks he's got nothing to lose." Jack looked her right in the eyes. "I want to tell him that's not the case."

"I don't know…" Petrovich closed her eyes again, as if digesting Jack's request. He was asking her to betray her ex-husband and put her own child in danger to protect the greater good. "I—"

"If you help me remove the knife from Oreshkin's throat, I can get her to withdraw Russian troops from Ukraine. Your homeland will be safe."

Her eyes opened, and they seemed to be burning with curiosity. "My son is in the Ukrainian Army…"

Jack spat out what might well turn out to be a lie. "I can keep him safe. Oreshkin wants to stop the assault on Ukraine, but some inside her cabinet won't let her. She's not strong enough to fight them while Kharlov has her daughter, but if we can find him and free the girl, it might be possible to stop the fighting."

"And Dmitry?" She looked at Jack with hope in her eyes then nodded when Jack didn't respond. She understood that Kharlov couldn't survive. It was a terrible arithmetic, every bit as brutal as Jack had found international diplomacy to be. She nodded. "Okay, his name is Vitali Dmitrovich. He's with the

Third Battalion. I think they're currently trying to retake Donetsk."

Jack frowned. "He's in the middle of a war zone?"

She nodded. "Yes."

"Thank you." Jack looked her right in the eye. "We're going to try our best to keep everyone safe. You've given us the chance to do so. You and your son will be looked after. I promise."

Jack stood and left the room. Gilleslee and the other two agents were standing in the hallway, where they'd been able to hear everything. Jack nodded at the lead CIA agent, and he led his men back into the room, where they would continue to keep an eye on Kharlov's ex-wife. She'd given up the treasure, and Jack had what he needed to stop Kharlov and get Oreshkin's daughter back.

He grabbed his cell phone out of his pocket and dialed McGhinnist. When the president answered, Jack explained the situation. He said he wanted to find Kharlov's son and use him to compel Kharlov to let Oreshkin's daughter go. He was certain that doing so would take the rogue arms dealer off the board, letting them focus on implementing the deal they'd agreed in London. His idea was crazy, but crazy might be their best chance.

"I don't mind the idea, but there are Russian troops in that town..." McGhinnist hesitated after Jack had explained his plan. "I can't risk using American assets to extract Kharlov's son. If there's any shooting between American and Russian troops, there'd be a war. This is just too dangerous."

Jack had been expecting that answer. "Fire me, sir."

"What?"

Jack smiled. "Fire me. I'm not an American citizen or

soldier. If you fire me, and I try to retrieve the kid, there's no connection to you at all. If I'm caught, it's on me."

McGhinnist grunted, but the long silence after that suggested he was thinking about it. Finally, he spoke. "It's dangerous, but it's our best chance. If we don't get Oreshkin's daughter back quickly, the prime minister is either going to die, resign, or do whatever Kharlov demands. If that happens, we lose the deal and gain absolute chaos."

"Precisely."

"Resignation accepted." McGhinnist had quickly processed the information and made a decision. "You'll need help, though."

Jack laughed. "I have just the person in mind."

ANNA CLOSED her eyes as the hot water ran over her body, enjoying the only small pleasure to be found in this godforsaken hellhole. Even though there were only two choices—scalding hot or freezing cold—the showers weren't bad, really. They sure beat the food, the beds, the leisure facilities, and the staff. In fact, pretty much everything else at Her Majesty's Prison Bronzefield was terrible except for the showers. Especially the company.

"Bitch." A female voice broke the moment of serenity. "Time to die."

Anna grunted as she was struck from behind and thrown forward. She managed to get her hands up in time to stop herself slamming face-first into the wall tiles, though her midriff did ram into the liquid soap dispenser. It didn't hurt very much, and it certainly had not taken her out of the fight.

She'd been waiting on the prison locals to try something on her, and clearly they'd chosen their time.

She pushed herself off the tiles and spun around, using the momentum to propel herself toward the woman who'd pushed her into the wall. The other woman was much larger, so when Anna's fist blew up her nose, she fell like a demolished skyscraper. The aggressor landed hard and cracked her head on the tiles, the blood from her nose mixing with the water from the showers.

Anna kept her eyes locked on the downed woman for a second, but when it was clear she was down for the count, Anna looked up again. Half a dozen other women had taken a step back after Anna's violent demonstration, while one other woman appeared confident enough to take a step forward. The self-appointed ringleader was a much fitter woman than the slab Anna had laid out on the floor.

Anna raised her guard and fixed the ringleader with a hard stare. "Do you ladies have a problem?"

The other woman gave an exaggerated laugh. A tough-looking woman in her thirties or forties, she seemed used to being top dog. "*You're* our problem."

Anna shrugged. "I haven't said a word to you, your friends, or anyone else. But I'm happy to teach you some manners."

"All of us?"

"If I have to."

"This is *our* prison." The ringleader spat at Anna's feet. "We're going to show you that respect must be paid."

Anna sighed. She'd tried to avoid such a confrontation, knowing that it would only complicate an already-complex situation. After taking out Popov, Anna had returned to the United Kingdom and been arrested upon landing. She'd been transported to a meeting with the MI6 director, Louise

Watkins, who'd chewed her out for going rogue then told her she would be held in prison without charge and without bail until MI6 decided what to do with her.

Since arriving at the prison, she'd kept to herself and skirted problems, but problems had come looking for her. The guards and other inmates had left her well enough alone for a while, but in the last day or so, Anna had felt a tension in the air. It had been subtle at first—sideways glances and whispers just out of earshot—but Anna's senses were more honed than most people's. Her training had told her there was a real problem. It also dictated how she should respond to a threat.

In one explosive motion, Anna turned sideways and used all her strength to pull the liquid soap dispenser from its holder. As the other woman guffawed, Anna aimed the pump at the thug's face and pressed down on it. A squirt of soap went into her eyes, and she staggered back, raising her hands to wipe the liquid from her eyes. The other woman watching the fight roared their disapproval at Anna's dirty tactics, but none of them tried to intervene.

"You're dead, bitch!" The woman with soap in her eyes hissed as she rubbed at them, only succeeded in making it worse. "You're a *fucking* dead woman!"

Anna almost gave her a warning, then she changed her mind. It was time to teach her a lesson. Anna took a step forward, delivered a brutal chop to the woman's throat, then took a step back. Her attacker was also blinded, and she couldn't breathe easily. She stumbled back and slipped on the wet floor. Landing hard, she coughed violently. Anna stomped on the woman's head and torso multiple times, adding some more damage into the mix.

As Anna was about to finish the destruction of her foe, sending a warning to the others to leave her be, the wail of an alarm filled her ears. Seconds later, prison guards swarmed into the shower block, shouting at the bystanders to get the hell out and surrounding Anna with a ring of muscle. The dozen or so guards did nothing to aid the two women she'd put down, focused instead on backing Anna against the wall and trying to intimidate her.

"Nice of you guys to show up." Anna didn't intimidate easily, not even when she was standing wet and naked, surrounded by prison guards. "What's the next step here?"

One of the guards pulled a pair of cuffs from his belt. "You're coming with us. If you don't resist, you won't fall down some stairs on the way to the warden's office."

Anna nodded and let them cuff her. Once she was secure, a guard grabbed her left arm, and another grabbed her right. Another guard radioed for someone to have clothes waiting in the warden's office. Then they set off. In addition to the guards holding her arms, two guards walked in front and two behind —a hefty security detail given she was cuffed and unarmed. The rest stayed behind to mop up after the fight.

Anna kept quiet as they walked to the warden's office, knowing it would do no good to resist. The guards were just following orders, and she would find the answers she wanted at the end of the walk. A few minutes later, they reached the warden's office, where a fresh set of clothing was waiting on one of the visitor's chairs. The guards uncuffed her so she could dress, then they restrained her again and ordered her to sit.

She stared into space and cleared her mind while she waited, until the door to the office opened and a woman stepped inside—a woman who wasn't the warden. Anna's eyes narrowed as Watkins rounded the warden's desk and sat on the other side to Anna's chair. At the same time, the guards who'd escorted Anna into the room left and closed the door behind them.

The MI6 director leaned forward, rested her elbows on the desk, and steepled her fingers in front of her. "I hear you're causing trouble."

"I wouldn't put it quite like that." Anna shrugged, holding the other woman's gaze. "I was putting down some feral dogs."

A hint of a smile showed at the edges of Watkins's lips. "I'm glad to hear you're upholding our reputation."

"I do my best."

The director laughed for a second then put a manila folder on the desk. "I'd like you to undertake a high-priority mission with no support and no cover if you're caught. The Americans requested your assistance specifically, and the PM wanted to support our friends. If you succeed, all charges against you will be dropped, and your record will be clean."

"And if I refuse?"

Watkins's features darkened. "You'll rot in prison until you're ready to atone. Don't underestimate how irritated we are by the death of Popov, Ms. Fowler. I'd suggest you think carefully about this opportunity, because you'll never get another. This is your yellow brick road back to redemption."

"My name isn't Dorothy." Anna took the folder. "But I'll do it anyway."

KHARLOV PRESSED the barrel of his pistol into the back of Sasha Oreshkin's skull at the same time as he whispered to the girl's father, "Be smart."

General Vladimir Oreshkin stared at Kharlov for a long few seconds, holding the handset of his desk phone to his ear.

He was on a phone call with the Kremlin, who'd finally called the base after several days of silence. One of Kharlov's men had answered the call, pretending to be the duty officer and insisting everything was okay, but the caller had insisted on speaking with the base commander. Kharlov had been forced to give the phone to General Oreshkin.

Finally, General Oreshkin saved his daughter's life by surrendering his only chance to summon help. "No, there's nothing else to report. We had a fire in our barracks and our chemical stores, but the fires are out, and we're working to repair the damage. The fires caused an issue with a chemical spill, so we're keeping the base on lockdown. We remain fully operational."

Despite the tension, Kharlov snorted at the truth in General Oreshkin's statement. Since taking the base, his men had increased their stranglehold on it. Some had donned uniforms, repaired the damage to the guardhouses, then manned them. Others had manned the security post, keeping a close eye on the base's network of cameras and its radar feed. The rest had kept watch on their prisoners. Nothing was happening on the base without Kharlov's knowledge.

Kharlov smiled and nodded at General Oreshkin as he exchanged a few more pleasantries, and even a joke, with the Kremlin official on the other end of the line. The danger had passed. If the general was going to reveal the base had been taken over, he would have done it already, but he kept the pistol pressed into the man's daughter anyway. It was important that lessons be consistent.

The second General Oreshkin ended the call, Kharlov started to deliver another lesson. He exploded with violence. He pushed Sasha Oreshkin out of the way, stepped closer to the general, and pistol whipped him. The other man grunted and stumbled to one knee, but he didn't try to fight back as Kharlov rained blows. Kharlov had already made it clear that to resist was a death sentence, so the general took his beating and slumped to the floor.

Kharlov craned his head to look at Sasha. She was screaming and trying to move to her father's side, but being held back by two of Kharlov's men. He smiled at her, turned back to General Oreshkin, and gave him one more hard kick to the midriff. That was enough. Though lessons needed to be learned, he couldn't go too far. He needed General Oreshkin alive for at least a little while longer.

"I would have thought a Russian soldier could take more than that." Kharlov poked General Oreshkin with his boot, looking down at the man with disgust. "Do not delay when I give you an order."

Kharlov laughed as General Oreshkin rolled onto his back. The other man's eyes were full of disdain and his teeth were bloodied, but he nodded. He understood the stakes and would play by the rules. Kharlov leaned down and held out a hand, offering to help the general to his feet. Oreshkin refused, returning to a seated position under his own power. Kharlov laughed and pulled his hand away, amused by the petty show of defiance.

"Now we can get back to business..." Kharlov smiled. "You were *just* going to tell me how to launch one of the missiles using the failsafe."

Before the phone call had come in, Kharlov was in the launch bunker with General Oreshkin, Sasha Oreshkin, and a couple of his men. The old man had been stubborn, refusing to reveal the method for launching, even though Kharlov knew there was one. He'd paid a great deal of money to learn that. The general had taken a number of vicious beatings for his refusal to reveal his secret, and Kharlov was almost ready to move on to more extreme measures.

"Fuck yourself." The general's voice was a snarl. "Nothing will cause me to reveal the secret that would allow you to end the world."

Kharlov sighed. He'd initially found General Oreshkin's dissent amusing, even charming, but his patience had come to an end. He nodded at his men then walked back out to the main courtyard. Close behind, he heard cursing and sounds of struggle as his men wrestled their two captives outside. He didn't look back because he trusted his men, unlike the general, to follow his instructions.

Kharlov looked out at his other prisoners. They were still huddled where they'd been when he'd first taken the base. They were tired, hungry, and dirty, forced to do their business where they sat. Kharlov's men were keeping watch, having already had to gun down several Russians who'd tried to escape. The conversation among the prisoners died down as they realized Kharlov was standing there.

"Your leader has a choice." Kharlov drew his pistol. "He's going to tell me what I want to know, or I'm going to kill a prisoner at random every ten seconds until he relents. There are twelve bullets in this gun. If he's still being stubborn after eleven of you are dead, the last bullet will go into his daughter."

Kharlov flicked off the safety as panic rumbled through the crowd of prisoners. One man tried to run for it and was cut down by a burst of submachine gun fire. Kharlov turned to General Oreshkin and raised an eyebrow. Vladimir Oreshkin stared back at him, a grim look on his face. Kharlov counted to ten in his head, and when it was clear General Oreshkin still wasn't going to spill it, he turned back to the crowd and shot the prisoner closest to him.

Ten more seconds passed. Kharlov shot another. Kharlov counted ten more seconds, then ten more, then ten more. With each milestone, another life was snuffed out. Kharlov took no joy in such killing, but he needed to deliver on his threat. He was surprised General Oreshkin was staying silent, watching his own people get slaughtered, but only the old man had the power to stop it.

"Stop it!" The general finally intervened, after seven of his people had been gunned down. "I'll tell you what you need to know."

Kharlov nodded, holstered his pistol, and looked out at the carnage for only a second. Seven more souls had passed to the afterlife, joining his wife and children in heaven or Nikolai Sokolov in hell, a terrible but necessary cost to unlock the secret he needed to finish his vengeance. Nothing could stop him now, not even God himself. He turned to the general and smiled. Veronika Oreshkin would die.

17

Russian Defense Ministry officials have refused to confirm an anonymous report that a nuclear missile base in the center of the country recently had a near miss with a chemical leak and a fire. When asked for comment, officials stated that Russia's nuclear deterrence remains strong and that they do not respond to American propaganda.

—*New York Standard*

Kharlov smiled as he surveyed the launch panel. All the lights were green, and he'd flipped the safety panel off the launch button. General Oreshkin's override had worked perfectly. Within minutes, he would use it to end the world, vaporizing Veronika Oreshkin and realizing his vengeance. He took a second to look at one of his men, but the other man kept a neutral expression on his face.

Kharlov really wanted Natalya by his side for this. He'd

radioed for her to join him, but she still hadn't arrived, and he was out of patience.

Since breaking the general and forcing him to reveal the launch process, Kharlov had painstakingly gone through the steps required. The missile was now ready to launch, thanks to the paranoia of Soviet leaders who were now all dead. Kharlov was a man of his word. He'd promised General Oreshkin he would spare his daughter, although he was about to rain fire down on the man's ex-wife.

Kharlov stabbed the button with his finger and closed his eyes, enjoying the euphoria of success. A split second later, an incessant beeping filled his ear and forced him to open his eyes again. The panel that controlled the launch had lit up like a Christmas tree, with red lights flashing across the board. He stared at the instrument panel for a long few seconds, not believing his perfectly planned and executed strategy had failed at its most critical point. The feeling of success turned into the sick bile of worry.

"Fuck!" Kharlov's bellow filled the room, and he mashed on the launch button several more times, but it was no good. He turned to his man. "Get me the chief engineer—now!"

Kharlov exhaled slowly through clenched teeth as his man went to carry out his orders. While he waited, Kharlov turned back to the panel to see if he could figure out what had gone wrong, but the displays and buttons may as well have been the controls for an alien spaceship. The general had told him how to launch, the chief engineer had readied the system, and everything should have worked. People were going to answer for their mistakes.

Kharlov's man returned, dragging the chief engineer, Alexei, into the room. Kharlov sneered at Alexei, who had a look of fear on his face. It changed to absolute terror when he glanced at the instrument panel. Alexei's eyes widened, and he opened his mouth to speak, but no words came out. Kharlov crossed the room, grabbed the man by the collar, and dragged him to the panel.

"What happened to the launch?" Kharlov shoved the man toward the instrument panel. "If you don't give me answers within the next minute, you're dead, and I'll find someone who can."

Kharlov watched Alexei nod then get to work. The frightened man read displays and pressed buttons, scrambling to figure out where things had gone wrong. The engineer made a few knowing sounds. Then he grunted and pressed more buttons. Nothing he was doing was giving Kharlov the answers he wanted as fast as he wanted them, though.

"You've got ten seconds left." Kharlov drew his pistol and aimed at Alexei. "Nine. Eight. Seven. Six. Five. Four. Thr—"

"Wait!" Alexei sounded relieved as he turned to face Kharlov. "There was nothing wrong with the launch authorization. It looks like there's some sort of problem in the silo itself. The missile's systems detected there wasn't enough fuel for a successful launch and shut the system down."

Kharlov's face curled up into a scowl. He stepped closer to Alexei and pistol-whipped him with the butt of the pistol. The man cried out in pain as he went flying away from the panel and crashed hard onto the floor. Absolute terror in his eyes, the engineer held his head and shuffled away from Kharlov, lucky the blow hadn't cracked his skull.

"Isn't it your job to make sure this fucking system works?" Kharlov's shout echoed through the launch command center. "Can it be fixed?"

"I... I don't know..." Alexei's voice was a whimper. "It should have been fueled up, so I'd need to get down into the silo to figure out what the exact problem is. Even if we can fix it, it will take some time to repair any damage, re-fuel the rocket, and get everything ready for another launch."

Kharlov turned and nodded to his man, who walked over to Alexei, grabbed him by the collar, and lifted him to his feet. The engineer pleaded and babbled some more as he was dragged to the exit, but Kharlov ignored him. He could trust his man to oversee the inspection down in the silo, so until he reported back, he didn't care about anything Alexei had to say.

Alone once again, Kharlov looked down at the display and sighed. Something that should have been so simple— and so satisfying—had disintegrated within seconds. He closed his eyes and allowed himself a moment of melancholy as his vengeance was delayed yet again. Then he opened his eyes again. He was filled with a renewed determination. If he couldn't destroy Veronika Oreshkin with nuclear fire, he would have to find another way to make her suffer.

He smiled as he thought of the perfect way to do so. Kharlov still needed Oreshkin's daughter as a hostage, to make sure she didn't assault the base. On the other hand, her husband had become surplus to requirements.

Fists clenched, he exited the launch bunker and walked briskly across the base to where Natalya was holding General Oreshkin. Though he spotted some of his men patrolling the base, they were smart enough to stay out of his way. He entered the general's residence and climbed the stairs. He pushed open the second-floor bedroom, ready to put a bullet in General Oreshkin.

Instead of Oreshkin, he found Natalya tied to the heavy steel bedframe, a sock stuffed into her mouth. Kharlov's mouth fell open, and he struggled for words for a moment.

Then he blinked a few times, pulled the sock from Natalya's mouth, and screamed at her, "Where the fuck is he?"

"Gone." Natalya swallowed. "He asked to use the bathroom, and I let him. When he came out, he hit me with a pipe. He must have had it stashed in there somewhere."

With a scream, Kharlov turned and left the room. He was enraged that Natalya had let him down for the first time ever and let General Oreshkin escape, but there was nothing to be gained from worrying about that. Instead, he tried to focus on finding his stray prisoner. Vladimir Oreshkin had the power to bring the Russian military down on Kharlov's head if he could alert Russian authorities that the base had been taken. Kharlov had to find and kill the man before that could happen.

VERONIKA SIGNED the last briefing paper from a stack that had towered over her desk, the ones her advisors had told her were routine and fine to sign without reading. She smiled at the thought. Although she'd only been prime minister for a few weeks, she'd been a senior politician for much longer than that. Veronika had learned long ago to read every single word of every single document she was asked to sign. Doing otherwise in Russian politics was signing her own death sentence.

She placed the final document gently on the top of the pile, put the lid on her pen and stood. It was the early hours of the morning, and her staff had all gone home, leaving her to work uninterrupted in her office. She'd worked through a great deal of her backlog, though it had caused her physical pain. Her back was killing her. She stretched then walked to the window and stared out at her country. It looked as dark as her current mood.

She sighed. Her mind wasn't on the job. It hadn't been since Kharlov called her on the London Eye. Although she'd struggled to focus on briefings about matters that seemed trivial in comparison to her daughter being held captive by a madman, she couldn't ignore the work completely. Her fragile alliance with Mikhailov and the hawks and the commitments she'd made to Emery and the Western leaders required attention. In return, she got to hold on to power and the support of American intelligence to find her daughter.

She'd heard from Emery the previous day. He'd found a lead—Kharlov had a son he didn't know existed. If Emery and the Americans could find him, Kharlov might trade Sasha for his son. Even if she still had to offer up her own life as part of the deal, Veronika was prepared to sacrifice herself. She would do anything to placate the madman and protect Sasha.

Veronika jumped a little when her ringing cell phone broke the silence of the night. She turned around and stared at the device for a moment, knowing there was a chance that Dmitry Kharlov was calling her again and that her daughter's life might be decided in the next sixty seconds. She swallowed hard, walked over to the phone, which was atop her desk, and answered it.

"Veronika…"

Her first instinct was to frown at the sound of her husband's voice, which she hadn't heard in a long time. A second later, her mind started to shout an alarm. He sounded weak. Broken. Though Veronika and her husband had shared turbulent times and hadn't spoken in almost a decade, the fact he sounded so pathetic struck at her core. Something else was wrong with her family.

"Vladimir? What's wrong?"

"He's using Sasha to force me..." He let out a hacking cough. It sounded like the cough of a dying man.

Stunned into a moment of silence, Veronika pressed a button on her desk that would summon her advisors. She'd known Kharlov had crossed the border into Russia, but she'd expected him to come straight to Moscow and try to take her life in the capital. Instead, he'd found her ex-husband, a tough man who'd commanded armies. A man who commanded...

Her eyes widened. "Kharlov has control of nuclear weapons?"

"He used Sasha to force me to show him how to launch the nukes without your command authority. It's an old Soviet-era failsafe, built into the launch system in case Moscow was taken out first by the Americans..." Vladimir paused, his voice getting softer. "I'm sorry, Veronika. I know I wasn't the best husband, but I've tried my best to protect Sasha."

"Forget all that," Veronika hissed, sick with worry for both of them. "Get her out!"

"I can't." Vladimir coughed again. "But I needed you to know he has nuclear weapons and Sasha. I love—"

A loud boom assaulted her ear, and Veronika flinched, pulling the phone away from her ear. She knew that sound. She cried out his name in outrage and agony, knowing her ex-husband was dead. The man she'd hated for the last decade and grown to love again in the last ten seconds had made the sacrifice she too was willing to make. Veronika put the phone back to her ear and cried out his name.

Instead of a voice, she heard laughter—long, deep, and evil. Then a familiar voice spoke. "It seems your husband was as poor at sticking to a bargain as you were, Veronika. He promised to cooperate, and in return, I promised your daughter would be safe. He lied. Just like you did when you promised to help keep my family safe."

"Dmitry, I—"

"No more talk. I have your daughter. I have nuclear weapons. I have the ability to launch them. You now have a choice."

"What choice?"

"You resign on national television, stick a gun to your head, and pull the trigger. If you do that, your daughter will live, and I won't launch the missiles. If you fail to do what I demand within twelve hours or if you attack the base, the launch goes ahead, and your daughter will pay the ultimate price."

Veronika was about to speak, but the call went dead. She lowered the cell phone and stared at it, her mind processing her anguish and fear. The stakes had been raised again. But at least she knew where he was and how much time she had to act. Although it was strange he'd given her time at all, she now had twelve hours to find another way to end his madness. If she failed, she would have to end herself to appease him.

JACK WASN'T A JEALOUS MAN, but the sight of Anna Fowler and the four British SAS men sleeping in the seats opposite him were enough make him feel green with envy. He turned his head to the left and saw that Gilleslee and another CIA agent were also sleeping. He was the only person in the plane's cavernous cargo hold who was failing to grab sleep when it was available.

"Jerks." Jack sighed.

He'd tried to sleep, but the sound of the big C-17 Globemaster's engines had been enough to keep him awake. It wasn't the ideal preparation for one of the most dangerous things he'd ever done, but he had little choice. The fact he had a chance to save the nuclear deal and Veronika Oreshkin's daughter was a miracle—lack of sleep or not—and it wasn't a shot he was going to squander.

From the CIA safehouse, Jack had traveled with Gilleslee and one other agent to a Ukrainian airbase, where a US Air Force C-17 had been fueled up and waiting to take them deeper into the hottest conflict zone in Ukraine—Donetsk. Anna Fowler and the SAS team who'd extracted them from Russia were along for the ride, because while the Ukrainians had agreed to hand over Kharlov's son, they'd also insisted he be extracted by Western forces.

It was only once he was in the air that Jack found out how *exactly* he was going to be getting onto the ground in the middle of the conflict zone. The fat-ass transport plane couldn't land nearby, which explained why the Pentagon had worked with British military commanders to assign the small SAS detachment to the mission. If Jack, Fowler, Gilleslee, and the other agent wanted to get to Kharlov's son, there was only one way down.

"Ten minutes to drop."

Jack swallowed hard as the pilot's voice boomed in his ears. Suddenly, he was six hundred seconds away from jumping out of a perfectly good plane. His stomach sank, and he felt his heart rate quicken, though he was glad the pilot's announcement had woken his companions. A few stirred, and they woke others, all of them instantly shifting into gear and starting to prepare for the jump.

Though Jack was scared, he was reassured by the fact that he was surrounded by professionals, and for them, the few minutes before a mission seemed as regular as breathing. He was only along for the ride. His job would begin when they found Kharlov's son, fighting somewhere in the city down below. Jack would need to convince him to help save the world by betraying his father.

"Mr. Emery, I've got the president on the line, sir." The pilot's voice filled Jack's headset, interrupting his thoughts. "I'm patching him through to you on a secure channel."

"Thanks." Jack sat up straighter in his chair. "I'm here, Bill. We drop in less than ten minutes. What do you need?"

"The situation has changed, Jack." McGhinnist's voice sounded distant and different in the headset, probably caused by the encryption or poor-quality line. "I wanted you to know."

Jack felt ashamed that he hoped the president was about to tell him the mission was off, that Kharlov had surrendered, or that they had figured out another way to stop him. "Know what, sir?"

"I've just received word that Kharlov has taken over a Russian nuclear base." McGhinnist's voice sounded grim. "He's still got Oreshkin's daughter, and he just killed her husband. He's told Oreshkin she has twelve hours to resign then kill herself live on television. If she doesn't, or if the base is attacked, he's going to launch the nukes."

Jack closed his eyes. He'd just gone from scared to terrified. "Do we have any proof that Kharlov is telling the truth and is able to launch?"

"Kharlov claims that the general revealed an old Soviet-era launch override that base commanders could use if Moscow was flattened." McGhinnist sighed. "Oreshkin tells me the override exists, and our people believe Kharlov's claims. We think it's likely he has the missiles and knows how to launch them."

Jack opened his eyes. Everyone else in the cargo hold was watching him intently. Though they couldn't hear his conversation, they'd apparently been able to read his body language easily enough. Jack tried to steel himself. "We stick to the plan, then. Our only hope is to find Kharlov's son."

"Jack..." McGhinnist paused. "Good luck to you and the others. I'll speak to you on the other side."

"Thanks, sir."

When the line went dead, Jack sighed and looked up at his companions. "President McGhinnist asked me to pass his best wishes. The situation just got more difficult."

The others nodded, but they didn't seem bothered by Jack's words. They were all used to life-or-death situations. They went back to gearing up and readying for the drop. Jack had no gear to ready. He had a pistol in a side holster and a headset that would let him communicate with the others. That was enough for him. Though he knew how to shoot, if such a highly credentialed team were relying on him to put a target down, they were in trouble.

Whatever Jack lacked in firepower, the SAS guys made up for. They were dressed all in black and had parachutes on their backs. They were kitted out with state-of-the-art tactical rigs and packing heavy weaponry—a mix of submachine guns and carbines. Anna had a submachine gun of her own, and the two CIA agents had pistols.

When the pilot warned they were three minutes out from the drop point, the cargo ramp at the back of the plane started to open. Jack unbuckled his seat harness and stood, careful to make sure he held on to something at all times. He'd wanted to stay out of the way while the professionals were preparing, but it was almost showtime. Jack had been buddied up with Daniel Sawyer, the same SAS trooper who'd extracted him from Moscow. He took a few steps closer to Sawyer and smiled.

"Don't shit yourself on the way down," Sawyer said over the comms network. "Ready?"

"As I'll ever be." Jack forced a smile then looked an Anna, who was standing next to her assigned SAS partner. "What are the chances this kid would be in the middle of one of the hottest conflicts on Earth? We never seem to catch a break on this kind of thing, do we?"

"The thugs down there are nothing." Anna laughed. "Some of the inmates I was hanging out with would scare the pants off anyone fighting down there."

"I'm glad you're out of there, Anna."

"I'm glad you *got* me out of there." She smirked. "We'll be fine, Jack."

He nodded right as the pilot started the one-minute countdown to drop. Jack let Sawyer manhandle him into the harness that would let them undertake a tandem parachute jump. Jack had never jumped out of a plane before, but the SAS trooper had reassured him before takeoff that there was nothing to worry about. He'd felt comfortable enough at the time, but once he was strapped to the other man, Jack suddenly didn't feel so sure.

"Go, go, go!" The pilot screamed the order to jump.

The SAS man urged him forward and over the ramp. As Sawyer jumped into the night, Jack hoped nobody else could hear him screaming.

18

In this week's deep dive on the crisis in Ukraine, we look at the city of Donetsk. An important industrial hub on the bank of the Kalmius River, the city has been the site of heavy fighting between Russia and Ukraine for the last two years. It does not seem like the city's two million residents will get any respite from the fighting in the foreseeable future, with Russia pouring more resources into taking the city following their success in Kharkov. Reports from the city paint a bleak picture for the defenders, with the Ukrainian forces ceding territory each day and running critically short on manpower and supplies.

—New York Standard

Jack grunted as he and Sawyer landed on the soccer field, stumbling and rolling as the parachute pulled them forward. He felt like he was stuck in a tumble until Sawyer managed to unclip the chute and send it flying off into the stands. Their momentum carried them forward a few more yards, then they came to a stop on the grass, watching as the other SAS men landed around them.

"I'm never doing that again!" Jack was breathless. "You bastards are the craziest motherfuckers on planet Earth!"

"Who dares wins, baby!" Sawyer grinned as he repeated his unit motto and gripped his weapon. "Welcome to the club. Now it's time to go to work."

Jack nodded as the last SAS soldier landed with Anna. Soon after, each pair of jumpers had shed their parachutes, and the four SAS soldiers had formed a defensive position— one man facing out from each corner of a square perimeter. The SAS communications officer radioed in to his commanders that they'd made it to the landing zone and were heading for the target. Then they moved out, walking in tight formation across the soccer field and into the city proper.

"Jesus..." Jack whispered as he took in the sight of the battered city. "They're not screwing around here, are they?"

Nobody answered him. They could surely see the damage as plainly as he could. A majority of the buildings had been burnt out or damaged, and the exterior of the stadium itself had also seen better days. Jack had been to Syria during the civil war, and the destruction in Donetsk was on par with anything he'd seen there. The scale of the destruction showed that Russia really wanted this place.

They walked for fifteen minutes in the direction of their target—the Third Battalion of the Ukrainian Army. The unit was bivouacked on the eastern side of the city, right on the front line, amid the thickest of the fighting. The Ukrainians had revealed the location, and Oreshkin had promised to get Russian troops to pull back while Jack and his small team were in the area. Jack wasn't as reassured by her promise as he should have been.

Despite it being in the early hours of the morning, the deeper they got into the heart of the city, the more refugees he saw streaming the other way. They were desperate people—traveling alone or in small groups—carrying whatever of their personal possessions they'd managed to salvage from their homes. They looked at Jack and his companions with empty eyes, seeing only more men with guns and not caring about the particulars.

Jack felt a lump rise in his throat at the sight of one family. An old woman was doing her best to drag a wheeled suitcase along the road while also carrying a baby in her arms. Alongside her, a boy who was about five years old was doing his best to keep up, despite the tears streaming down his cheeks. None of the other refugees offered to help, focused instead on their own survival.

An immense feeling of guilt overwhelmed Jack. Although he hadn't orchestrated the Russian invasion of Ukraine, he had helped to broker the deal that traded the territory for a global nuclear deal. Seeing the old woman and the children struggle, it felt like he'd been a party to an atrocity against the people of Ukraine. He didn't know the family's story, but theirs would be one of millions of pain and displacement resulting from the conflict.

"Jack, we need to keep moving. We've got a job to do." Anna gripped Jack's arm and gave it a squeeze. "Shit happens, okay?"

Jack looked at the family for another long second, then he swallowed and looked at Anna. He knew it wasn't okay, and her face revealed she did, too, but he nodded anyway. "Let's go."

Jack made it four steps before gunfire boomed.

"Ambush! Shooters on the rooft—" The shout of one of the SAS soldiers was cut off as he grunted and dropped, his head turned into a bloody mess.

Jack crouched low as the street exploded with action. Gunfire rained down on them, and the rest of Jack's team returned fire at the rooftops of multiple buildings. Jack knew his pistol was impossibly outclassed, so he looked around for cover and spotted a trashed sedan that was his best shot. He ran at a full sprint toward it, until he saw the old woman from a moment ago scream and fall to the ground, the baby landing hard on the road.

Jack made a split-second decision. He changed his course, ran toward the children, and scooped them up. As gunfire roared around him the toddler kicked out, but Jack gripped him tighter and focused on getting off the street. He locked eyes on a storefront that had been blown out and ran straight for it, jumping through the front window that had no glass covering it. The second he landed back on his feet, he started to fall.

Jack screamed as the floor gave out from under him, and he fell down to the basement level of the burned-out store. He tried his best to protect the baby and the toddler from the weight of his body. He landed on his back. The force was enough to drive all the air from his lungs. As he struggled to suck in one breath of precious air, the toddler started to scream, and the young boy cried even louder.

Though gunfire continued to roar on the street above, when Jack finally managed to get a breath, he sat up and focused on the boy. "It's okay. You're safe."

Jack sighed when the boy stared back at him blankly. The kid clearly didn't understand what he was saying, but his crying did ease off a little. He looked down at Jack's gun then back up at his face, as if assessing whether the strange armed man speaking another language could be trusted.

"Jack?" Anna's voice had a hint of concern as she spoke over the comms network. "Where the hell are you?"

Jack groaned and climbed to his feet, glad the gunfire from the street had stopped and that she'd survived. He keyed his microphone. "Deli. Basement. The floor gave out."

"Hang tight."

Jack smiled, helped the kids to their feet, and started to look around for a staircase that would lead him back up to street level. He found it quickly enough, but when he tested out the first stair, it crumbled beneath his feet. The wooden stairs were rotted through, a sign the basement hadn't been used for generations. He and the children were trapped in a giant hole without an obvious way out—until Anna jumped down to the basement, landing on her feet like a cat.

"That's one way of avoiding the fight, Jack." She smiled with relief when she saw him, then her features darkened. "We lost two guys—one CIA, one SAS—but we dealt with the ambush."

"More death." Jack sighed. "We need to get these kids out of here. Their grandmother was taken out by the shooters."

"That's a waste of time, sir." Gilleslee spoke from the level above, staring down at them. "We need to keep moving."

Jack looked up at Gilleslee. "We're going to help these kids back up to the street and make sure they're safe, *then* we can contin—"

"Sir, I must insist." Gilleslee cut Jack off mid-sentence. "The operation must come before a pair of civilians."

"We're going to help these kids! That's a *fucking* order. And if I need to call to get the president to tell you that, I'll waste even *more* time doing so."

Jack held Gilleslee's gaze, and they stared at each other for a long few seconds, then the CIA agent sighed, put down his gun, and waved for Jack to pass the children up. A few moments later, Jack was boosting up Anna, and she was in turn lifting up the children to Gilleslee. The CIA agent was gentle with the children, showing no more signs that he thought it was a waste of time.

When the kids were safe back up on the street, Jack intertwined his fingers together, crouched low, and smiled at Anna. She nodded and put her foot on his hand. On the count of three, Jack used all of his strength to lift her high enough up the wall to reach the outstretched hands of Gilleslee. The other man grabbed onto Anna and hauled her up to the top, relieving Jack of the weight, and leaving him alone at the bottom of the wall.

"You're up next, Jack." Gilleslee knelt and reached down again. "Get a run-up and try to reach my hand."

Jack nodded and walked away from the wall, then ran back at it and tried to jump high enough to grab Gilleslee's outstretched hands. Falling short, he grunted as he landed heavily on the ground. Gilleslee shouted down at him to try again, so Jack dusted himself off and ran at the wall once more. It went about as well as the first time. It was no good. Jack wasn't getting to the top of the wall any time soon.

"Lancer, this is Overwatch." A new voice in Jack's ears interrupted his attempts to get back to street level. "Be advised, a Russian armored column is three blocks from you and closing from the southeast. Recommend that you seek to avoid contact and continue onto the target by heading northeast. Over."

"Fuck." Jack muttered under his breath, annoyed at the Russian interference after Oreshkin had committed to withdrawing troops but glad they had drones overhead watching over them. He looked up at Gilleslee and Fowler. "You guys need to leave me. Get out of here and find Vitali Dmitrovich. I'll figure a way out of here and join you when I can."

"Not a chance, Jack. If you stay down there, you're a sitting duck." Anna's voice was strong and firm. "We go together or not at all."

Jack shook his head. He wasn't keen to sacrifice himself, but there was no choice. If the others stayed, they would die. The mission would fail. He couldn't allow that. He'd asked McGhinnist to invest everything in his cause, so he couldn't balk when the situation demanded he pay the same price. The only way to beat Kharlov, a man who'd lost everything, was to push all in and put everything on the line.

"Find him and end this." Jack gave Anna a sad smile. "There's not another thing in this entire world that matters a damn."

"Target down." Anna whispered into her headset as the sentry she'd shot in the head dropped at the same time as his three patrol mates.

"Move up." Sawyer's clipped command came over the comms network one second after they'd downed all four targets. "One hundred yards to the brick fence on the edge of the park."

Anna responded to Sawyer's command by darting from the car she was sheltered behind and advancing up the devastated street, trailing the three SAS guys, with Gilleslee pulling up the rear. Though she hadn't worked with any of these people before, the caliber of the SAS troops made it easy to follow their lead. They were ruthless, efficient, and whisper quiet.

Anna passed the corpses of the Russian troops they'd just taken down and kept moving to Sawyer's rendezvous point. She hoped they'd seen the last of the Russian troops who would be in their way, because despite Veronika Oreshkin's promise to pull Russian troops back from the front lines, the reality on the ground had been very different. And the continued presence of Russian troops in the city wasn't even their biggest problem. They'd lost contact with Emery.

Since they'd left Emery behind in the basement and continued on to find Vitali Dmitrovich, they'd stayed in contact. But just before engaging the latest group of hostiles, Emery had broadcast a warning then gone silent. Anna wasn't sure if the comms system had failed or if something had taken him out, but they'd gone from being in regular contact to hearing nothing but silence.

She'd hated leaving Emery behind and felt even worse about it afterward. Though her choice of career demanded an ability to compartmentalize—to force feelings down into the deepest pit of her soul so she could keep going and get the job done—she was struggling. A few times, Anna had to strongly resist the urge to go back for Jack, but she knew the consequences of that decision would be too great. There was no choice but to press on with the others.

She reached the waist-high brick wall and crouched behind it, right next to her allies. On the other side, a large park spread as far as the eye could see. The Third Battalion was bivouacked inside the park, being pressed on all sides by the encroaching Russian troops, despite Oreshkin's promise to pull them back. Somewhere up ahead, Anna knew she would find Kharlov's son.

Anna waited while Sawyer and the other two SAS men stood and made their way over the fence, then she and Gilleslee followed, all of them keeping their eyes peeled and their guns at the ready. They pushed deeper into the park— one hundred yards, then two hundred yards, then three hundred yards—until someone shouted at them in Ukrainian.

Anna and her people stopped their advance and took cover behind trees, then she shouted the code word. "Sorrow!"

"Happiness!" A man with a Ukrainian accent shouted back in heavily accented English. "Move forward slowly."

Although the code words told Anna it was safe to proceed, she still felt uneasy leaving cover and advancing toward a Ukrainian Army position. She kept her weapon high over her head as she moved forward, until she could see the Ukrainian Army platoon dug into shallow trenches on the park's lawn. Twenty assault rifles were pointed at her, held by men who were probably nervous about the situation and angry that their country had been invaded.

Thankfully, one man had lowered his weapon and was waiting with a smile on his face. "You're late."

She nodded at him. "You guys are almost surrounded by Russian troops. We had to fight our way through some of their advance forces."

"We know." The soldier's smile vanished. "We're pulling out to the north the moment we hand Vitali Dmitrovich over to you, so let's get to it."

Anna nodded, communicated with her team, and followed the soldier behind the lines. The Ukrainian encampment was a mess. Wounded soldiers leaned against trees and against vehicles, while the dead had been secured in body bags then simply covered by blankets when they'd run out of bags. It was clear the unit had paid a huge price to hold out until Anna and her makeshift team arrived.

And when Anna was taken to the man—a boy, really—it was obvious why they had been forced to travel to him. He was asleep on a camp stretcher, a thin blanket covering his legs and bloodied bandages covering his torso. She wasn't sure what had happened to Dmitrovich, but he was severely wounded.

Anna inhaled sharply. "What's wrong with him?"

"He was wounded before we received word of his... importance." The soldier shrugged. "We got him behind the lines and stabilized him, but he wasn't stable enough to move."

Anna nodded. Though it was clear they didn't understand the exact reason why the enlisted soldier was in such demand, they'd obviously been told he was key to ending the war.

Anna forced herself to look away from Vitali Dmitrovich and back to the soldier who'd escorted her to him. "Is it safe to move him now?"

"Probably not." He shrugged, and his voice was deadpan. "But there's no choice. We have enough men and ammunition to hold this position for one more hour, then we withdraw."

Anna nodded. It was time to call in the cavalry. She keyed her headset. "Overwatch, this is Lancer 4. We've secured the target."

"Confirmed, Lancer 4. What's your status?"

"The target is wounded, the defenders are barely holding on, we're surrounded, and Lancer is also down three casualties. Requesting evacuation by helicopter."

"Not possible, Lancer 4. The airspace is too hot." There was a pause. "There's a thin northern corridor that's still open. That's your best option."

"Confirmed, Overwatch." Anna forced the words out, even though she wanted to tell the man on the other end what she really thought. "We'll figure it out."

Anna sighed. As Sawyer headed for the truck and the other SAS men lifted Vitali Dmitrovich's stretcher, Anna tried to think of another way. The defenders were exhausted, the Russians had them surrounded, and they clearly hadn't heeded Oreshkin's order to stand down. Worse, if they couldn't get Kharlov's son out of the vise they were in, there would be no way to stop the nuclear launch.

She reached into her pocket, pulled out her cell phone, and dialed a number she'd memorized. She put the phone to her ear and smiled when a Russian woman answered. "Prime Minister Oreshkin? This is Anna Fowler. I'm on the team with Jack Emery, trying to get Kharlov's son out of danger..."

There was a very long pause on the other end of the line, then Oreshkin spoke. "What do you need from me, Ms. Fowler?"

"I need you to get the Russian troops that are currently pushing into Donetsk to get the hell off my ass." Anna paused. "With all due respect, of course."

VERONIKA WAS TAKEN ABACK by Anna Fowler's boldness, though in the short time she'd known the British agent, she'd learned to expect it. "There are no Russian troops remaining in the city at all, Ms. Fowler. My generals have assured me that all Russian forces have pulled out."

Fowler scoffed on the other end of the line. "Tell that to the Ukrainian battalion that's been through the meat grinder trying to keep the kid safe. Or my guys who're dead. Or Jack Emery."

Veronika sat up taller in her chair, a flash of fear passing through her body like lightning. "Is Jack all right?"

"I don't think so." Fowler's voice sounded as hurt as Veronika felt. "We had to leave him behind or risk being overrun by *your* troops. We've lost contact with him."

"I'm sorry. I've been betrayed." Veronika barely whispered the words, she was so overwhelmed by anger. "I promise the troops will start withdrawing soon."

"Don't take too long. We're holding on by our fingernails here."

The line went dead. Veronika removed the handset from her ear and stared at it, as if waiting for answers to spew out of it. When Emery had contacted her about Kharlov having a living son, she'd agreed with him and the American president that securing that boy was the best chance of making a deal with Kharlov to secure her daughter and stave off a catastrophic nuclear launch.

McGhinnist and Emery had promised to get the boy. All she'd had to do was order her troops back. Except the troops hadn't pulled back.

Veronika walked out of her office, past her army of administrative staff, and down the hallway to where her cabinet ministers had their offices. A few who had their doors open looked up from their own desks as she passed, but Veronika ignored them all. She had one target in mind. Nothing would stop her or divert her path. She was a heat-seeking missile of anger and outrage.

When she reached the door to Yevgeny Mikhailov's office, she pounded on the heavy oak door ceaselessly until it opened and she was face-to-face with him. As a loyal ally, she'd appointed him defense minister after Popov's death, but she'd been betrayed. Mikhailov raised an eyebrow, stepped back inside the office, and retreated behind his desk. As he sat and stared at her, Veronika slammed the door behind her and stalked forward to confront him.

"I just received word that the Army is still advancing in Donetsk, Yevgeny." Veronika's voice was sub-zero, cold enough to freeze molten lava. "Explain."

He sized her up for a few moments, then he smiled. "I decided your order was illegitimate, given your personal conflict. Pulling our troops out of there would have reversed hard-won gains paid for in the blood of young Russian boys, all so that their prime minister could save her daughter from a terrorist plot."

Veronika's eyes flared, and she balled her fists beside her. "You'll spend the rest of your life inside a cell, you fat toad. I—"

"You don't recognize your place in all of this. You were a tool, a moderate fig leaf covering the true power in the government. I'm not satisfied with the deal you made with the Americans or the concessions you got in return. We're going to take all of Ukraine, and news of an attempted nuclear strike by a Ukrainian terrorist will be the invitation we need."

"You're insane. I—"

"You'll *what*, Veronika?" His laughter was mocking. "Without Kharlov's son as a bargaining chip, you'll have an impossible choice. If you kill yourself, there's no nuclear launch, and you're out of my way. If you don't, we'll do it ourselves and make a deal with Kharlov. Either way, you're finished."

Veronika exhaled slowly, trying to bring her anger under control. She'd been a fool to trust a former puppet of Sokolov.

He'd betrayed her, humiliated her, and gone very close to costing her the only hope she had of stopping Kharlov, saving her daughter's life, and preventing a nuclear launch.

Her anger welled up and exploded. Veronika took a step around his desk, grabbed a letter opener off his desk, then lunged at him with it. Mikhailov's eyes bulged in shock as she plunged it into his stomach, her muscles and her fury driving the implement deep. She stabbed him with it repeatedly, and by the time he pushed her away, it was too late. He was bleeding from a half dozen places, his white shirt turning crimson.

"You cow." He spat the words at her as he pressed his palm into the wounds, trying to staunch the bleeding. "I'm going to stick that thing down your throat."

Veronika stepped back as he stood to attack her. She tried to stab out with the letter opener again, but he used his superior strength to grab her wrist and twist it until she let go of the weapon. Then he pushed her onto the floor and bent down to retrieve the letter opener. Veronika retreated from him, trying to keep her distance while at the same time screaming for help at the top of her voice.

Veronika kept screaming until Mikhailov dived on top of her and tried to stab her with the letter opener. She felt the blade penetrate her hand, and she could smell his rancid breath. No matter how hard she fought, he was stronger. He sat up on top of her, restricting her ability to slap him away or buck him off. He raised the letter opener. Veronika could see the blade. She cried out as it came toward her face. Then the room exploded with noise.

Veronika squealed as the letter opener fell from Mikhailov's hand—only inches from her face—and he slumped forward on top of her. She didn't stop screaming until she saw a soldier standing in the doorway, looking down the sights of his rifle. The soldier lowered the rifle and stared at Veronika, seemingly waiting for her to say something, to validate the action he'd taken.

Although she was shaking in fear, she was happy to oblige for the man who'd saved her life. She swallowed hard and tried to summon up some shred of authority. "Thank you for your assistance. He attacked me, and I couldn't fight him off. You saved my life. I won't forget this. Please stand guard outside this office while I make some calls."

The soldier nodded, exited the office, and closed the door behind him. Veronika exhaled slowly, glad her attack on Mikhailov would be considered self-defense. The soldier wouldn't question her version of events, and there would be no evidence that she'd attacked first. The man who'd betrayed her was dead. One more hawk from Sokolov's cabal had been shot from the sky.

Veronika pushed Mikhailov off her. He was heavy, especially as a dead weight, but she was still so full of adrenaline that she easily pushed him onto the floor. Veronika climbed to her feet and stared down at him for a second, feeling her anger slowly subside and her mind return to business. There was more work to do than ever before. She sat in Mikhailov's chair, picked up his phone, and dialed.

The phone was answered after only a few rings. "This is General Bovromich. How can I help you, Minister?"

"This is the prime minister." Veronika leaned back in the chair. "If you're not in Yevgeny Mikhailov's office in five minutes, you'll be relieved of your command."

Veronika slammed down the phone and waited. To his credit, General Bovromich arrived in three minutes. He knocked gently on the door, entered the office, and closed the door behind him. Veronika watched him with cold, calculating eyes as he crossed the room and stood in front of the desk. She didn't know if this man was part of the treason against her—part of putting her daughter and the world at risk—but she was going to find out.

Bovromich didn't even look down at Mikhailov's corpse. He kept his eyes locked on her. "How can I help?"

"I want you to call whoever you need to call to get the troops in Donetsk to immediately cease firing and withdraw from the city."

Veronika waited while the general nodded and left to carry out her orders, then she stood from the chair and glanced down at Mikhailov's body. She allowed herself a moment of relief, knowing that she'd survived a battle to the death and foiled a man who'd betrayed her at every turn. Then she exited the office and asked the soldier standing outside to arrange for the police to be called.

She returned to her own office, closed the door, and sat in the chair behind her desk. She used her cell phone to call Anna Fowler. She forced the thought of losing Jack Emery to the back of her mind.

"This is Fowler." The British woman's voice was laced with stress, and there were muffled explosions in the background. "I hope you've got some good news for me, Prime Minister."

Veronika smiled. "There was a kink in the chain of command that has now been fixed. The Russian forces will start withdrawing momentarily."

"Glad to hear it." Fowler sounded relieved. "Now we've secured Vitali Dmitrovich, what's the plan?"

"We call his father." Veronika removed the cell phone from her ear, selected the option to connect another person to the call, and dialed another number. This time, the call was answered quickly. "It's me."

"Veronika!" Dmitry Kharlov's voice was full of false cheer. "I hope you're calling to tell me to tune in to watch you blow your brains out, because the clock is ticking."

"Not exactly..." Veronika smiled, anticipating his reaction to her next statement. "There's someone else on the line— Anna Fowler. She's currently with your son."

"Is this some sort of sick joke?" His response was acidic. "My son is dead and you're playing with the life of your daughter. I—"

"It's true." Fowler cut him off. "His name is Vitali Dmitrovich. Anya Petrovich is his mother. You're his father."

Veronika pressed the phone into her ear and held her breath as she waited for him to respond. It felt like her entire life had led to this second. There were a million ways the next few seconds could go, but there was only one outcome she was hoping for—only one that would save her daughter and avert nuclear annihilation. She was about to find out if Dmitry Kharlov's love for his family—even a family he didn't know he had—was enough to stave off his madness.

"I don't know what possessed you to try such trickery." Kharlov gave a short laugh. "You have signed your daughter's death warrant."

Veronika cried out. "No, I—"

"You expect me to simply believe your lies? You want me to believe that a woman I loved and who loved me kept news of a child from me?" he hissed. "It was your lies that led to this situation in the first place, Veronika. Your failure to tell me that Merefa was in danger is what led to the death of my *real* family."

"I..." Veronika had no answer. She'd failed. She felt her

eyes well up, and she squeezed them closed, though not before a tear escaped and fell down her cheek.

Then she heard a muffled male voice. And a gasp. And laughter.

"Jack!"

19

Our correspondent in Donetsk is reporting that Russian troops are beginning a withdrawal from the city, disengaging from firefights, and leaving forward positions. The move is particularly shocking because all reports indicated that Russia was only hours away from seizing total control of the city, having won several comprehensive victories against the Ukrainian defenders in recent days. The withdrawal can only have come at the order of Russian leadership, although it remains to be seen if this is part of a broader softening of the Russian push.

—New York Standard

Jack jumped down from the back of the truck he'd been riding in and smiled at Fowler, who was staring at him with wide eyes and holding a phone to her ear. "Miss me?"

Her mouth fell open, and she was speechless, until she

remembered she was still on the phone. "Prime Minister, Jack Emery is here. I'm going to put him on the phone."

Jack held out his hand and took the phone, a quizzical look on his face. He put the phone to his ear. "Hello?"

"Jack!" Oreshkin's voice was filled with relief. "You're also on the line with Dmitry Kharlov. I've told him about his son, but he doesn't believe he had a child with Anya Petrovich."

Jack looked around at the mention of Kharlov's son and saw the rest of his team standing around a uniformed Ukrainian soldier lying on a stretcher. Jack assumed the kid was Kharlov's son. He was unconscious, and his torso was bloody, but none of that mattered. They'd found the kid, so they had a chance to barter with Kharlov.

Jack returned his focus to the conversation. "You there, Kharlov?"

"I'm here, but not for long." Kharlov's voice was like a rumble from the pits of hell. "You've got ten seconds before I hang up and prepare for launch."

Jack took a deep breath. He had one shot. "I met Anya. She told me she used to call you her dormant volcano. She also told me you were the father of her son."

With each passing second of silence, the chances of Kharlov accepting some kind of deal increased. Anya had told him that only she and Kharlov knew she used to call him that, a pet name for happier times, when the safety of the world hadn't been in jeopardy. Jack hoped her little pet name for Kharlov was the ace he needed to win this game they were playing.

"There's no way you could have known that without speaking to Anya." Kharlov finally spoke after almost a full minute. "You've got until midnight to get the boy to me. Fly him to the front entrance of the base in a helicopter, and both of you exit after landing. If I'm satisfied you're telling the truth, I'll trade Oreshkin's daughter for my son, and I won't launch the nukes."

Jack smiled. "I—"

"I'm not finished." Kharlov cut Jack off. "Even if I believe that it is my son and the trade goes off without a hitch, I'll still require Oreshkin to resign and kill herself on national television. That combination of things—bringing me my only remaining family member and the suicide of the person responsible for the rest of them dying—is what will stop me flattening Moscow."

Jack kept silent. He could deliver Dmitrovich, but only Oreshkin could accept the second part of Kharlov's terms. Jack knew there would be no more bargaining with Kharlov. He'd given his terms, and everyone on the call was waiting to see what Veronika Oreshkin would decide. It was a bargain with the devil, an impossible choice for the Russian prime minister.

"Agreed." Oreshkin spoke a few seconds later. "I'll do what is necessary to keep my daughter safe."

"We have a deal." Kharlov sounded delighted. "You have until midnight."

Jack exhaled when Kharlov exited the call. "Veronika, are you willing to do what you need to when the time comes?"

"Of course. Any parent would do the same." The response was instant, although Oreshkin's voice did waver. "If you can get Sasha to safety, I'll do what I need to do to avert the launch."

"Leave it with me. We'll get Dmitrovich ready to move and take a plane into Russia. We'll need to land and switch to a chopper to fly the last little way to the base."

"Okay." Oreshkin exhaled slowly. "Let me get started on the preparations on my end. Call me in an hour."

Jack ended the call. "We need to get Kharlov's son to the base and trade him for Oreshkin's daughter. If we can do that, she's willing to do what needs to be done to prevent the launch."

"Forget that for just one second." Fowler scoffed. "How the hell did you survive back there, Jack?"

Jack laughed. "Well, it's a funny story…"

He spent a minute explaining how he'd been found by Russian troops who'd taken him prisoner. He hadn't been able to understand a word they were saying, but he'd been afraid for his life. They'd cuffed him, thrown him in the back of a truck, and started to drive away.

Only a few minutes later, the Russian troops had set the prisoners loose. A Russian who spoke broken English had told Jack it was their lucky day, because Russian troops were withdrawing from the city and had no interest in taking prisoners with them. Jack and his fellow prisoners had been pointed in the direction of the main Ukrainian encampment. After passing through the frontlines and into the Ukrainian rear area, Jack had found Fowler.

"You're the luckiest bastard on Earth." Fowler patted him on the shoulder. "You better call McGhinnist and let him know what's going on. I'll get Dmitrovich and the others ready to go."

Jack split off from the group and took a second to compose himself. He reached into his pocket for his cell phone and dialed the president. When McGhinnist answered, Jack smiled. "It's good to hear your voice, sir."

"I was starting to worry I wouldn't hear yours again, Jack." The deep rumble of McGhinnist's voice was like thunder on a stormy night. "What's the situation?"

Jack left out the operational details but explained that

Kharlov had agreed to a trade. What the president was really asking was what would come next. He wanted to know what Jack had in the bag to save the world.

"There's only one problem, sir." Jack sighed. "The kid isn't in great shape. He's got a chest wound, and he's lost a lot of blood."

McGhinnist was quiet for a few moments, then he said, "There's no choice but to proceed. I'll get on the phone with Oreshkin while you're in the air and see what I can figure out."

"Okay." Jack nodded. "We better get moving. We need to get the kid to the missile base by midnight."

"Good luck, Jack. I'll speak to you when you're in the air."

The line went dead, and Jack removed the phone from his ear. He stared down at it for a long second, wondering if he should call Celeste while Anna and the others got ready to move. Then he thought better of it. If he called her, she would only worry. It was better to let her think that everything was going to plan and call her when everything was over. He clenched his teeth and put the phone back in his pocket. It was time to finish this.

KHARLOV OPENED his eyes and was instantly awake. He gripped the pistol that was lying on the bed next to him, then he locked eyes on Natalya. "Is it time?"

She nodded. "It's time. We've picked up a helicopter on the long-range radar, and Emery just texted your phone to say they're fifteen minutes out."

"Okay."

Kharlov climbed out of bed, not bothering to wait for Natalya to leave the room. He dressed, pulled on his boots, and grabbed his pistol. On his way out of the room, he stopped to glance at the alarm clock and framed photo on the bedside table. It hadn't occurred to him before that he'd gone to sleep in the bed of Vladimir Oreshkin, but the family photo of the deceased general, the Russian prime minister, and their daughter drove the fact home. He'd impacted their family as much as they had his.

Smiling, he left the room without thinking more about it. He had to focus, which was why he'd slept a few hours after making the deal with Emery. He felt rested and primed for whatever else came his way. Kharlov felt butterflies at the thought of meeting the only family he had left in the whole world, a son he hadn't known existed until a few hours ago.

Kharlov had always loved Anya, but she'd told him to leave. Eventually, he'd given up and moved on. He'd kept depositing large sums of money into her account to make sure she would be okay. His business had expanded, and he'd met his wife. They'd started a family not long after, a family that had been taken from him. But now he had a chance to reunite with the only family he had left.

"You should reconsider, Dmitry." Natalya cut off his thoughts as they walked. "We came here to avenge your family, not to make a deal to get our hands on someone you've never met. We can't trust them. What's to say they won't level the base the moment we give them Oreshkin's daughter?"

Kharlov stopped walking and placed a hand on each of Natalya's shoulders. "I understand the risks, but I can't turn my back on this. If I have any family left, I must fight for them."

She sighed. "Dmitry, I—"

Kharlov cut her off. "If you or any of the others want to leave, you've got fifteen minutes to get out of here. Take a truck and go with my blessing. I think you all have a better chance of survival here than elsewhere, though. Even when we trade Oreshkin's daughter for my son, we still have nuclear weapons and the ability to use them..."

She simply nodded. "I'm with you until the end, Dmitry. While you're undertaking the swap, I'll be ready to launch the missiles if there's any kind of treachery."

Kharlov smiled. He was glad she was sticking by him. Though he wasn't sure if she totally accepted his reasoning, he didn't care. He was moments away from meeting his son, and she was going to be his dead man's switch.

He exited General Oreshkin's residence and stood on the stairs, glancing at the hostages for a moment. They were all hungry, exhausted, and growing increasingly desperate as the hope of a Russian military intervention lessened. If some of his men were going to depart from the base, he wanted to make sure the prisoners couldn't cause him any problems. Natalya was right. The soldiers he'd taken captive were no longer useful to him. He locked eyes with the man he had in charge of the prisoners and ran a finger across his throat.

Kharlov didn't wait for acknowledgement. Without waiting for his orders to be carried out, he stepped closer to Oreshkin's daughter, who he'd kept handcuffed to a pillar out front of General Oreshkin's residence since he'd captured the base. The girl stared at him blankly. She'd long ago given up trying to resist. She simply watched as he uncuffed her and waited for whatever came next.

Kharlov drew his pistol, dug it into her ribs, and pushed her in the direction he wanted to walk—toward the base's front gate.

"Where are we going?" Sasha asked when the gate was in sight. "What's happening to me?"

Kharlov smiled. "You're going home to your mother, so long as neither of you try to do anything stupid."

He ignored the girl from then on, focusing on Emery and the helicopter. He took her to the front gate and waved at the two men he had inside of it. Both of them were heavily armed, and they were fine men to have at his back if Kharlov was facing a double cross. One of the men waved back, and a second later, the gate started to grind open.

Kharlov took four steps outside the gate, stopped, and pressed the pistol against Oreshkin's skull. "Get down on your knees and don't move an inch. I'll tell you when it's time to move again."

He relaxed a little when she nodded and complied. He looked up to the horizon, above the tree line in which he and his men had hidden prior to taking the base. A large gray helicopter appeared and slowly approached. Kharlov watched the helicopter come in for landing with all the grace of a flying bathtub. It was a military model, armed to the teeth with guns and rockets. Yet despite the firepower the chopper boasted, Kharlov wasn't worried. If the Russians wanted to attack the base, they would have sent more firepower than one chopper, and he would send a nuclear missile flying right back at them.

The helicopter landed gently on its struts, the side door opened, and two men stepped out—Jack Emery and a young man that Kharlov assumed was his son. They kept their heads down and their eyes shielded as they moved away from the helicopter, trying to avoid the dust and dirt kicked up by the chopper's rotor wash. Only when they were fifty yards clear of the chopper did the two men stop and look at Kharlov. It was time to make a deal. Or the last chance to back out of it.

Kharlov knew the minute he gave up Oreshkin's daughter, there would be nothing stopping the Russians from assaulting the base. He was sure they were coiled and ready to strike. He had to rely on their fear of a nuclear launch being enough to keep him in command of the situation, though it was possible the Russians would try their luck. There was no alternative, because he simply couldn't pass up the chance to meet his son.

Kharlov raised hand into the air and gave a thumbs-up. In response, Emery raised his hand and did the same thing. The deal was on.

"Get up and walk to the other man." Kharlov removed the pistol from the girl's head, gripped her blouse, and pulled her to her feet. "Don't run. Don't look back. Don't do anything stupid."

He waited until she nodded, then he let go of her blouse. She walked like a robot at first, stiff and cautious, clearly focused on following his instructions exactly. Kharlov watched her closely until she was twenty yards away, then he shifted his attention to Emery and his son.

He remembered Jack Emery from Castle Montjuic. Wearing black combat fatigues and a holstered pistol, Emery walked alongside a soldier in a Ukrainian Army uniform. He followed Emery one foot to the left and one behind. About twenty years old, he was a strapping young man who stood tall and proud as he walked across no-man's land between Kharlov and Emery.

Kharlov smiled as hope filled his heart. Everything was going to plan. There was no shooting or shouting. Kharlov's son and Oreshkin's daughter passed by each other without stopping. They didn't even look at each other. As his son got closer, he dared to hope that he might have a family again. It didn't fix the gaping hole that the loss of his wife and his other two children had left in his soul, but it went some way toward it.

When Oreshkin's daughter and his own son were three-quarters of the way to their respective destinations, Kharlov breathed a sigh of relief. His faith in the Russian prime minister's self-interest had been correct. She hadn't wanted to put her daughter in danger while the transfer took place, and the minute Kharlov had his son inside the base, he would be protected again. He would be in a bunker with nukes, ready to demand Oreshkin kill herself.

Then Natalya's voice filled his ears over the communications network and ruined everything. Her voice was breathless, panicked. "Dmitry... we've run this man's face through the Russian Army database. There was a hit. He's a Russian soldier dressed as a Ukrainian."

Kharlov squeezed his hand around the grip of his pistol until he thought the steel might bend. He was outraged that Oreshkin had tried to betray him yet again. Once again, her betrayal had cost him his family.

Kharlov looked down at the weapon and saw his knuckles were white with the rage coursing through him. He looked back up at his "son," who had a wide smile on his face. His hands held wide, he stepped closer to Kharlov. He looked like a son who was about to meet his father for the first time, when in reality, he was a Trojan horse that had sprung a wheel before getting inside the gates. Kharlov smiled back at the imposter, raised the pistol, and shot him in the face.

"FUCK!" Jack screamed as the Russian plant fell to the ground. "We're blown!"

Jack ignored the half-dozen voices that spewed out of his earpiece. He was focused on nothing else except getting Sasha

Oreshkin away from harm. He held out his hand to the young woman as she froze in place, not daring to turn around to look for the source of the gunfire but not advancing on the helicopter, either.

"Sasha!" Jack shouted over the sound of the helicopter's rotors powering up again. "You need to move!"

He waved her closer. She locked eyes on him, breaking the trance she'd been in. She started to run, getting closer to safety with each second. Jack drew his pistol and fired at Kharlov while a shooter inside the helicopter tried his luck with a rifle —but Kharlov had retreated back inside the base.

The Russian soldier was a volunteer who'd been tasked with killing Dmitry Kharlov. Kharlov's son had succumbed to his serious chest wound during the journey. Forced to think on the fly, Jack and his allies had scrambled into action. The soldier had rendezvoused with them at the airfield, where they'd worked up a plan to kill Kharlov before boarding the chopper. Something or someone must have warned Kharlov.

"I was told I was seeing my mother!" Her cry was in broken English with a heavy Russian accent. "What's going on?"

"The world has just gone to hell." Jack grabbed her hand. "We need to get out of here right now."

Jack pulled her in the direction of the chopper. With each passing second, he expected to be shot in the back or to hear a rocket with a nuclear warhead launching from the base, but all he could hear was the *thump-thump-thump* sound of the helicopter's rotors. The rhythmic beat was like the pounding of his heart, the drumbeat to his desperate run for safety.

Twenty yards… it felt like he was running through molasses. Ten yards… Five yards…

Jack pushed Sasha onto the helicopter. The Russian soldier inside took her hand, pulled her on board roughly, then held out a hand for Jack to grab. He clenched the soldier's hand and climbed aboard, barely getting his feet off the ground before the chopper lifted off. He felt nauseous as the helicopter climbed far quicker than he was used to, but he was glad to be on the way to safety.

Jack glanced at Oreshkin's daughter to check that she was seated and strapped in, then he focused on doing the same himself. Once he had settled in, his heart rate slowed, and his breathing returned to normal. Only then did he start to focus on what was going on around him: the excited chatter of the people involved in the mission, the pilot climbing as fast as he could to avoid Kharlov's weaponry, and the woman who was coming to terms with the cost of her release.

Oreshkin spoke once she was given a headset and patched into the helicopter's communications system. "That man died for me, didn't he?"

"He did his job." Jack shrugged and pressed his lips together for a second before deciding to give her more. "Your mother moved heaven and earth to get you back—you should focus on that. The soldier volunteered to try to take down Kharlov, but it's not always possible to succeed in that business."

"I'll make it up to his family." She seemed content with Jack's response, then she smiled at him. "Thank you."

Jack nodded and closed his eyes, focusing on the chatter in his ear and trying to get a grip on exactly what had happened. He knew nothing of the wider situation, of what was currently happening inside the base.

Then Anna Fowler's voice came over the network. "The drones monitoring the base are showing movement out the rear gate. We think some of Kharlov's men are bailing on him."

Jack's eyes opened, and he cracked a smile. If Kharlov's

men were getting the hell out, then it was over. "That's fantastic. Tell Oreshkin her daughter is safe. I—"

"It's not good news, Jack." Fowler's voice sounded tense as she cut him off. "The drones are also showing dozens of bodies in the main courtyard of the base and signs of activity around the launch bunker and missile silos. We think they wiped out the prisoners and are preparing to launch if Oreshkin doesn't kill herself on national television."

"No..." Jack shook his head. With voices in his ear and Oreshkin's daughter staring at him intently, it felt like a giant piece of the puzzle was inching to fall into place in his head. Then it struck him like a blow. The evidence had been there since the beginning. Kharlov had called Oreshkin to tell her that he had her daughter then called her *again* to tell her he had her husband and control of a nuclear base.

If simply forcing Oreshkin to kill herself would have been enough to satisfy him, there would have been no need to take the nuclear base and make the second call. Oreshkin would have done anything for her daughter, including end her own life. No, Kharlov wanted more. He'd taken the base because he wanted the nuclear weapons, and he'd taken General Oreshkin because he knew how to conduct the launch. Kharlov had planned to launch all along.

"He's going to launch." Jack cut off the others. "He's been planning it from the beginning. He's just been playing for time."

There was a pause as everyone else on the network digested the news. It wasn't every day the world faced a nuclear launch, and this time, Jack had no way of stopping it. In the United Kingdom, he'd faced a fight to the death to prevent a launch, but now he was on a helicopter, flying away from a heavily fortified military base that'd been taken over by terrorists. He couldn't act. All he could do was help others to act.

"We need to stop him." Jack filled the silence. "Veronika, Bill, do we have anything that can stop him from launching?"

McGhinnist came over the line. "We don't have any assets that can intervene in time. We could flatten the base after the fact, but it's not going to stop Moscow from being leveled. The only option is for Russia to attack the base as quickly as possible, but that seems unlikely to succeed."

"There's one other option," Oreshkin said. "It will put an end to our hopes for a nuclear deal though, Jack..."

Jack's eyes widened. "Veronika, you can't!" Jack's shout was visceral, his voice filled with poison. "A nuke hasn't been dropped for eighty years! This will start a chain-reaction of launches!"

"I've had jets on station in case this intervention was required." She sighed. "I'm sorry, everyone. I wanted the deal as much as the rest of you, but I can't let him flatten Moscow."

Jack shouted her name a few more times, but she'd stopped talking. He wasn't even sure she was listening anymore. She was going to hit the base with a nuclear weapon to prevent Kharlov from doing the same to Moscow. Jack's mind strained to think of another solution, but McGhinnist had nothing up his sleeve, and Jack was strapped into a helicopter flying away from the base.

Jack swallowed. There was a lump in his throat. The launch couldn't be stopped, and he had to come to terms with that. After a deep breath, he switched his mind to protecting the world from the consequences of the launch, isolating the situation from the broader disaster it could cause. He'd failed to eradicate the threat of nuclear weapons, but he had to again make sure they didn't end the world.

"Bill, Caleb—you guys there?" Jack paused until the president and the national security advisor had responded. "You guys need to work the phones right the hell now. All the nuclear powers from biggest to smallest need to be told that there's an incident in Russia and that nobody should launch in response to it."

"Good thinking, Jack." McGhinnist sounded strong and determined. "We'll get onto it right aw—"

The rest of the president's statement was replaced by the sound of an explosion unlike any horror Jack had ever experienced before. It sounded like the Earth was being ripped open. It sounded like failure. He knew well enough that he shouldn't look out the window at the sight of the nuclear explosion, so he squeezed his eyes closed and hoped it wasn't the end of everything.

He expected to be turned into a cinder or for the chopper to fall out of the sky. Death by nuclear fire would be the ultimate irony for a man who'd tried to extinguish the weapons from the planet. Worse, McGhinnist and Davidson hadn't had time to make the calls. It was possible that Oreshkin's order to flatten the base would lead to further launches from other jittery nuclear powers who thought missiles were coming their way.

One second passed... Then two... Three... The end didn't come.

Jack opened his eyes and stared out the window with wide eyes. Amazed eyes. Confused eyes. Terrified eyes. A small gray mushroom cloud was rising up into the sky from where the base had been. It wasn't as large as the ones he remembered from movies and documentaries about Hiroshima and Nagasaki, but it was impressive. Nothing at its base could have survived.

Jack exhaled slowly through clenched teeth. He'd failed. Nukes had once again been used in anger. But his failure could have been a hell of a lot larger—Moscow could have been flattened, a global launch could have been triggered, and all of his loved ones could have been vaporized. Though he knew that, he wasn't sure he could accept it just yet. He wasn't sure he could ever accept it.

He sighed. "Did Kharlov launch?"

"No, Jack." McGhinnist's voice was grave. "We detected no launch before the detonation."

"Then I hope he rests in peace with his family."

Jack took off his headphones and tossed them on the floor of the helicopter. He'd heard enough. He'd had enough. Kharlov was dead, the world wasn't at nuclear war, and everyone was safe. It was a victory, but it was a pyrrhic one. The cause he'd fought so hard for was hopeless, and the deadly tools he'd hoped to bury deep in history had sprung forth into the present. What the future held was anyone's guess.

EPILOGUE

Jack stood with his arms crossed, leaning against the wall of the cavernous White House ballroom, keeping the paintings on the wall company. Nobody else was standing near him. They were all seated ahead of him, engrossed in the history being made at the front of the room—the official return of large slabs of Ukrainian territory by Russia. He sighed. He'd wanted to hold a similar event to mark the start of a world free of nuclear weapons. Instead, the nuclear genie was once again out of the bottle.

After the nuclear explosion had leveled the base and extinguished Dmitry Kharlov's campaign of hate, Jack had landed at a military base and handed over Sasha Oreshkin to Russian authorities. After all the drama of the girl's rescue, her farewell had been anticlimactic. She'd tearfully thanked him then been whisked away by a small army to be reunited with her mother.

While Jack was making his way back to the United States, he'd watched the world go to hell. Though the other nuclear powers had quickly been reassured that Russia wasn't launching a global nuclear strike, everyone now knew Russia had unleashed a tactical battlefield nuclear weapon. Publicly, all the other nuclear powers were making no comment, calling it a Russian nuclear test. Privately, they were furious Russia had dropped the bomb. The chance of a nuclear deal was as dead as Kharlov and his men.

More promising was the consolidation of Oreshkin's power and the complete withdrawal of Russian troops from Ukraine. Amid the confusion of the nuclear explosion, Oreshkin had purged the ultra-nationalists from her government, her bureaucracy, and her military. Her loyalists had rounded up anyone involved in attacking Ukraine over the previous few years. Officers, intelligence officials, bureaucrats, and politicians had been arrested en masse.

With her leadership secure, Oreshkin had ordered an immediate withdrawal of Russian troops from all occupied territories and ceased support for the pro-Russian partisans. Though there were still spot fires burning in a dozen locations, for the most part, the borders were back to normal. Russian troops had returned to their corner, Western troops had resumed a wary watch, and Ukrainian troops had moved to reclaim territory lost throughout the war. The event at the White House, despite all the pomp and ceremony, was simply making official what had already happened.

Jack sighed again as the Ukrainian prime minister finished speaking and McGhinnist took the stage. Although the president put a positive spin on the events of the last few months, every word his boss spoke simply felt to Jack like failure. He'd returned to McGhinnist's government to achieve one thing, and he'd failed completely. Before leaving his office to attend the event, Jack had put his resignation letter on McGhinnist's desk. He was merely waiting to say goodbye.

He remained lost in his own thoughts until the end of the speeches, then he pushed himself off the wall and walked to the front of the room. Others tried to stop him and make conversation, but Jack politely excused himself and kept moving. Once he was through the crowd, he saw McGhinnist and Oreshkin clustered together, looking like old friends. It was further proof that the world had changed forever in the past few months.

Jack waited on the periphery of the conversation, observing protocol despite his relationship with both McGhinnist and Oreshkin. They remained in conversation for another minute or so, smiling and making animated hand gestures, then Oreshkin noticed Jack waiting to speak with them. After she flashed a warm smile at Jack, both she and the president walked closer to him.

"Mr. President, Ms. Prime Minister." Jack forced a smile. "Excellent speeches today, both of you."

"Always so formal." Oreshkin laughed. "Jack, I wanted to thank you in person for getting my daughter back. I can never repay you."

"My pleasure." Jack's smile became more genuine. "I'm glad Sasha is safe and that we could get her out of there."

"She's safe and back at school, although she has some trauma to work through..." Oreshkin's voice trailed off, and her face clouded over. "But that's enough of my problems. I believe there's a dinner tonight where we can all talk more, but I'm sure the two of you have much to discuss, as always."

Jack smiled at her then waited while she exchanged pleasantries with McGhinnist and departed. As he watched her leave with her security detail, he wondered what she had in store for Russia and what Russia had in store for her. Either way, he didn't think he'd heard the last of Veronika Oreshkin, though she'd probably heard the last of him. His days at the big table of international affairs were over.

"How are you, Jack?" McGhinnist finally spoke when Oreshkin was out of earshot. "I know you're having a hard time, so we can talk in private if you want."

"No." Jack shook his head. "I appreciate it, but I just wanted to say goodbye. I'm flying home for a while."

"Home..." McGhinnist's eyes narrowed. "To New York?"

Jack shook his head. "No. Celeste is taking some time off, as well. We're going to fly to Australia to get married and get away from here for a while."

"You're leaving?" McGhinnist exhaled loudly, clearly frustrated. "If this is about the nuclear deal or the bomb going off, then don't be so hard on yourself. The deal was always a long shot. You saved Oreshkin's daughter and freed her up to hit the base. Without that, Moscow might have been glassed."

"I—"

"No, Jack." McGhinnist held up a hand. "You need to hear this. Do you think the outcome would have been any different if Moscow was flattened? The outcome was terrible for the deal, sure, but it would have been terrible for the whole planet if it'd gone differently. You need to remember that. Kharlov is dead. The detonation has been contained. The good guys won."

Jack opened his mouth to argue then closed it again. He'd spent the last year trying to protect the world from the scourge of nuclear weapons. He'd foiled terrorists and stopped Dmitry Kharlov, but in the end, the only way to do so had been for Oreshkin to order a nuclear strike herself.

Jack had worked for McGhinnist for every minute of his

presidency, and the two men had a close relationship. They'd disagreed before, but each man had always understood and respected the other's position. Not this time. McGhinnist clearly couldn't understand why Jack was so flat and why he felt like he'd failed at the most important thing he'd ever attempted. Or why he felt like he had to walk away.

McGhinnist sighed when Jack didn't relent. "Go have your vacation, Jack. But after that, do you intend to return to work?"

Jack looked at McGhinnist for a long few seconds. The two men had a conversation with their eyes that didn't require words, then Jack shook his head. "No."

"You said that last time." McGhinnist tried to force a smile. "You'll be back, but if not, then I want you to know it's been a hell of a ride, Jack. I've loved every minute working with you."

Jack nodded, and they shook hands. Then Jack turned his back and walked away.

ACKNOWLEDGMENTS

Well, we made it. It has been a torturously long time since Jack Emery saved the world.

As always, first and biggest thanks to my wife, Vanessa. A large dose also goes to my beta readers, Gerard Burg, Dave Sinclair and Janice Harris.

My production crew are the best in the business - Stuart Bache with the cover and Stef Spangler-Buswell with the edit. Thanks to both of them for the polish and the coat of paint.

Lastly, thanks to you, the reader, for your patience between drinks on this series. I'll keep writing them as long as you keep reading them.

ABOUT THE AUTHOR

Steve P. Vincent is the USA Today Bestselling Author of the Jack Emery and Mitch Herron conspiracy thriller series.

Steve has a degree in political science, a thesis on global terrorism, a decade as a policy advisor and training from the FBI and Australian Army in his conspiracy kit bag.

When he's not writing, Steve enjoys whisky, sports and travel.

You can contact Steve at all the usual places:
stevepvincent.com
steve@stevepvincent.com

One Minute to Midnight

Cover design by Stuart Bache

Edited by Stefanie Spangler-Buswell

www.ingramcontent.com/pod-product-compliance
Lightning Source LLC
Chambersburg PA
CBHW021405110726
47901CB00008B/2067